THE SHARPSHOOTER BLUES

Also by Lewis Nordan

THE SHARPSHOOTER BLUES

a novel by
Lewis Nordan

Algonquin Books of Chapel Hill
1995

Published by
ALGONQUIN BOOKS OF CHAPEL HILL
Post Office Box 2225
Chapel Hill, North Carolina 27515-2225

a division of
WORKMAN PUBLISHING COMPANY, INC.
708 Broadway
New York, New York 10003

This is a work of fiction. While, as in all fiction, the literary perceptions and insights are based on experience, all names, characters, places, and incidents are either products of the author's imagination or are used fictitiously. No reference to any real person is intended or should be inferred.

Library of Congress Cataloging-in-Publication Data
Nordan, Lewis.
    The sharpshooter blues : a novel / by Lewis Nordan.
      p.   cm.
    ISBN 1-56512-083-3 (hardcover)
    I. Title.
  PS3564.O55S53   1995
  813'.54—dc20   95–15306
                                                              CIP

10 9 8 7 6 5 4 3 2 1
First Edition

for you, Mama
Sara Hightower Bayles

The author wishes to thank the Virginia Center for the Creative Arts for a fellowship which made the writing of this book possible.

THE SHARPSHOOTER BLUES

1

The island where Mr. Raney had his fishcamp was a strip of high ground far out in a strange bayou, the vast, unbounded backwaters of many lakes and rivers; from underground, somewhere, salt water, brackish at least, mineral salts, filled up the swamp and broadened it far across the Delta. The water seemed limitless, everywhere, even to a boy who grew up on the island; it was a black mirror, colored by the tannic acid that seeped into it from the knees of cypress trees.

Beavers had felled the trees, a few trees anyway, sweetgum and tupelo, and built dams and houses as big as igloos, or tepees; and they swam in and out, the size of collies.

Turkey buzzards floated above the swamp like prayers and admired their own reflections in the water. Blue herons and cranes and snowy egrets stood on long legs and ate snakes and minnows in the shallows. Cottonmouth moccasins hung in the willow branches, turtles sat on the logs, alligators lounged in their big nests, which smelled of sugarcane and sorghum and rice and fish. Rats the size of yellow dogs clung to the bark of trees by their toenails and yapped like puppies and then dropped into the water and held their noses up above the flood and swam to high ground where they sat and howled at the moon by night.

Somehow dolphins, porpoises, whatever they were, had

1

made their way up here to the Delta, to this vast water, all the way from the Gulf of Mexico—who knows how, or why, up rivers and canals, to this inland sea—and they swam and bred and gave birth and fed upon the million carp and mullet and the other bony fish that populated the swamp. Minerals in the fresh water made it somehow fit habitation for these sea creatures, no one understood quite how. Scientists were forever arriving here from Jackson and Biloxi, with water-testing equipment; maybe they knew.

Mr. Raney named the porpoises—Sister Woman, and Renford, and Lamar, and St. Elmo—and could recognize them, and call each by its name, even at night, six feet long some of them, with a million sharp teeth and a naughty grin. Often when he floated past in the boat and watched their playful wheeling, in and out among the cypress knees, he called out to them, "Lamar, we are all alone in the world!" or "Renford, cork is an export product of India!"

The echo of his voice across the wide water of the bayou was like a heartbreaking song, a music of the swamp.

Hydro said, one time, many times, "Do they understand what you tell them?"

Mr. Raney said, each time, "Nobody knows."

Sometimes they had this exchange, father and son, but not tonight. Tonight the bloody deaths of the boy and girl at the William Tell Grocery occupied their minds, the two of them.

Hydro was quiet, quiet in the front of the boat. He thought it might be a good idea to jump in the water and drown, he was not sure why. He sat in the bow of the little boat like a mermaid carved out of wood in the prow of a sailing vessel, eyes forward and watchful of the sea.

The waters were wide, they stretched far out across the Delta. In some places the deep-water trenches were bottomless, or seemed so; and nearly a hundred years ago, ironclad vessels floated here, warships of the Confederate and Union navies. Men died in the swamp for reasons that must have seemed good at the time, and women waited for them in vain, and children grew up without daddies. People said these deep-water trenches were caused by an earthquake, a long time ago, but nobody knew for sure when, and nobody knew for sure if it was true, it could have been. The scientists from Jackson, maybe they knew.

In the front of the boat, Hydro thought of what it would be like to slip over the side, into the black water, through the looking glass. He imagined that he could breathe there and be happy, swimming among the bluegills, laughing with St. Elmo, his smiling face. He believed he might find the boy and the girl there, beneath the surface, the lovely children, alive again, and that they would love him and speak to him of Texas and tortillas and love and Dinty Moore. They might be happy there, underwater, the three of them together, his head might be a normal size, no longer large, he might be smart, with no atrophy of the brain, they might not call him names. This was the deep water that he imagined, the excellent world on the other side of the mirror of the lake.

At times the surface of the water broke, though, and Hydro saw a little face, wet whiskers shining in the moonlight. Here and there muskrats swam and dived and sur-faced, smiling like rich children in the blue water of the Leflore city swimming pool, beneath the diving board, beneath the lifeguard stand where a bronze young man sat with a steel whistle on a lanyard around his neck, above the benches where Hydro had been allowed to sit and watch but never to dress in a swimsuit or to swim, it was so dangerous, his daddy would have worried about him.

In these swampy places, these wide shallows, a man in chest-waders might walk long distances, twenty-five miles, without ever stepping in over his head. Sometimes scientists did do this, walked so far, men from Jackson, looking for an ancient flock of buzzards that lived there, far back in the woods, trying to take their pictures.

Hydro would not look to the back of the boat at his daddy. He did not look right or left, only straight ahead into the dark swamp. He wished his daddy would fall out into the water and drown. He imagined this, hoped for it, so that finally everything would be lost, there would be no more waiting.

He looked above him, for parrots, whatever they were, wild birds, of jungle colors, red heads and curved yellow beaks and long green tails, seen nowhere else in Mississippi, not even on the Gulf of Mexico, that sailed through the skies at morning, and cried out in African-sounding voices. He saw only the moon, only the stars above. There were no parrots tonight, no jungle birds. Were there ever, had he ever really seen parrots, had he ever loved anyone, even his daddy?

In the deepest swamp, where now the boat pushed on,

outwards, towards the island, wild monkeys leaped from tree to tree, and rested in the shade and nibbled upon the tender leaves and the beards of Spanish moss. Hydro looked up in the treetops and saw them there, asleep beneath the big moon, little families with daddies and little child-monkeys, and even mamas who loved them. Somebody said these monkeys came from a pair of tame creatures, pets, who escaped from a one-man band, long ago.

Except for the fishcamp on Raney's Island, there were no houses anywhere nearby. Mr. Roy, once a week, delivered mail, in a flat-bottomed motor launch, and sometimes stayed talking with Mr. Raney too late to be confident he could find his way back to the mainland without getting lost in the dark, or hitting a stob and shearing a pin in the launch's propeller, and so he spent those nights in the camp, telling old stories until late at night, and ate fried fish for breakfast, with hushpuppies and catsup and Tabasco sauce, and then he motored out across the wide water, towards Arrow Catcher, until he saw the Roebuck bridge and the flagpole down at the post office.

Mr. Roy was handsome enough to go to Hollywood, everybody said so, and it was true. He could easily break into show business, if he decided to. He wore his uniform wherever he went, gray slacks and white shirt with patches, and billed cap, even on Sundays when he went to church, even when he and Mrs. Roy went out to a café, a supper club they called it, and ate and drank bonded whiskey over ice, and sometimes mixed it with a Coke or Seven-Up, on a Saturday night. Mrs. Roy said she could never resist a man in uniform and she didn't see no reason to start resisting now. This was a joke they shared and they always laughed together, and always, always seemed to be in love.

When Mr. Roy pushed off in the morning, after he had delivered the mail and told the old stories and spent the night, like the story about the snake he thought he killed with a flashlight but it turned out to be his own arm, gone to sleep and he beat it to a bloody pulp, Mr. Raney would be standing on the dock, ready to say goodbye. He might wave to Mr. Roy as the launch pulled out.

Mr. Raney might say, "Bring me out some wanted posters next time. Them with the pitchers on them. My boy likes to look at them ones with the pitchers."

Hydro would be standing on the dock waving goodbye, too.

Mr. Roy might say, "Hydro, what you need with a wanted poster?"

Hydro said, "I don't know."

Mr. Roy said, "You don't know."

Mr. Raney said, "He plays a game. He plays like the men in the pitchers are folks he knows. He makes up stories about them. He plays like the women are his mama."

Mr. Roy said, "Well, ain't that nice."

Hydro said, "That ain't all, though."

Mr. Roy said, "It ain't?"

Hydro said, "I might catch me one of them desperate criminals."

Mr. Roy said, "You might catch you a desperate criminal?"

Hydro said, "I might."

Mr. Roy said, "What you going to do with a desperate criminal when you catch him?"

Hydro said, "I might turn him in. I might get me a reward. I might get us a new mama."

Mr. Roy said, "Get you a new mama! Oo la la!"

Mr. Raney said, "Don't tease the boy, Mr. Roy."

Mr. Roy said, "Well, wanted posters can be educational, I grant you that. Very educational, sure now. You can learn a-plenty from a wanted poster, sure can. Wanted posters can be as good as school. I always said so. And, well, I don't know, they might help you meet people, too, interesting people, somebody you might want to, I don't know, invite home and make her your mama. I'm trying to take you serious, Hydro, but I ain't altogether sure how you mean that about a new mama."

Hydro said, "I was just pretending. I was just telling a story. You can go oo la la, if you want to."

Mr. Roy said, "Well, and it's a good one, too. A fine story. A reward, a new mama, off a wanted poster. That truly is a good one, Hydro. You had me going there for a minute. You had me fooled. Oo la la."

Hydro said, "It might be true."

Mr. Roy said, "Well, that's a fact, it might be. I ain't ruling that out neither, I ain't ruling nothing out. It could be true."

Mr. Raney said, "Don't tease the boy."

Mr. Roy said, "What else can I do, Raney? I'm doing the best I can, talking about wanted posters."

There was not much other traffic in the deep bayou, not tonight, under the starlight, not ever.

Mr. Raney called out to Hydro over the rattle of the engine: "Look yonder."

He was pointing at a big tree, with construction materials up in the top of it.

Hydro didn't look back, didn't look side to side. He knew what his daddy was pointing to. He always pointed to it. The tree house, what was left of it, a three-story tree house, that still had a dinette set sitting up on the top layer of plywood.

A long time ago, when Hydro was just a baby boy, a family lived there, in that tree house, an elaborate construction of plywood and ropes and pulleys and corrugated metal and trapdoors, away out here in the swamp, only a few miles from the camp. A man and his wife and their three children, white folks, lived in it. His daddy said they did, Hydro guessed it was true, he never did meet none of them.

They fished and they trapped water birds and gathered dock and wild onions and poke salad and parboiled it and ate it and didn't get diarrhea, they was used to it, not like normal folks like Hydro and his daddy. Wild vegetables would have sent Mr. Raney to the slopjar and kept him there a week, if he just boiled and ate them, right out of the swamp. They poached electricity, the tree house family, from the hot wires that passed through the trees to light Mr. Raney's place. It was dangerous but they did it, and it worked too, they burned lights, Mr. Raney paid the extra nickels and dimes it cost him on the monthly bill.

On the weekends, Mr. Roy delivered the Sunday newspaper to them, and in the evening the man and his wife, wearing overalls, sat up in the trees in overstuffed chairs, reading *Alley Oop* and *Little Orphan Annie* and *The Katzenjammer Kids* and listening to *Amos 'n' Andy* on the radio. One of the children kept a pet, a dog or a cat, nobody remembered which. It was rumored that they ate monkey meat, their long-tailed neighbors who lived nearby, in the trees, which some people thought was cannibal behavior, a scandal they said, a crime and a shame, a long, long time ago, probably not even true, nobody knew for sure, it might just be a story, like so much else in the world.

Hydro one time said, "How do they go doodies?"

Mr. Raney said, "Well, pretty much the same as anybody else, would be my guess."

Tonight Hydro would have liked to have asked again, but he didn't intend to give his daddy the satisfaction. He knew they went doodies like everybody else—how did they get it down out of the tree?

They were gone now, the tree people, and only the tree house remained, fragments of it. Nobody knew the whole story. Hydro said he never saw them, he couldn't remember.

His daddy said, "Sure you can."

He said, "I don't."

Sometimes a game warden motored out, too, once or twice a year. He checked Mr. Raney's licenses, renewed them when necessary. He brought saltlicks for the deer on the island. He usually stayed a day and a night and brought along a casting rod and a Lucky 13 and got some fishing done.

Once, in an unusual winter, cold as the North Pole, the

swamp froze solid, ice as far as you could see, and the game warden drove his Jeep all the way out to the island, across the ice, and let Hydro shoot his pistol. Everybody in Arrow Catcher remembered that day and talked about it for a long time.

Mostly Mr. Raney and Hydro spent their days alone. They didn't get much company, so far out, like they was. Hydro liked to be sung to, love songs mainly, so they did that, a lot of tunes from the olden days, especially "Let These Red Lips Kiss Your Blues Away," but also a couple of new songs by Elvis Presley, "Blue Moon over Kentucky" and "When My Blue Moon Turns to Gold Again."

Hydro said, "How can the moon be blue?"

Mr. Raney said, "Nobody knows."

Hydro said, "What is Kentucky?"

Mr. Raney said, "Nobody knows that neither."

Hydro said, "They don't? Nobody knows what Kentucky is? It's a state, that's what I heard."

Mr. Raney said, "Hush up, if you want me to sing you any more songs."

Or Mr. Raney told Hydro about the olden days, when he was a boy and there were many families of tree people, and still a few wild Indians who tamed the looseherds, and rode wild ponies without no saddles and carried bows and arrows across their backs, and when all the sidewalks were made of wood, and about the time when wild bison roamed the Delta, even out on Runnymede plantation.

Hydro said, "Daddy, was you a real cowboy?"

Mr. Raney said, "Well—"

Hydro said, "It's just a story, ain't it? Just for fun."

Mr. Raney said, "Well—"

Sometimes Hydro thought he made the stories up; other times, when a small herd of swamp elves clattered out of the cane and disappeared in a flash into the deep bayou, he didn't know, he thought maybe there were looseherds of wild horses and herds of buffalo, not so long ago, and maybe a wild Indian or two, the stories might be true.

Mr. Raney tried to teach him many things, gentleness for one, and to talk about how it felt to hear people make fun of his big head, and not to be too scared of the fire whistle when it blew, and not to chase cars when they went into Arrow Catcher, and to identify fish, by color and shape and fin and gill, bream and crappie and bass and buffalo and carp and a fish his father called a chinquapin, after the trees they nested near, and to understand tail, and how it made Mr. Raney love Hydro's mama even more, when she was alive and they once in a while knocked off a piece in the afternoon, just for fun.

Each evening Mr. Raney iced down a cargo of fish, which he pulled up in wide nets from the swamp and threw a heavy tarpaulin over them while they were still flopping, and fired up the little Evinrude and hauled the fish into Arrow Catcher in his boat and sold them for pennies on a low pier alongside the Roebuck bridge and then baled ice water out of the boat with a rusty lard bucket, before setting out across the bayou, on the way back home.

This night, though, the night that Hydro killed the two lovely children after confession at William Tell, shot them square between the eyes like a sharpshooter in a circus sideshow, Hydro and his daddy did not call to the dolphins, did not speak of fish or love or the looseherds or gentleness or Kentucky or the wild buffalo. For the first time in a long time, Mr. Raney just didn't know what to say. He did not know what to say.

The island came into sight, a light on the pier, and another up in the main house. Mr. Raney cut off the Evinrude and let the boat drift in to the dock. It made a small sound like ka-chunk, wood against wood, when it struck there.

Hydro stood up in the bow and took the length of hemp rope that was tied to a steel ring and looped it around a piling and pulled them in tight and cinched the rope up against the post so the stern could swing around. Water lapped up against the boat and made the sound of waves against wood.

Mr. Raney said, "You go on and get out first."

So Hydro got out, stepped up on the dock and steadied himself.

Hydro looked back over his shoulder in his daddy's direction, but he didn't seem to see his daddy.

Mr. Raney said, "I'm fine, jess fine, no help wanted, thank you, thank you very much."

Hydro turned away.

Mr. Raney started to climb up out of the boat.

Hydro walked on ahead, towards the house.

His daddy said, "Well, you go on to bed, honey. You're tired. You just go right ahead on. I'll finish up down here."

Hydro kept on walking.

His daddy said, "You go on to bed, son, you're tired."

While his daddy was down at the dock, securing the boat for the night, Hydro climbed up the ladder and crawled up through the trapdoor that led into their house. He came out on the upper porch, where he stood for a moment and listened. He heard jungle sounds across the swamp, the gators calling like old cows, a parrot somewhere far off, the final nighttime chatter of a sleepless family of monkeys. Nothing told him the secret that might save him from this pain.

He passed through the kitchen, with the huge old Chambers range, where his daddy baked peach pies and fried fish, and with the two refrigerators, one full of bullet holes. A cypress tree grew up through the kitchen, and the roof was open above him where the great silver-trunked tree spread upwards, out into the summer air, and stretched its limbs and leaves like a canopy above him. During the long hard Delta rains, in April and September, the rain fell into the house and the floor was slick here for a month at a time and had to be mopped each day.

Down below, he heard the paddle and the little anchor make their familiar sounds, as his daddy secured the boat. For the first time in his life, he did not want his daddy to sing him to sleep. He thought of taking the boat out alone, in the dark middle of the night. He thought of floating far, far away.

He went into the room where his bed stood beside a screened wall. Cypress limbs outside brushed up against the screen. The room was called the sleeping-porch, and the bed was really a sort of divan, wide and flat and comfortable, not like the little army cot at William Tell. His daddy kept clean sheets on the bed, and big feather pillows with white pillow cases. There was a patchwork quilt somebody made, always pulled back and folded over in the summertime.

Hydro sat on the side of the bed and took off his shoes and looked at them, inspecting for blood stains, and saw none. He dropped each shoe on the floor, and then pulled off his socks, one at a time, from the toe, and stuffed them into his shoes. He kept on sitting there. He heard his daddy come up the ladder.

Mr. Raney said, "Good night, son."

Hydro looked at him.

Mr. Raney said, "I wouldn't worry too much about Morgan killing them two lovely children, if I was you."

Hydro said, "I don't want no songs tonight." Nobody but Hydro knew who really killed the two lovely children. Everybody else thought it had to be the sharpshooter, the young gunslinger whose real name was Morgan. Nobody believed it could be sweet, simple Hydro. Mr. Raney brightened up some at the sound of his son's voice. He said, "Well, no, I wouldn't think so, sure wouldn't, I agree. You're too tired. It's been—well, it's been a long day." Hydro didn't say anything else. Mr. Raney said, "Well—" There was nothing left to say, nothing Mr. Raney could think of anyhow. Finally, he said, "You don't want no songs."

Hydro was still sitting on the divan-bed. He held up his hand in front of his face and looked at it in the moonlight that filtered through the screened wall. The right hand, the one that had held the gun. He inspected it, first one side and then the other. He was surprised at the long blunt-end fingers, the blue veins in the back, the creases in the palm. It was a man's hand. He had expected to see a child's hand, for some reason. He looked at the finger that had pulled the trigger. He put his hand to his nose and breathed in, to discover its smell. There was nothing. No gunpowder, no death, no sex. What had happened tonight? What was that ancient noise inside his head?

He held up the other hand, the left hand, and inspected it as well. He compared the two, to see whether there was any difference. One hand had killed a boy and a girl, the other hand—well, where had it been? It might as well have been on another planet, as far as Hydro remembered. He had forgotten he had another hand. His left hand had been invisible while the right did its bloody murder. And yet it looked just the same as the hand that had held the pistol. He could tell no difference, none at all. He wondered whether this was because of his atrophied brain, the fluid inside his skull. Sometimes he almost wished his daddy never had explained that part to him so good.

Far across the swamp Hydro listened for the sound of some voice that would tell him the secrets that others must already know, the whispered words that would explain what had happened to him this night, or about life and death and hope for the future, of which he believed there was none, or even African animals, and tree people, which he wasn't so sure he believed in neither.

He heard his daddy, first out in the kitchen, then at the other end of the fishshack, taking off his own shoes, getting ready for bed. Hydro thought about his mother. He tried to imagine her face, or at least her dress, or her arm, or hand, which never killed nobody, her little shoe.

But for all the stories he had heard of her—skinning a catfish, riding a wild horse, making fig preserves in jars with paraffin lids, reaching a hand in a bee tree for a honeycomb, knocking off a piece of tail in the afternoon, just for fun, stomping a rat, sewing on a button—he could not see her. She was not there. She never had been. He suddenly understood that he had no mother, that he never had had a mother, that he had never known her or seen her and never would know or see her, no matter how hard his daddy tried to keep her alive in their hearts. He was a motherless child. That was what he was today, just as he had been on the day of his birth. No matter how old he became, or how many people he killed, he would always be that, maybe always only that, a motherless child, all alone.

Maybe he even killed his mother, as tonight he had imagined killing his daddy, and as he had surely drawn a bead and, with a steady hand, fired bullets into the brains of the two lovely children, who, unlike himself, did have mothers somewhere who loved them and whose hearts broke for their absence, even before they knew what had happened to them, even before they received a phone call from a man who looked like a giant in the circus telling them that some big-headed idiot like himself had pulled the trigger of a gun, careless of their babies' health and safety, and selfishly, because he was so scared, had taken away their dear lives forever.

Hydro went to sleep then, a sudden, hard sleep; you wouldn't have thought he could have a dream in a sleep as deep and quick, but he did, and it was almost real. He didn't take off the rest of his clothes, he didn't even stretch out. He just leaned over onto the big pillows, with his feet still on the floor, and laid his big old head down, and dreamed his mama was a porpoise, swimming as graceful as a water angel in the bayou, and so Hydro tried to holler out to her from the boat, "I am all alone in the world, Mama," but the words got all scrambled up in his head and so what came out of his mouth was, "Cork is an export product of India," and then he woke up thinking about wild Indians and looseherds and the wild buffalo, and he screamed out loud and sent strange echoes through the swamp and woke up a parrot somewhere, far away, and he wished that he could die. The parrot screamed, "Bloody murder!"

He sat up in bed, then, and looked around the sleeping-porch and let his eyes get adjusted again to the moonlight, and finally he saw where he was, in his own home, in the fishhouse, and so he calmed down a little bit. He said, "Wild parrots cain't talk." He got up then and undressed and went back to bed and got under the sheet.

In a minute his daddy came in the room. He stood by the door and said, "Did you have a bad dream, peaches?"

Hydro was lying on his pillows, staring up through the roof. He said, "I killed them two lovely children, Daddy. I'm the one done the shooting at William Tell."

His daddy was just wearing his drawers, nothing else. He walked over to the bed and sat beside Hydro.

He said, "Okay, peaches, okay, honey. You calm down. You just had a bad dream, that's all. Ain't nothing going to hurt my baby. It was all just a dream, just only a bad dream, that's all it was."

Hydro said, "It wont a dream."

Mr. Raney said, "Was you dreaming about parrots? I heard you hollering."

Hydro said, "No! It wont no dream. I done the murder. A wild parrot said I done it too, said, 'Murder!'"

Mr. Raney tried to take Hydro's hand, to stroke it, but Hydro pulled away. Mr. Raney said, "Maybe you need to go see Dr. McNaughton tomorrow, sweetening. Why don't we take the boat in and talk to the doctor tomorrow."

Hydro said, "I hate you! I hate you, I hate you!"

His daddy said, "Peaches—?"

He was screaming. He was crying. He was crying his guts out. Mr. Raney hadn't seen his son lose control like this for a long time.

His daddy said, "Let me sing you a couple of tunes. How about I sing you a verse or two of 'Sixty Minute Man,' darling, see don't it calm you down a little bit."

Hydro said, "The Prince of Darkness ain't no madman. The Prince of Darkness is the onliest person in town what'll say the truth. I'll live forever with the blood of them two lovely children on my hands and wont nobody even let on that I done it."

His daddy's voice was tinny and thin with grief and confusion. He sang, *There'll be fifteen minutes of squeezin', and fifteen minutes of teasin'* . . .

At the mention of sex, Hydro began to scream. He screamed and screamed, like his daddy had never heard, not even in the old days before the medication. Hydro screamed and kept on screaming. He would not be comforted.

His daddy said, "Oh baby, oh sweet baby—"

The screaming went on. It got worse. The lake echoed with Hydro's screams. Swamp animals woke up, in their dens and nests. Parrots and jungle birds screamed back. Monkeys chattered in the trees.

Mr. Raney said, "Oh baby, oh gentle boy, oh honey-lamb—"

Hydro would not be consoled. He listened to nothing, heard nothing.

Mr. Raney tried to sing to calm him. He sang "Salty Dog," he sang "Candy Man," he sang "Honey Hush."

Hydro stopped screaming. He looked at his daddy. The glare in his eyes was as violent as a spotlight. His daddy shut his mouth, in fear and amazement. The silence was long; it was more frightening than the screaming.

Hydro said, "Shut your stupid mouth, you stupid moth-erfucker, you stupid son-of-a-bitch."

Mr. Raney said, "Oh, punkin—"

Hydro said, "Morgan ain't killed nobody. Morgan has got too much hope in his heart to be killing nobody. I'm hope-less. I might shoot somebody else. My pitcher ought to be up on the wall in the post office. I ought to have my very own wanted poster. Somebody ought to be offering a reward."

Mr. Raney said, "I'll just lay down here beside you till you can drop off again. I won't sing no more songs, I promise. I'll be here, I'll just be laying here, in case you have another bad dream. Marshal Webber Chisholm has some bad dreams, too. Did you know that?"

Hydro was finished. Now he only cried. He cried for a long time without stopping. Deep sobs, and lots of tears, and then more quietly. He got snot all over his pillowcase. Finally he quit a little bit.

He just kept lying there. He pulled the pillow over his head. Mr. Raney didn't know what to do, what to say. A long time passed.

Finally Hydro did speak. He said, "Marshal Chisholm does?"

It caught Mr. Raney a little by surprise; then he said, "Well, sure now. Webber Chisholm suffers turrible from nightmares. I hate to think about how he's doing tonight. He's tossing and turning. He's crying just like you. The Prince of Darkness probably made him wash them lovely children's hair tonight. At least you didn't have to wash their hair."

Hydro lay still. He whimpered a little, and every now and then he flinched and sucked in a quick breath, but it was mostly over now. Mr. Raney went into the next room to get him his medication and a glass of water.

When he came back, he said, "You close your eyes, sweetening. You drift on off to sleep, if you can. I'll stay here, I'll be right here all night, you just wake me up if you want to talk, if you get scared."

Hydro stretched out on the divan and turned over on his side, away from Mr. Raney.

Mr. Raney sang in his low, gravelly voice, *I'm drinking TNT, I'm smoking dynamite—*

After a while Mr. Raney thought Hydro must be asleep, so he eased out of the bed and went into a farther room, where he dropped off to sleep, content in the belief that when he woke up, he would see the morning sun, and know what to say to his boy.

2

Before Hydro killed the two lovely children, he had been having a pretty good day, this one day, a Sunday, excellent in fact. Hydro was about twenty and didn't have real good sense, but he did a pretty good job looking after Mr. William Tell's store. Mr. William Tell said he couldn't complain. First thing he did the day of the killing, even before his friend Louis got there, was he ate a peach pie, the whole thing, with a big steel spoon, which his daddy packed in his lunch bucket. Deep dish, crust tough as a saddle. Fresh peaches, too, grown on stunted little black peach trees out on the island, beyond the fishshack, gathered in peck-sized baskets.

Then, after Hydro ate his pie and rinsed off his spoon (wrenched it off, he said), he pumped a few gallons worth of red gas, one dollar two dollar, off and on, all day long, for whoever came by. He sold a few half-pints of Mr. William Tell's whiskey, some bonded, some white, including some potato whiskey that smelled like coal oil.

After that was when Hydro's best friend, little Louis McNaughton, came out to visit with him and read some comic books. Louis was not but ten years old and fat as a butterball, wore round pink-rimmed glasses. Louis was the doctor's boy. Louis could stay gone from home all day and nobody would miss him. Louis was back in the pantry, where Mr. William Tell stored the bootleg, sitting on the floor, reading old *Gerald McBoing Boings* and *Tales from the Crypt.* Nobody in Mississippi had a comic book collection that could beat Hydro's.

Hydro hollered, "Louis, you want some Dinty Moore?"

Dinty Moore stew was for special days only, like today. Confession day.

That's another reason this day looked like it was going to be a good one. Leonard Reel had come out to William Tell to confess his sins to Almighty God. Leonard Reel was an extra-fat melancholy man. He kept quails in a chicken house in his backyard and picked up truck drivers at the Shell station out by Fort Pemberton and usually wanted to kill himself after sex with them. It was a pretty good confession, first few times you heard it, but then it got tiresome after a while. That was Hydro's opinion, anyway.

Louis hollered, "Okay." He meant he would have some stew with Hydro and the others. Hydro knew Louis wouldn't be getting any supper at home, he might as well eat out here.

Hydro said, "But if you eat stew, you have to listen to Leonard confessing. It's one of Mr. William Tell's rules."

Louis said, "Is Mr. Magoo Gerald McBoing Boing's daddy or granddaddy or what?"

Preacher Roe was in the store, of course, to listen to Leonard confess. He wore a black shirt and backwards collar, almost like a Catholic. He was tall and smart and wore an eye patch.

Two blues singers were out at the William Tell for a while, Blue John Jackson, the big man, and The Rider, the albino. They said they were headed on over to the knife fight in Holcomb, they would have to skip the confession today.

Preacher Roe looked up. He said, "There's a knife fight in Holcomb?"

Hydro served up the stew and Leonard Reel confessed. There wasn't much to tell, but he gave it all he had. Leonard said he peeked in a shower stall and saw a truck driver lathering up. He drew the story out as well as he could, but there wasn't much more to it than that.

Preacher Roe looked a little disgusted. He said, "You mean to say all you did was peek at him?" He looked to Hydro like he would rather have been at the knife fight, if that's all he had to confess.

Before confession was over one more person showed up, Morgan, the sharpshooter, in the pickup he got when he was living down in Texas. Morgan was tiny as a midget, almost. He was a foundling, got raised up by a hoodoo woman, and it stunted his growth. He looked like a department store dummy, perfectly shaped. Nineteen years old, with yellow hair and rosy cheeks and red lips. Ever since he got back from Texas Morgan wore white shirts and a black leather vest and cowboy boots. He had stopped by the William Tell Grocery to pick up oil for his truck, it was smoking pretty bad.

Preacher Roe said, "Hey, Morgan."

Morgan just looked at him.

Preacher Roe said, "I don't guess you got anything you want to confess."

Morgan looked away, and so Preacher Roe dropped the subject.

Out behind William Tell, just beyond the back stoop, a sugarcane field stretched far out across the Delta, under the golden sun, all the way to the flatwoods. The sugarcane was fenced off from the backyard of the store by four strands of barbed wire. Large, kitelike birds circled high above the swamp. Hydro was having a good day.

After confession, the sharpshooter looked out the back door of the store across the sugarcane. There was a big watermelon sitting on the back porch of the store. He said, "Hydro, what'll you take for that watermelon?"

Hydro said, "That's Mr. William Tell's personal watermelon."

Morgan was carrying his silvery pistol in his hand.

Morgan said, "It'd be some good dessert, to top off that stew."

Morgan opened up his pistol, and the cylinder gate flipped out with what you might call a hush of oiled nickel. He checked to see was it loaded. Then he snapped the cylinder back into place.

Hydro said, "I guess it would, at that."

Morgan stuck his pistol in the front of his pants. He said, "That wasn't no real confession we just listened to, I hope y'all realize that."

Louis finished his stew and went back in the pantry to read some more comic books.

Leonard said, "Turn that light on in there, Louis, you going to put out your eyes, reading in the dark."

Preacher Roe said, "You're probably thinking about Mexican confession." He was talking to Morgan.

Morgan spun the pistol on his finger. He flipped it over to his left hand and spun it again. He shrugged and didn't say anything else.

Hydro picked up all the dirty plates and ran some water in the sink and squirted in some Joy and made it foam up.

Morgan asked if Hydro wanted to see some pistol-shooting.

Hydro said okay. He said his daddy, out on the island, loved to shoot a pistol in the house, it was one of his favorite things.

Everybody else thought watching some pistol-shooting would be okay, too, even Louis.

Morgan said, "I heard your daddy shoots the refrigerator. Don't it melt the ice cream?"

Hydro said, "He don't keep frozen goods in the one he shoots."

Somebody said sharpshooting was about the only thing that could tear Louis away from *Plastic Man*.

Louis McNaughton could hear them out there, from where he sat in the pantry. He had plenty of good reason to hate the sharpshooter, and everybody knew it, but Louis didn't say anything. He just laid his comic books aside and followed the others out the door.

Hydro went out in back of the store and lugged the watermelon down the steps, a big green-striped number, and dumped it into a wheelbarrow and rolled it over to the barbed-wire fence on the edge of the sugarcane field.

It took him a while, but he was finally able to wedge the melon between the top two strands of barbed wire, like the sharpshooter showed him. It just hung there in between the strands of wire. He pushed the wheelbarrow off a little to the side.

Morgan said, "I'll give you two bits for them cantaloupes I seen in the store."

Hydro went back inside for the cantaloupes.

Leonard Reel said, "Ain't you hot?" Talking to the preacher about his black shirt.

Preacher Roe said, "It's for the Lord."

Hydro came back outside with the cantaloupes. He looked across the sugarcane field in the direction of Roebuck Lake, where he knew his daddy was cleaning fish on the island, far away. He wished his daddy was here to see some trick-shooting. He missed his daddy when he was away from him too long.

Preacher Roe said, "That's a mighty fine looking pistol, Morgan. Truly it is. That would be a genuine Texas six-shooter, it looks like, now, wouldn't it?"

Morgan held the big pistol up and let the afternoon sunlight catch the chrome like a mirror. He twirled it on his finger.

He said, "It takes some practice."

Leonard said, "I wouldn't mind shooting a pistol like that myself."

Preacher Roe said, "You don't know the first thing about a pistol, Leonard."

Hydro's friend Louis, the little fat boy, pushed his glasses up on his nose. Louis said, "Let me hold that pistol."

Everybody looked at Louis. Morgan especially looked at him. He said, "Not today, Junior."

The sharpshooter turned to the others now. He told Hydro, "Balance one of them cantaloupes up on a fence post, down to the right of the watermelon. Just hold on to the other one."

Hydro put the cantaloupe on the fence post and walked back up on the porch with the other three men. Hydro said, "Is this going to be some trickshooting? Is this going to be some Wild West Show shooting, Morgan?"

Morgan spun the pistol so fast it looked like a hubcap. He said, "You know, I took that oil-burning pickup of mine away from a Mexican."

Everybody nodded their heads, they knew about it.

Hydro said, "Is this another confession?" Morgan didn't answer so he decided to shut up.

Leonard said, "You stole it from him?"

Nobody wanted to ask if he killed the Mexican.

Morgan said, "What's a wetback doing with a truck in the first place?"

The others nodded. That's right, sure is, right as rain. Hydro still thought it would make a fine confession.

There was no remembering Morgan's hand moving from his side, or the silvery pistol leaving his belt. Everybody was watching, even the boy, and especially Hydro, but they just didn't see it. There was no slow motion, or stop-action, none of the usual ways of seeing a thing that you can't see except in the memory of it. No blur, even, no glint of chrome in the afternoon light.

Only, one moment, Morgan standing at ease on the back porch, with his hands by his side and speaking of his truck, and the next moment a roar, an explosion of high caliber ammunition, and a streak of fire a foot long blazing out of the end of the barrel.

In Hydro's memory, the explosion in Morgan's hand was a single report, boom, like a cannon, loud enough to cause a lengthy echo and cause the circling birds overhead, above the sugarcane, to tilt in the air from the sound as it reached them, but in fact what he heard was not one shot but six, faster, closer together, than he could imagine a trigger being pulled twice, or even once, let alone six times in succession. Hydro stood there in amazement and love.

The first bullet hit the cantaloupe dead center, and before the spray of juice could even reach the outside air, the second bullet struck, and before the fissure in the cantaloupe rind could open up, the third bullet hit, and the little melon exploded, rind and meat and seeds and guts, and blew apart backwards into the sugarcane.

The other three shots hit the ponderous old green-striped watermelon, suspended above the earth in barbed wire, and broke it apart. It collapsed into a low ditch in three big ugly pieces, like a fat man falling down and breaking apart, the meat as red as guts. The big dark birds circling above the swamp, tilting at the sound of the gunfire, neither gained nor lost altitude, and only kept circling and circling above the trees and cane.

Hydro fell in love with the sharpshooter. He didn't love him as much as he loved his daddy, who shot the refrigerator for love and a memory of the heart; and Hydro's bones didn't ache for him the way they ached for his mama, who he never knew, a long time gone; and he didn't even love him as much as he loved Louis, the strange child who was the doctor's boy and who shared *Wonder Woman* and *Green Hornet*—but you couldn't watch anything as beautiful as two melons busting open and slick seeds blowing out into a sugarcane field without falling in love.

The sharpshooter released the cylinder and ejected the spent shells. He reached into his pants pocket and took six new cartridges from a small, green pasteboard box and reloaded the silvery handgun and put the little box of bullets back into his pocket.

He handed the spent casings to the child. He said, "Little souvenir for you, sport."

Louis took the bullet casings and stuck them in his pocket and rattled them like loose change and suppressed his hatred of the sharpshooter.

Nobody said anything much for a few minutes. The sharpshooter put the gun back in the front of his pants. Hydro was still holding onto the second cantaloupe, shifting it in his hands, first one hand and then the other. He wanted to say something to the sharpshooter, to ask him the meaning of guns, or of love, but even Hydro knew he didn't have good sense and wouldn't have no idea what to say, what was the right question to ask.

After a while Preacher Roe stepped down off the porch and walked out to the fence where the pieces of the striped melon lay. He took a Barlow knife out of his pocket and bent over and cut a big hunk of heart out of the busted melon and scraped the seeds off with the blade and then wiped the blade on his pants.

He put a piece of melon in his mouth and the juice ran down his chin. He said, "Sweet as sugar candy." He cut out another hunk and brought it over to Louis.

Leonard Reel stepped down off the porch then. He said, "Long as you got your knife out, Preacher Roe, why don't you cut me off a stalk of that cane?"

Preacher Roe reached his arm through the barbed wire as far out as he could and snagged a stalk of sugarcane and bent it towards him. When it was bent down pretty good, he cut through it with his Barlow knife and pulled the whole stalk back through the fence.

He cut off a length of cane about six inches long and stripped away the hard green bark and handed it to Leonard.

Leonard chewed and sucked on the cane.

Preacher Roe said, "Don't let that sugarcane be reminding you of nothing Leonard."

The two men smiled together at the small joke. Leonard held up the shank of cane. He said, "I ain't going to need to confess over this."

The men were quiet for a while. Louis's hands were sticky from the melon. Leonard offered a stalk of sugarcane to Louis, but he shook his head.

In a minute, Morgan said, "Hydro, stand out yonder by the fence."

Hydro would do anything Morgan told him. He didn't even say, "How come?"

Hydro walked down the steps, off the porch, and stood out by the fence. He was still carrying the second cantaloupe.

Morgan said, "See can you balance that lope up on your old melon head."

Hydro said, "Balance it?"

Morgan said, "Go on."

Hydro lifted the cantaloupe up and put it on top of his head, but it wouldn't stay. When he started to let go of it with his hand, it rolled off. He had to catch it and try again.

Hydro said, "It's kindly round-bottomed."

Morgan said, "Don't drop it."

Hydro stood out by the fence holding the cantaloupe on his head with one hand. His other hand hung down by his side.

He said, "You are a crack shot, ain't you, Morgan?"

Morgan took out his pistol. He looked at Leonard, and then he looked at Preacher Roe.

He said, "I don't know which one of them melons to aim at, the one on top or the one on bottom."

The four men chuckled a little, Hydro too. Hydro didn't mind being the butt of a joke, now and then. It was all part of a good day, today.

Hydro said, "I'd say the one on top."

The men laughed again, and Hydro realized he had made a joke.

The sharpshooter turned to the others. He said, "Who wants first shot?"

Preacher Roe and Leonard just stood there.

Morgan looked at Leonard. He said, "Have you ever shot a pistol?"

Leonard said, "Well, no."

Morgan held out the pistol for him to take. He said, "Hold it with both hands, then. To steady it good."

The pistol passed between the two men, and Leonard stood there holding it.

Morgan said, "Go on."

Leonard said, "Go on?"

Preacher Roe said, "Be careful. Aim a little high, maybe, just to be safe."

Leonard said, "You want me to—?" He looked out at Hydro, with the cantaloupe on his head.

Hydro called, "Try not to shoot me in the head."

Leonard held the pistol out in front of him with both hands.

He cut his eyes over at Morgan, and then looked back at Hydro. He said, "You know what? This thing feels fine."

Preacher Roe said, "Aim a little high, Leonard. This might not be such a great idea."

Hydro called out again, "Try not to shoot me in the head, okay?"

Morgan said, "Cock back the hammer first."

Leonard did as he was instructed.

Just then the pistol went off. It sounded like a car running up on a metal bridge across the swamp, ba-rong.

Everybody looked at Hydro, who hadn't moved.

Morgan said, "Goddamn! Excuse my French, but give a person some warning."

Hydro was still holding the cantaloupe on his head.

Morgan said, "Lemme see that gun, Leonard."

Just then Leonard cocked the pistol, held it out in front of him again, and fired off another shot.

The men looked at Hydro again. He still hadn't moved.

Hydro said, "I heard that one in the air, it come whizzing past my ear."

The sharpshooter took the pistol from Leonard.

Leonard said, "That's pretty good for a first try."

Preacher Roe said, "Beginner's luck."

Morgan handed the pistol to Preacher Roe.

Preacher Roe took it and held it in his hand for a minute. He said, "It's warm as toast."

Morgan said, "Your turn, Preacher."

Preacher Roe said, "I never claimed I could hit anything with a pistol."

He held the heavy pistol out in front of him. Hydro smiled like he was having his picture taken. The preacher pulled the trigger, one time, two times, blam, blam, and missed both times.

Hydro kept standing by the fence. He called out, "My arm's getting tired."

Leonard said, "Did you hear the bullets, Hydro?"

Hydro said, "No, sure didn't."

Leonard gave the preacher a look. Preacher Roe said, "I aimed a little high, just to be safe."

Morgan took the gun away from Preacher Roe.

Morgan walked out to where Hydro was standing. He said, "Okay, Hydro, give it here."

Hydro took the cantaloupe off his head and held it in front of him in both hands, like a bowling ball.

He said, "My arm was getting tired."

He handed the cantaloupe to the sharpshooter. Morgan took the melon and handed the pistol to Hydro.

Morgan said, "You shoot it."

Morgan bent over and pounded one end of the cantaloupe down on the ground and flattened it. He put it up on his head and held it for a minute until it stayed. He stood out by the fence with the lope balanced up on his head. Morgan was so short the canteloupe made him look normal height.

Hydro said, "Me?"

He said, "Get back over there by the porch."

Hydro walked over to the porch and turned back around, with the pistol dangling by his side.

Hydro said, "Morgan—"

The sharpshooter shouted, "What?"

He said, "I don't think I want to do this."

Morgan yelled, "Shoot it." Hydro started to raise the gun, then dropped his hand by his side again.

Morgan shouted, "There is no hope, Hydro. Do it because we're all alone in the world."

Hydro said, "Don't talk like that, Morgan. Please don't."

Morgan yelled, "Do it because your daddy's going to die some day. Do it because you won't ever see him again, you won't be able to live at the fishcamp."

Hydro raised the pistol out in front of him and cocked the hammer. He had started to cry. The gun was heavy but it did not tremble in his hands.

He said, "Don't tell me bad things, Morgan."

Morgan yelled, "Do it, Hydro. Shoot the fucking cantaloupe. Shoot it now."

Leonard and Preacher Roe weren't even watching as the cantaloupe exploded on Morgan's head, seeds and meat and rind. They were already walking back inside the store. They might play some checkers. Mr. William Tell had Chinese checkers, if Hydro hadn't lost all the marbles.

Louis was watching, though, the child. Louis was transfixed. He saw everything, surface and core. He watched as the big chrome revolver jumped in Hydro's hand, fire and white smoke from the barrel, cordite in his nostrils. He watched as the melon took the bullet into itself like oxygen into healthy lungs, took it like milk into a baby's mouth from a mother's breast, swallowed it and made it a good part of its good self.

The melon blew backwards off of Morgan's head, weightless almost, as if it had been a dustbunny swept away with a straw broom. Louis knew, without knowing, that the power of bullets was meaningless illusion, like movies, like card tricks and ventriloquism. Cantaloupe parts went everywhere, meat and seed and rind and sugar water, a million droplets, fragments, into the air. The air around Morgan's head, where the cantaloupe burst, was like a golden aura, a halo of cantaloupe juice.

Morgan didn't even look back at the cantaloupe, where it lay in the weeds behind him. He walked to Hydro and took the pistol and shucked out the empties and handed them to

Louis and reloaded and stuck the pistol back in his pants. He grabbed the bottom of the leather vest with his hands and snapped it like a whip.

He said to Louis, the little fat boy with pink-rimmed glasses, "Hydro can shoot like a motherfucker, cain't he, four-eyes?"

THAT WAS all that happened for a while. Later on, after the sun went down, Hydro turned on a light out by the pumps. Morgan's truck needed four quarts of oil. The four men and Louis stood together in the driveway while Hydro raised the hood and filled up the crankcase. Louis thought of his mother and father and his little sister Katy at home. Hydro thought of his daddy, out on the island at the fishcamp. Hydro didn't hold it against Morgan for talking so mean, for saying those things about his daddy dying. He knew it was just a way of talking, just a way of wishing you were dead.

Morgan walked around his truck, kicking his tires, hanging around. He wiped off his hands on Hydro's oily rag and handed it back to Hydro.

He said, "One time, late at night, I went in this diner, down in El Paso."

Hydro loved to hear a story. He said, "What's a diner?"

Preacher Roe said, "It's like a café in a streetcar."

Hydro said, "What's a streetcar?"

Preacher Roe said, "Hush up, Hydro."

Morgan walked around in back of the truck. He said,

"I'm going to pump me two dollars' worth of red gas, while I'm at it."

Leonard said, "You need to get out more, Hydro. Get your daddy to take you to Greenville some time."

Hydro checked the dipstick one more time and slipped it back in the tube. He screwed the crankcase cap back in place and slammed down the hood. He wiped his hands on an oily rag and went back and took the hose from Morgan and pumped the gas.

The day was about over. Preacher Roe said, "Well, I got to be going. You coming with me, Leonard?"

Leonard said to Morgan, "What about the diner in El Paso? You're not going to leave us hanging, now are you?"

Morgan said, "It was this boy and girl, sitting together in a booth. That's all. That's all I meant to say. They were just sitting there, eating tortillas."

Leonard said, "Hydro, don't go asking what a tortilla is. I mean it."

Preacher Roe said, "I got to be moving on down the line. Thanks for the Dinty Moore, Hydro. Let's go, Leonard. You coming or not?"

Leonard said, "Are you sleeping out here at William Tell these days, Hydro?"

Hydro said, "Mostly weekends."

Preacher Roe said, "Mr. William Tell, he's good to you, isn't he?"

Hydro said, "He's okay."

Leonard said, "Yeah, I'm coming. I got to go feed my quails. They'll be wondering where I'm at, about now."

Preacher Roe said, "Well, get in the car, then. Let's go. I'll drive you by the house."

Preacher Roe said, "Flies'll be getting in that watermelon, out by the fence."

Hydro said, "I'll clean it up. I'll bury it in the sugarcane field."

Leonard said, "Bye."

Preacher Roe said, "Leonard, we all loved the part about you sneaking a look at that truck driver in the Shell station showers."

Hydro said, "I liked the part where you wanted to die. That was my favorite."

Preacher Roe said, "Okay, y'all take it easy, we're taking off now."

Preacher Roe and Leonard drove off in the preacher's car. The others watched it move on down the road, out of sight.

Morgan turned to the little boy. He said, "Get in the truck, short stuff. I'll drop you off at your house. I know where you live."

Hydro said, "Ain't you going stay out here with me, Louis? I got *Gerald McBoing Boing*."

Morgan said, "Ain't no skin off my ass."

The truck was smoking when it pulled away, up the gravel drive towards the highway. Through the rear window you could just barely see the back of the sharpshooter's head, he sat so low in the seat.

Louis said, "You got the new *Gerald McBoing Boing*?"

Hydro said, "Did you get enough supper? I got some hot tamales and crackers, if you're still hungry."

3

The sun had set now. Supper dishes were stacked in the sink, the hotplate was unplugged, like Mr. William Tell showed Hydro he must always do. Hydro was standing out by the pumps looking across the sugarcane fields. The Delta sky was streaked with red and gold. Louis was inside William Tell, sitting on the floor of the pantry, reading *Mr. Magoo*.

Hydro went in the store and mashed the No Sale key and opened up the cash drawer of the register and pulled out the bills and counted them and turned them so the faces were all looking out in the same direction, like Mr. Tell showed him, and smoothed them flat with his hand.

He said, "Louis, you doing okay?"

Louis said, "Uh-huh." He sounded like he was in a cave, back in the pantry, with the groceries and whiskey and the broom and the mop and dustpan and buckets.

Hydro counted up the change and wrote down the numbers on a little pad with the date. He folded the bills up and bound them with a rubber band and put the heavy change in a leather pouch with a drawstring and then stuck them both in a metal cash box with a lock and key and put the strongbox in the false bottom of a steamer trunk. He felt like a regular storekeeper. Mr. Tell was nice as he could be, but particular about his money. He told Hydro, "Don't let nobody steal my money."

Back behind the counter Hydro reached up and pulled a string on a light cord and a bare light bulb blazed on, no telling how many watts, and sent shadows running all around the store. It was dark outside now.

Hydro took the shovel with him, out in back of the store, and crossed the fence into the sugarcane field, and spaded him a hole in the ground between cane rows and shoveled the watermelon and the cantaloupes into the hole and then put dirt on top again.

There were still a few things to do, though. He washed the few dishes and the pan he'd used to heat up the stew in, and put them on a rack to dry, like Mr. Tell showed him.

He went up to the front of the store and looked out the door to see was anybody coming. He pulled the door shut and shot the bolt, goodnight, Irene, I'll see you in my dreams. Sometimes Hydro's daddy came out and sang to him.

Hydro knew Louis had most of the *Gerald McBoing Boings* with him in the pantry, but that was all right. Hydro had him a stack of comic books up underneath his army cot, *Heckle and Jeckle* and *Little LuLu* and *Casper the Friendly Ghost*. He had some more in a bound trunk of Mr. William Tell's. He didn't keep scary comic books out at William Tell, *The Crypt* and *Ghoulish Tales*. Casper was scary enough for Hydro.

He looked in his basket to see was there another peach pie in there, but they wasn't. It was a shame, since all of his spoons were clean. He wondered if Plastic Man wasn't Gerald McBoing Boing's daddy in real life. It did make sense, if you thought about it.

About the time Hydro got good and settled in, though, here came somebody up the gravel driveway in a car, a 1953 Mercury with Hollywood mufflers and headlights blaring all through the front windows. Happy Hour's done come and went, he hoped whoever it was understood that.

He listened to the car stop and to the deep throat of the glasspacks shut down, out by the pumps. Hydro walked out into the front part of the store and peeped out the window to see who it was.

When he saw them, all dressed up in black like they was, girl and a boy, he thought, Well I declare. What are them two doing in Arrow Catcher, Mississippi? He couldn't believe his own two eyes. This must be Morgan's Texas friends, from the diner.

Hydro stood beside the front window, real quiet, just watching them. The boy flung his door open and got out of the car and stood there. He stretched himself real good. He walked back and forth in the gravel a little bit and looked at the gas pump and then said something back into the car, to the girl in there.

The boy was dressed in a baggy black suit of some kind, looked like a zoot suit, with blousey legs and wide lapels. He had his hair well-greased and slicked back like a Mexican.

Hydro wished he could tell what they were talking about. He once read a little bitty advertisement about a lip-reading school. You could order lip-reading lessons by mail from the back of a *Gerald McBoing Boing* comic book. He wished now he'd written off for it.

He'd ordered plenty of other things, including a ventriloquist's dummy that he named Joseph of Arimethea, but he never could make it talk, so he traded it to old Mr. O'Kelly in Arrow Catcher for one of his soap carvings of wild animals. He got him a yellow Dial soap lion but forgot and left it out in the rain and it foamed up and melted and got ruined. You couldn't tell if it was a lion or a dog. Now poor old Mr. O'Kelly believed Joseph of Arimethea was his grandson. Ain't you glad you use Dial soap? Don't you wish ever-body did?

The other door of the car opened up and the girl stepped out in the gravel and stretched herself, too. The girl was dressed up in black, same as the boy, hot as it was, and had red lips.

Black skirt, black turtleneck, black stockings, even a little black hat of some kind, although Hydro couldn't think of the name for her hat. What was it called? It might be a boo-ray, or maybe boo-kay, something another.

Hydro shot the bolt and opened the front door to greet them. It startled them a little bit, looked like.

Hydro said, "I ain't got no tortillas. We plumb out of tortillas." He thought he'd bring up the subject real gradual, then pop the question: What is a tortilla, anyhow?

The boy and girl looked at each other, and then back at Hydro.

Hydro said, "Morgan ain't here. He's done already went home."

For a while the boy and girl still didn't talk.

The boy said, "Let me see if I have this straight. You ain't got no tortillas and Morgan has done gone home."

The girl with the red lips giggled when he said this.

Hydro said, "That's it, that's right."

The girl said, "You open?"

Hydro said, "I was just fixing to read *Heckle and Jeckle*."

The boy said, "We need some gas. Pump us some gas."

Hydro said, "Oh. Okay."

He went out to the car and took the hose off the pump.

He said, "How much?"

The boy said, "Fill it up."

Hydro never had filled up a tank all the way to the top before. He was more used to selling gas in one-dollar two-dollar installments. Sometimes one-gallon, two-gallon.

Hydro said, "Say which?"

The boy gave him a look. Then he turned away and talked to the girl some more.

When the tank was full, Hydro was amazed at how much it cost. He never had seen such a big gas bill.

The boy opened up the screened door of the store and went on in, uninvited, while Hydro was still out by the pump. The girl followed him inside.

Well, Mr. Tell wouldn't like it, strangers inside the store while he was out at the pumps, but Hydro guessed it was all right this one time.

Hydro wiped off the windows with a rag and checked the oil and checked the radiator and the air pressure in the tires.

He remembered a couple of cans of hot tamales on the shelf in the pantry. He'd have to disturb Louis. That boy ought to be headed on home, anyway; it was after dark. So, anyway, he could fix them the tamales, fire up the hot plate, if they wanted it. Maybe open up some saltines and a bottle of Tabasco sauce.

When Hydro walked inside the store to explain about the tamales and saltines, the boy and girl were standing behind the counter with the cash drawer of the register wide open. They looked up when he came inside.

The girl said, "Where is the money?"

Hydro said, "I won't charge y'all what the pump says. It's too much. A couple of dollars ought to about cover it."

Hydro came walking on up to the counter where they were standing.

The next time the girl spoke, she was holding a pistol in Hydro's face.

She said, "Listen to me, you fucking moron."

Hydro said, "I shot a lope off Morgan's head because I'm so hopeless. We all are."

The girl said, "You're hopeless all right."

The boy said, "Where do you keep the money? We know you've got money in here somewhere."

The girl said, "I'm just aching to cover these walls with hair."

Hydro said, "Hair?"

WILLIAM TELL was way out in the country, beneath starry-starry skies, and between wide Delta fields of fragrant sugar-cane, and so on a Sunday night, when the roads were all quiet except for a pulpwood truck crossing between Money and the river, where the wood would be loaded onto a barge and floated down to Vicksburg to a papermill, or New Orleans, and the sun had gone down and the golden moon was just beginning to rise up out of the gum and cypress trees in the loblollies in the flatwoods, you could hear far away, if the wind was just right, like it was tonight, the big farm bell ringing vespers in the parish yard of St. George by the Lake, a deep clear distant sound, like a dream, or a memory, or a prayer.

Hydro was listening to this sweet music while looking down a gun barrel at the counter of William Tell Grocery, as the big yellow light bulb above his cot swayed and cast comic shadows across the faces of Gerald McBoing Boing and Mr. McGoo and the bare boards of the floor. Back in the darkness, down at the end of the gun barrel, Hydro thought he could see his mama, who was a long time dead.

AND HYDRO'S daddy, Mr. Raney, far away, out at the fish-camp on the island in Roebuck Lake, beneath the same rising moon, heard the Sunday music, too, just as Hydro was hearing it.

Mr. Raney was cleaning fish, out on the island, where the fishhouse stood. The lake below him, where he looked down between his feet, through worn planks, was like a black mirror catching gold and silver traces of lamp light from the pier and moonlight and starlight from the sky.

Each fish in its turn Mr. Raney laid on the cleaning table beneath his knife and bore down and took the head off with a single stroke and a soft crush of severed bone. He turned each fish, and split it up the bottom, from the tail to the head, and reached into the cavity with his fingers and brought out the bright guts and eggs and slung them off his fingers, over the rail and into the water.

With the knife blade then, he scrape-scrape-scraped a fish, first one side and then the other, until it was clean of scales, and then dropped it into a great tub of chipped ice with the other cleaned fish. His arms were covered with the scales of crappie and bluegill, and in the moonlight they looked like silver.

He thought about taking a small mess of fish out to Hydro at William Tell. They could dig a pit out in back of the store and open a can of lard and a bag of cornmeal and chop up an onion and stir up a batch of hushpuppies and have a regular fish fry. He could sing a song or two.

Well, no, not tonight. It was late. Hydro had already eaten, probably. But maybe it wasn't too late to go out and sing to him, though. Maybe that's what he would do instead.

HYDRO SAID, "Y'all ain't from El Paso, are you?"

The boy said, "He saw the Texas plates."

The girl said, "He won't be talking to anybody."

She cocked the hammer of the pistol.

She said, "Where do you hide the money?"

Hydro said, "In the trunk."

She said, "In the trunk?"

He said, "Mr. Tell's trunk, over yonder."

The boy said, "Open it up."

Hydro walked over to the trunk and unbuckled the belts around it and opened the latches.

When it was open, the three of them stood looking at Hydro's stash of comic books.

Hydro said, "Plastic Man is Gerald McBoing Boing's daddy. It's a theory I've got."

The boy took the pistol away from the girl and held it to Hydro's head.

He said, "Listen here. We want the money. Where is it?"

Hydro said, "Pull out the shelf. It's got a bottom up underneath the bottom."

The boy said, "You pull it out."

Before Hydro could move, the girl ripped the comic books out of the top of the trunk and flung them all over the store. She jerked the false bottom out of the trunk and revealed the roll of bills and the bag of change.

Back in the pantry, Louis heard this and laid down his comic book and peeked around the edge of the half-open door.

The girl said, "Jackpot."

Hydro looked around at the comic books, where they lay in pieces on the floor. Louis eased the door shut and stepped back inside the pantry. He saw the pistol the boy was holding. He reached up and turned the switch on a hanging light bulb and made the pantry dark. He listened at the door again.

Hydro said, "Mr. McGoo ain't Gerald's daddy. Some people might say he is, but he ain't."

The girl took the money out of the trunk and snapped

the rubber band off the roll. She wet her thumb and peeled off bills, counting them.

She said, "There's a lot of money in bootlegging, looks like."

The boy said, "Get a couple of cases of whiskey and some food while you're at it."

The girl said, "You get it."

The boy was still holding the gun. He looked at her.

She threw the roll of loose bills down in the bottom of the trunk and dropped the bag of silver down beside them. She picked up a clean croaker sack from a stack and started raking canned goods off the shelves into it. She took peanut butter and cheese and sardines, too. She found a drawer with ammunition in it, and picked out all the boxes of .38 caliber cartridges and put them in the sack.

Hydro said, "That Dinty Moore is extra tasty."

The boy said, "Have you got a shovel?"

Hydro said, "I buried a watermelon this evening."

The boy said, "You going to be burying something bigger than a watermelon tonight."

Louis eased back inside the pantry again and tried to make his breathing more regular.

The girl said, "Have you got a can opener?"

Hydro said, "Yessum."

He reached in a drawer and pulled out the can opener.

The boy fidgeted with the pistol. He was nervous watching Hydro open a drawer.

Hydro handed the can opener over to the girl.

She took it out of his hand.

She said, "We ain't got time to be digging a hole."

She took a loaf of bread and some cold beers and that filled up the second croaker sack.

She said, "Bring the money. And the whiskey. I can't carry a case of whiskey and all these groceries."

The boy followed her out of the store, both of them loaded down, and they put the supplies in the trunk of the car.

Hydro followed them out the front door and tagged along out to the car.

Louis stayed in the pantry. He didn't know what to do.

Hydro said, "I never did understand what a streetcar was."

The girl slammed the trunk shut and looked at Hydro.

She said, "A streetcar?"

Hydro said, "Look like all cars are streetcars."

The girl and the boy looked at each other.

The boy said, "Let's do it. We got to get out of here."

The girl said, "Can a big-headed idiot like this get it up, do you suppose?"

The boy said, "If we don't have time to dig a grave, we sure as hell don't have no time for you to be pulling down your pants for this fool."

The girl said to Hydro, "Do you know what sex is?"

Hydro said, "A grave?"

The boy said, "Let's go. I'll take him out back and do it, and then we'll go." He said to Hydro, "Get back in the store. Get moving, right now."

The girl said, "I'll do it."

The boy stopped. He said, "You want to do it?"

She said, "Give me the gun. I'll do it."

The boy handed over the gun.

He said, "What else are you going to do?"

She said, "You wait in the car."

He said, "We don't have time for this, Cheryl."

She said, "You've given him my name and address, why don't you give him my telephone number, too."

He said, "We got to get moving."

She said, "You keep watch over these groceries. Me and Gerald McBoing Boing here got some talking to do."

He said, "Be sure he's dead."

MR. RANEY finished up work out on the pier and turned on the water at the spigot and stuck his hands and arms up under the stream and let the fish scales wash away. Up on the railing there was a thin red sliver of Lifebuoy soap, which he took and lathered up under the cold water as well as he could and used that to wash off more of the scales and fish slime.

When he was finished he slung the water off his hands and was careful not to wipe his hands on his overalls, so he wouldn't have to start all over washing them again. He went inside the fishhouse then, and stepped out of his boots and then out of the overalls and hung them on a nail and pulled on his regular boots, the brogans. He was wearing clean khakis and a white shirt underneath his overalls. He checked himself in a cracked piece of mirror hanging up on the fishhouse wall and ran his fingers through what was left of his hair.

He had a little pistol that he kept on the sideboard, .25

caliber, so he picked it up now and fired off a couple of shots into the refrigerator, up against the wall. It was an old refrigerator, unplugged, worthless. Shooting it once or twice a day was just something Mr. Raney liked to do. It relaxed him, made him remember the old days, when his mama and daddy were still alive.

He had one more peach pie in the good refrigerator, the one that worked, so he took the pie out and put it in a burlap bag and stuck the pan of newly cleaned fish in the lower part of the icebox and then switched off all the lights in the fishhouse and headed down the stairs to the landing. It wouldn't hurt Hydro to have an extra peach pie on hand, if he woke up hungry.

Darkness had fallen across the Delta, and it was especially dark down on the landing, near the boats and under the trees, where the moon didn't shed much light, but Mr. Raney knew the way, he didn't stumble. There was a board sidewalk, made out of washed-out, silver-gray two-by-fours, down to the water, onto the dock. Sometimes it was slick, but not tonight.

He made his way along the walk, in the dark, carrying the peach pie in the sack. He might sing "Rescue the Perishing" to Hydro. It was Sunday, after all. Maybe not. Hydro wasn't partial to church music. He might sing "Money Honey" or "Sixty Minute Man" instead.

He knew where the boat was, the one he would take through the bayou over to the mainland, the leaky old wood boat with nets and poles and tackle boxes and his daddy's little motor on the back. It was dark, dark down by the water.

He couldn't see much. He said, "Where are you, boat?"
He bent down and felt around in the dark, this way and that
way, until he found the bow. He said, "Here you are."

He pulled it up alongside the landing and stepped in the
front end. He unwound the rope from a spar on a creosoted
post and picked up a Feather paddle in the bottom of the
boat and poled along in the shallow water until he couldn't
reach bottom anymore, then he sculled behind the boat with
the paddle.

The dark lake water buoyed him up and lapped softly
against the gunwales, as he drifted backwards into the
moonlight and rocked back and forth like a baby in a cradle.

He found the pull-rope for the little Evinrude engine,
down in the floorboards, and wrapped it around the crankshaft, one-two-three, and set the throttle and pulled out the
choke and leaned back and gave the rope a good yank.

The little motor started up on the first pull, putt-putt-
putt, rattle-rattle-rattle. A fragrant, familiar mixture of warm
oil and gasoline filled his nostrils.

Mr. Raney turned the bow out into the bayou and
pushed the throttle over to High and set out in a cloud of
oily smoke, slow as a turtle, under the moon and stars,
across the swamp and towards the Runnymede bridge and
town.

In the narrow channel he had to steer a little. He slid
around a cypress knee, he avoided a stob sticking up out of
a bream bed, he slid alongside a trotline and didn't get it
tangled up in the propeller.

Then, out in the wide bayou, he drifted past a log filled

with sleeping turtles, past alligator nests and snowy egrets and blue herons sleeping on one foot out in the bulrushes and willows, a water moccasin swimming, gar rolling in the moonlight.

For a little while two small dolphins slid in alongside the boat and swam as slow as he was going. Then they swam far out from the boat, they rolled like wheels and showed their oily humps, they dived, they disappeared, they surfaced near him, they swam in circles around him, and then they were gone.

In a minute he saw the Roebuck bridge, and then before long he was tying his boat to one of the stanchions, and laying the pie on the front seat of his pickup truck, which he left up on Harper's Road every day where nobody ever bothered it.

He reached up under the seat and found the ignition key, right where he left it, and started up his truck and headed out Highway 49 to William Tell.

THE BOY in the zoot suit saw the lights of Mr. Raney's truck coming, as it pulled off the highway and headed down the gravel road to the store.

He said, "Shit."

He flung open the car door and went running up past the gas pumps and then up the steps and inside William Tell.

He said, "Somebody's coming."

Cheryl was naked, standing beside the cot where Hydro lay. Hydro was naked too, not looking at her, or at anything.

Louis could see this from behind the pantry door. He was

trembling. He took off his little pink-rimmed glasses and cleaned the lenses on his shirt and put them back on. He stared at Cheryl. The sight of her nakedness, this girl's flesh and bones, her milky skin, her skeleton-thin frame and tiny breasts, the wide, womanly patch of hair between her legs, broke his heart. He tried to ease away from the door again, but he was so nervous he pushed too hard and it closed with a click of the lock.

The boy in the zoot suit looked up.

Cheryl was holding the pistol to Hydro's head, his temple, where he lay on the cot. The hammer of the pistol was cocked.

She turned away from Hydro and looked at the boy in the zoot suit.

She said, "What?"

He said, "Did you hear something?"

She said, "What?"

Louis was standing in black darkness.

He said, "A truck. Somebody just pulled up, out front."

She said, "Shit."

She lowered the gun, and let the hammer down, real careful, with her thumb. She didn't dress yet, she only moved swiftly past the boy, around the counter.

She hurried across the store to the front window and looked out. There was somebody coming, all right. It was an old pickup, bouncing serenely down the road from the highway with its headlights jiggling.

She said, "Goddamn."

The boy trailed behind her to the window and looked

out, too, but now she was already gone, already moving. She raced back to the rear of the store. Louis could hear her standing just outside the closed pantry door. He knew she was naked. He was afraid she would try to hide in the pantry.

Hydro had not moved.

Cheryl laid the gun on a chair and started pulling on her clothes.

The boy said, "If you'd gone on and done it, we'd be out of here by now."

She said, "Put your clothes on." Talking to Hydro.

She grabbed up Hydro's pants and shirt and threw them in his face.

Hydro did not move, did not seem to have heard her.

She said, "Somebody's coming. Get moving. You're going to see who it is."

The truck stopped out in front of the store. The tires ground to a halt in the gravel when the brakes were applied, and then something in the bed of the truck seemed to shift forward, a toolbox or an ice chest, something heavy, and made a loud metallic sound when it did, a scraping, and then a thump, or clunk, when it stopped.

The girl said to Hydro, "Put your clothes on. Right now."

Hydro pulled on his pants, then his shirt.

Louis hoped to get one more look at the naked girl. He opened the pantry door again and peeked around the side.

Just then a light turned on in the little store, where Hydro and the boy and girl stood. The light was as bright as the sun. The whole store lit up. You never saw such an amazing and sudden light. It might as well have been the center ring of the bigtop at the Ringling Brothers and Barnum & Bailey Circus, it got so bright in that little grocery and whiskey store, William Tell. It was like the spotlight at the air show, one time, when two-winged cropdusters did loops and turns above the fairgrounds at night.

What an incredible and magical light, like sunshine! Louis felt almost good about his life, peeking around the doorjamb and seeing such a light. Cobwebs in the ceiling corners, the labels on soup cans, a broom that had been lost, misplaced, days before—everything became visible, all of a sudden. Nothing in that store was hidden anymore when that light turned on.

That's what seemed like had happened, when the first shot was fired. Not just Louis thought this, either. The boy in the zoot suit thought it, too. He thought somebody had turned on a bright light, or maybe that the sun had started to shine indoors all of a sudden.

Partly this was because a flame a foot long leaped out of the end of the gun barrel. It did provide a certain amount of sudden and unexpected illumination, that was the truth.

And partly, also, it was because only sudden light, or maybe sudden insight, was ever so startling as the sound of that elemental and unexpected explosion in this small room, especially in this well-dressed boy's mind, in his ringing ears.

Everything became suddenly so clear to him, so crystal clear. Things the boy had never understood were now, all of a sudden, plain as day, past and present, the meaning of life and death, how to break into show business. Suddenly, and for the first time, he understood the expression "This sheds a whole new light on things."

He turned just in time to see the back of Cheryl's head blow off and go flying past him, blood and hair and bone, and onto the wall of the store, in amongst the canned goods. Louis saw this, too. It was almost like Plastic Man's head was stretched halfway across the room. Cheryl didn't fall backwards, though, and not even forwards. Louis all of a sudden remembered that expression "fell in a heap." He remembered the expression "like a sack of potatoes." That was Cheryl. That was how she died. With a bullet between her eyes and her hair all over the walls and Vienna sausages, and then, flop, like a heap of potatoes.

Louis opened the pantry door all the way. He might as well get a good look at this. He wiped his glasses on his shirttail again, and then fitted the earpieces around his ears and pushed the glasses up on his nose.

The boy in the zoot suit imagined another bright light then, and more clear vision and lucid insights into the past and present and future, and for maybe one one-millionth of a second he thought he might have heard a repetition of the phrase "We are plumb out of tortillas."

And then he even imagined his own hair all over the walls, and another sack of potatoes in a heap, similar to Cheryl, but he may have been mistaken about most of this. In fact he probably was, because before he could have heard or seen anything like it, Hydro, the big-headed lover of peach pie who had just killed Cheryl, had already turned a few degrees to his left, in his hopeless way, and had already swung the pistol around, out in front of him, straight-armed. The hammer was already cocked again.

And in fact, the boy in the zoot suit was already dead with a bullet in his forehead, so there is little chance that he might have had these insights, no matter how clear they might have seemed. The boy in the zoot suit was dead before the light and shape of the foot-long flame of the second shot could have registered on his optical nerve; his brain pan was already resting among the canned corn beef and Dinty Moore and Campbell's pork and beans before any such insights or even firelight might have reached it for interpretation.

Louis saw it, though, and regretted that he had no one to tell this to. This was by far the most interesting thing that he had ever seen, and it seemed to him impossible that the sight of it would not ruin his whole life forever if he did not tell someone. He could tell his sister Katy, except just hearing it might ruin her life too, he supposed.

Hydro wondered how an elephant might feel at the end of a long day, after toting all that extra weight around with him. He's just got to be tired, don't he? That's how tired Hydro was. Tired as a durn elephant. He felt like his legs all by theyself must weight two three tons.

He was still holding the pistol out in front of him, but now he let his arm ease down, real slow, to his side. He turned again, another few degrees, and faced the front door of the store. The gun was just hanging there on his fingers for a minute, while Hydro let his breathing become regular.

It didn't fall, though, the pistol, he didn't let it drop to the floor.

Hydro was dressed, in a careless sort of way. He was still barefoot. Just standing there, with the gun dangling by his side, as if at ease. The whole store smelled like cordite and burned gunpowder. The air seemed thick with something, maybe smoke, maybe only portent. There was another smell, too—blood, he thought. He hadn't given the first thought to how much blood there would be when he pulled the trigger, let alone what it would smell like.

Hydro held onto the pistol and didn't let it fall out of his hand, because he wasn't quite done with it yet. He was about to use it one more time. He had heard the truck pull up out front. He didn't recognize the sound of it. Don't blame Hydro for not recognizing his daddy's pickup truck. He didn't recognize much of nothing. He was under a right smart amount of stress.

He didn't know who was coming up the drive, in the store. It could be anybody. It might be friends of the boy and the girl. Well, see, that was the thing. He wasn't planning on taking any chances. Hydro was fixing to shoot the next person who walked through the door of William Tell.

He heard the pickup door open and slam shut. He heard steps in the gravel. He heard boots on the wood steps. He cocked the pistol a third time and held it out in front of him, aimed at the door. Come right in, can I help you? We are plumb out of tortillas.

MR. RANEY, coming down the drive-road in his truck, had heard the two shots, loud, too. He saw the flash. It looked like lightning inside the store.

He was already pumping on the brakes, hoping he could get this sorry old truck stopped. Morgan or some of the other boys from Arrow Catcher must be out here visiting, keeping Hydro company, wasn't that nice. They were shooting up the store a bit, having some fun.

But even before that, before he heard the shots or saw the flash, Mr. Raney saw the boy in the black zoot suit, scurrying out of a strange car with Texas plates, and in through the front door of the store.

Well, wasn't that nice, too. You don't see many zoot suits in this modern day and age of ours. He might ask this boy for some fashion tips, pass them along to Hydro. You couldn't go wrong befriending a man in a zoot suit. That was Mr. Raney's own personal appraisal of the current fashion scene.

Then he saw what looked like two faces inside the front window of the store, neither of them Hydro.

Mr. Raney thought Hydro was pretty lucky to have friends with a pistol, every man needed a friend, it didn't matter how big his head was. A friend with a firearm was a special blessing. And a zoot suit! He couldn't remember the last time he saw one. Hydro himself would look mighty fine in an excellent suit of clothes like that.

Mr. Raney carried a gun, too, and not just the little .25 on the sideboard. A big gun, ten-inch barrel. He kept it in a locked toolbox out in the bed of his truck. So he knew first-hand the value of firepower in friendship.

Sometimes there was just nothing as satisfying as shooting a gun inside a house. It didn't have to involve a refrigerator. It relieved stress. It cemented relationships, strangers or partners in marriage. It helped most anybody, the least of these my brethren, as Preacher Roe might say. It cleared the air.

You wouldn't want to be careless with it, you wouldn't want to hurt anybody, but to fire a shot out your bedroom window, say, into a neighbor's garage, or in your own kitchen, into a large appliance, maybe, or just through the ceiling, when you were singing the blues, when you had lost your dear wife in childbirth and your only son had come out a waterhead, well, there was not a thing in the world to criticize about shooting off a pistol in that case, now was there, nothing but a good idea to spread a few rounds through the house, nail a few nails in the wall, so to speak, melt a little ice cream.

When Mr. Raney was a boy he worked behind the soda fountain in old Mr. Durham's drug store. There was a man back then named Childe Harold who Mr. Raney used to admire greatly, lived in Arrow Catcher in a house called The Green Door, for some reason, out near the dump.

Childe Harold was a fat man, with a long white beard, and sweated bad. He smelled like Korea, once he got started sweating. He wore a red bandanna around his neck, and for some unknown reason, he wore a silk stocking tied around one ankle.

Every day when Childe Harold came into the drug store, with Red Man stains in his beard, and had flopped his big old sweaty fat butt down in a booth, Mr. Raney, just a boy working behind the big marble soda fountain, would go up to him and he'd say, "Can I get you some coffee, Mr. Childe Harold?"

Childe Harold would stroke his beard with one hand and give his silk stocking a good yank with the other hand, and then he'd drag his enormous old fat ass out of the little booth, pulling and straining, heaving and puffing, sweating, and the gun in his holster would be swinging this way and that way, knocking up against the booth, getting stuck up underneath his leg and poking him in the butt.

He talked through his nose. He would say, "Goddamn."

Then, once he did finally get himself pulled out of the booth, he'd yank the pistol out of the holster, ten-inch barrel Colt .45, fully loaded, and hold it out in front of him. He did this every day.

In his nasal way, Childe Harold would say, "Hold my gun, son, I got to shit."

Dooney Man Drake, the town lawyer, wrote Mr. Raney a letter one day, when he was still in high school, told him Childe Harold was dead, died of a heart attack, and Mr. Raney had inherited his pistol. Dooney Man said in the letter he hated for a bearded man to die and never learn to talk right.

Mr. Raney's daddy said, "A letter? You got a letter?"

His mama said, "Well, but ain't that nice, though."

They were more interested in the letter than in the inheritance.

Later on, Mr. Raney showed the pistol itself to his folks.

His daddy said, "And a letter to boot. I swanee goodness."

His mama said, "Don't shoot it off in the house without asking first, honey."

His daddy said, "A schoolboy—*my* boy—receiving his very own letter, through the United States Post Office. I'm just so proud of you, son, I could almost cry."

When Mr. Raney thought these old friendly thoughts of his childhood, he also thought, well, he might as well get in on the fun. He wouldn't shoot another man's refrigerator, even an old friend's, that could be considered pushy, he understood that, but it sure couldn't hurt nothing to put a plug in one of Mr. William Tell's cans of pork and beans, now would it, nobody could blame you for shooting the pork and beans.

So he reached back in the bed of the truck and dragged the heavy old toolbox over to the side and opened it up and reached around in the dark and found the leather bag.

The pistol was so big, it was about the only thing that would fit in the toolbox, though there were a few other things in there, a couple of wrenches anyway, a half-pint of whiskey, a claw hammer, and a box of ten penny nails. He hauled the leather bag out and pulled open the drawstring.

He took the pistol out of the bag, real careful, because it was covered with grease, packed in it, and he didn't want to get grease all over his shirt. He pulled a big rag out of his back pocket and wrapped the pistol in it and rubbed it good, to get some of the grease off.

He wiped the long blue barrel and the checkered handle grip; he seesawed the rag through the trigger guard. It was still pretty greasy, but you could handle it. He wiped grease off the hammer.

He let the cylinder drop, to see if the gun was loaded; the sound of metal on metal was like the sound of silk on silk. He wiped grease off the cylinder too, and the gate, and clicked it back in place and gave it a spin, for good measure.

He stomped on the board steps on his way into the store; he pounded each step hard, in case there was still some mud from the island caked onto his boots. He didn't want to be tracking up Mr. William Tell's floor with gumbo.

WHEN THE front door of the store opened, Hydro was already holding the dead girl's pistol out in front of him, straight-armed. It was no small caliber weapon itself. The hammer was already cocked. His hand did not tremble. The large figure that filled up the door frame was unrecognizable to Hydro.

The first shot was Hydro's. He let the hammer fall. It was like simultaneous lightning and thunder.

The second shot was Mr. Raney's, Childe Harold's ancient enormous sidearm, and the sound and blaze that erupted from it were even more elemental, essential, volcanic than the crash and yellow illumination of the pistol in Hydro's hand.

The report from this ancient weapon was so large, so impressive and heartfelt, you had to say it was historical, it was geological, geographical, it was the Army Corps of Engineers, it was the dam on Grenada Lake with the locks open, it was so loud, and the light it produced was the hydroelectric generators in the dam as they turned on all the electricity in Grenada County, or Buffalo, New York, with one switch, lights on. The echo lasted a century, it seemed like; eyes that saw the fire from the barrel were seared permanently, like eyes that had looked straight into the sun. The sulphur and cordite, burning, might have come from the bowels of hell, they stunk so bad, they produced such a cloud of noxious smoke.

There were no other shots, only those two. The firefight was finished.

Far across the sugarcane fields, across acres of water, deep in the swamp, wild creatures heard the gunfire. Some of them might have thought it was thunder, the innocent didappers who looked for rain, the gentle alligators who were too bored to care, the nutrias who stood on gum stumps and shook water out of their fur like slinging silver coins in many directions at once.

But turkey vultures, roosting in the tops of dead trees in sight of the Indian mound, where stone-age civilizations lay quiet for so long, they heard it and opened one eye, perhaps, and shrugged their big poultry shoulders, shivered, as if to shake off a bad dream, and slept again.

Sly foxes heard it, and wrapped their red tails across their half-sleeping eyes and crept an inch deeper into their dens.

Wild dogs heard it, and dreamed of armadillos without shells.

Louis McNaughton heard it, the fat little boy with pink-rimmed glasses, and stepped back into the pantry and turned on the overhead light. He wished there were more choices for a person whose life had probably just been ruined by what he had seen. If there were choices, he couldn't think what they were right now. He sat down again to try to finish reading *Gerald McBoing Boing*.

Mr. Raney said, "What a racket! Wasn't that something special! My eyes are still seeing black spots."

Hydro said, "Daddy?"

Mr. Raney said, "Let's get some lights on in here. Let's see what we hit. I probably should have warned you about shooting Mr. William Tell's refrigerator. Them things are expensive."

Hydro said, "Daddy? Are you all right?"

Mr. Raney said, "I'm not promising nothing about my marksmanship. I was only half-remembering where them pork and beans used to set. No telling what I put a plug in."

Hydro dropped the gun to the floor. It sounded like a tire iron.

Mr. Raney said, "Turn on some lights, son. Let's see what we got here. If I hit one of them cans of Campbell pork and beans, I'll buy you a Co-Cola."

Hydro said, "I missed you. How did I miss you?"

Hydro reached up above him and yanked on the light cord. The door directly behind his father had a piece missing as big as a wedge of pie.

Mr. Raney's eyes were still getting adjusted to the light. He said, "Introduce me to your friends, son, let's don't be rude. I saw them through the window. I got to tell you, I admire your young man's sense of style, sure do."

It wasn't until right then that Mr. Raney noticed that

Hydro was barefooted and there might be some dead folks in the room.

Mr. Raney said, "Sugarplum?"

He walked through the store, closer to Hydro.

Mr. Raney said, "What has happened? Why are these two lovely children laying here dead on the floor with their heads blowed off? Where are your shoes?"

4

Mr. Raney took the scratchy wool army blanket and laid it over the girl so she wouldn't look so pitiful. The blood smelled like a big raccoon in the house.

He sat down next to Hydro on the army cot.

After a while, Mr. Raney got up and walked over to the shelf where the canned vegetables sat. The whole back side of a lard bucket had split wide open where his bullet came out.

There was a pay telephone out on the wall, outside, up under the shed.

Mr. Raney felt around in his pants pockets, looking for change for the phone box.

Hydro said, "Morgan said I was hopeless."

Mr. Raney looked at his son. He said, "Was the sharpshooter out here? Did he do this?"

Hydro said, "I buried a watermelon."

Mr. Raney didn't know what to say. He thought for a minute. He said, "Well, that's all right."

Hydro didn't say anything. He seemed to be looking at something far off, somewhere.

Mr. Raney looked at the dead bodies, the bullet holes between the eyes.

He said, "So Morgan done the shooting and then run off, did he?"

Hydro still didn't say anything. Hydro was tired of

talking now. All of a sudden, he just couldn't say another word.

Mr. Raney waited for a minute.

Hydro was staring at the wall.

Mr. Raney said, "I can understand you not being in a talkative mood."

Mr. Raney went outside and put a nickel in the phone box. He said, "Webber, this is Mr. Raney."

On the other end of the line Marshal Chisholm said, "This phone is just for official use, that's all."

This meant the marshal was watching his new Philco television set and didn't want to talk.

Mr. Raney said, "There's two dead people laying out in William Tell. Morgan killed them, it looks like."

There was a silence on the line. A TV set was playing in the background.

Webber said, "Dead? Are you sure?"

Mr. Raney said, "Oh, they're dead all right."

Webber said, "Two people, you say?"

Mr. Raney said, "Two lovely children."

He said, "Who are they?"

Mr. Raney said, "Strangers. A boy and a girl."

Mr. Raney could hear the music from the Philco. He knew Webber was watching some program.

He said, "Webber, are you there?"

Mr. Raney hung up the phone and went back inside the store. He sat on the cot beside Hydro.

He put his hand on Hydro's knee and gave it a pat.

THEY KEPT on sitting there for a while. A long time passed.

The marshal was taking forever to get out to William Tell. Mr. Raney said, "What I ought to have done was slung this pair up in the back of the pickup and drove them into town. We are going to have buzzards nesting on the lard buckets before Webber ever gets his lazy self out here."

Hydro laid his big head on his daddy's shoulder, and Mr. Raney held his boy and rocked him in his arms, sitting on the army cot.

Mr. Raney kissed Hydro's hair and rocked him in his arms. He hummed a little lullaby.

In the pantry Louis heard the humming and put down his comic book and listened.

Mr. Raney sang, *Sixty minute man, they call me Lovin' Dan.*

He sang, *Money, honey, if you want to get along with me.*

He sang, *Come ride with me in my Rocket 88.*

He sang, *Honey, hush.*

Hydro said, "She said she never did tail with no retard. She said it made her want to throw up, she was so disgusted with herself."

Back in the pantry, Louis thought about his mama and daddy, at home in Arrow Catcher.

Hydro's daddy looked at his son. He said, "Tail?"

About that time, Marshal Chisholm drove up in his Jeep and so Mr. Raney got up and stepped over the bodies and went out to the front of the store.

He hollered out the front door, "Hey, Webber. We're in here."

The marshal was adjusting his pistol belt beneath his

stomach as he stepped down out of the Jeep. He looked up and squinted in the direction of the light.

He said, "Who's talking?"

Mr. Raney said, "Mr. Raney."

He kicked mud off his boots on the porch steps and came on in the store. He said to Hydro, "You was mighty durn lucky you had a sharpshooter as a visitor."

Hydro said, "I buried the watermelon."

Mr. Raney said, "That reminds me, I ought to put this old thing back in its bag in the toolbox." Talking about his pistol with the ten-inch barrel. He said, "I store it in mutton."

The marshal said, "Just to keep the record straight, Mr. Raney, you ain't shot nobody tonight yourself, have you?"

Mr. Raney said, "I ain't shot nothing but a lard can. I pretty well greased Mr. William Tell's floor."

The two men laughed quietly.

Hydro said, "I done it."

Both men looked at him.

They stood around the store for a couple of minutes.

Louis McNaughton came out of the pantry.

Mr. Raney said, "Hoo!"

He said, "Louis, you like to scared me half to death."

Louis said, "Sorry."

Webber Chisholm said, "Hey, Louis."

Mr. Raney said, "Did you see Morgan kill these two lovely children?"

Louis looked at Hydro. He thought about this.

Webber Chisholm said, "Morgan is the Lone Ranger, ain't he?"

Mr. Raney said, "He cleaned up Dodge and rode out of town."

The marshal said, "Who was that masked man?"

Louis said, "Hi-yo, Silver."

Everybody looked at Louis.

Mr. Raney said, "That's a good one. Hi-yo, Silver. You sharp, Louis."

Webber Chisholm said, "You all right, Louis?"

He said, "I guess so."

Webber said, "You know who you look a little bit like, Louis. You kind of favor Mr. Peepers. You know. On the TV show."

Louis said, "Uh huh."

Webber Chisholm said, "It's the glasses, I think. A little bit owlish, you know."

Louis said, "Yessir."

The four of them stood around for a few minutes and stared at the bodies.

Webber said, "Well, I sure do hate to call the Prince of Darkness, this time of night."

Mr. Raney said, "I don't know how that man stays in business, with his attitude."

Webber said, "Business keeps coming."

Mr. Raney said, "Ain't nothing certain but death and taxes."

Webber said, "This was some solid-gold shooting Morgan done here."

Mr. Raney said, "He saved my boy's life."

Webber said, "Well, I'll talk to him tonight or tomorrow."

Mr. Raney said, "Give him my thanks."

Webber said, "Well—"

Mr. Raney said, "I'll call the Prince of Darkness for the ambulance if you want me too."

Webber said, "No, it is my job."

Mr. Raney said, "Another idea might be, we could sling these two lovely children up in the bed of my truck and drive them in our ownself."

Webber said, "That's a thought."

Mr. Raney said, "Okay, then, why don't we do that. I'll take that old metal toolbox out of the bed and stick it in the floorboards of the cab, so it don't go slamming up against them. Not that it's going to make much difference to these two." He said, "Hydro, I brought along an extra peach pie if all this excitement made you hungry."

Webber said, "They wouldn't hardly fit in the Jeep. I thought about taking them back in the Jeep. We'd have to set them up in the seats, though. It would be disrespectful."

Mr. Raney said, "The pickup would be more dignified."

Webber said, "It's not exactly the Prince of Darkness's Cadillac hearse, though, is it?"

Webber looked over at Hydro, who looked a little pale.

Mr. Raney said, "Are you all right, son?"

Webber said, "Set down, Hydro, take a load off, why don't you. Have a seat on the cot."

Mr. Raney went out to the pickup and let down the tail-gate.

Webber took the army blanket off the girl's body and spread it out like a pallet alongside her. He said, "Step back,

Louis. Set over there on the cot next to Hydro." He rolled her over onto the blanket and straightened out her legs and arranged her arms at her sides.

He folded the blanket up over the girl and took hold of one end. He said, "Mr. Raney, you take the head end."

In this way they dragged the girl's body across the floor, and down the steps and across the graveled lot and around to the back of the truck. They positioned themselves at the tailgate.

Hydro watched, and then he eased out the back door and stood by the fence and puked real good.

Louis walked out to the truck to watch.

Webber said, "Ready?"

Mr. Raney said, "Whenever you are."

They said, "One two three," and slung the blanket and the girl like throwing sandbags up on the levee. The body landed up in the bed of the truck, flop.

Mr. Raney got up in the truck and pulled the blanket with the body in it up to the front end, to make room for the boy, when it came his turn. He had to roll the girl out of the blanket, so he could use it in the same way, one more time. She spilled out like tent poles out of a rolled-up tent.

The dead boy was a little heavier, but not bad. The two men worked a little better together the second time around.

Hydro had some color back in his cheeks now. He came out and stood next to Louis.

Mr. Raney slammed the heavy tailgate up and secured it in place with two metal hooks, one on each side. He and Webber were both blowing pretty hard by now.

Webber said, "I'll put on the light. No need for the siren. You follow me to the Prince of Darkness Funeral Parlor."

Mr. Raney said, "I got to catch my breath."

He put the big pistol back in the mutton-greased leather bag, and he and Hydro climbed up in the cab and slammed the heavy doors shut.

Webber said, "Louis, you come on with me."

Louis said, "Can I ride back in the bed?"

Webber said, "Come on with me. Mr. Raney might have to stop real sudden."

Louis said, "Nobody ever lets me ride in the bed."

Webber said, "Not tonight, honey, come on."

Louis said, "Can I blow the siren?"

Webber said, "Come on, I'll let you turn on the light."

Louis got in the patrol car, and Webber Chisholm eased it out onto the highway and turned towards Arrow Catcher, with his siren silent and his red light going zoop-zoop-zoop. Mr. Raney and Hydro drove slow behind the patrol car in Mr. Raney's pickup, real careful, so the bodies in the back wouldn't slide around too much. Hydro looked straight ahead and didn't talk. Mr. Raney couldn't think of anything to talk about either. Louis could have ridden back there in the bed tonight, slow as Mr. Raney was driving.

THE PRINCE of Darkness was a skinny baldheaded man in a black suit; he had big dark bags underneath his eyes, and bony hands. He was raised from the dead when he was just a young man, a boy really. That was the story, anyway.

He came to the back door when Webber rang the bell. He

said, "Pull up next to the spigot, you can use the hose to wash out Raney's truck."

The Prince of Darkness sang bass at St. George by the Lake Episcopal Church and looked like one of his own customers. You hated to see the Prince of Darkness in the middle of the night at a funeral parlor. It wasn't quite as bad for Mr. Raney, who had known him all his life, ever since Mrs. Mitchum's kindergarten, down in the basement of the old Arrow Catcher community house, when he and Mr. Raney were children.

The Prince of Darkness waved out the back door to Hydro, who was standing out by his daddy's truck. He hollered to him, in his odd old nasal mortuary voice, "Hydro, you'll live forever with the blood of these two children on your hands. Come by here and talk about it sometime, if you want to." Then he said, "Hey, Louis."

He closed the door and went back inside. Hydro did not see him again.

Mr. Raney said, "It was Morgan that did the shooting."

The Prince of Darkness wasn't in a talkative mood. He gave Mr. Raney a look. The looks the Prince of Darkness gave you were black, black.

Mr. Raney said, "Well, we got to get on back out to the island. It's late."

Webber said, "I guess I ought to hang around for a while. There might be some more paperwork."

Mr. Raney drove his truck around to the back of the funeral parlor and hosed the blood out of the bed.

He said, "Good night, Webber."

Webber said, "Good night. Good night, Hydro."

Mr. Raney said, "Louis, you want me to drop you at your house?"

Louis said, "Can I ride in the bed?"

Webber Chisholm said, "I don't want you riding in the bed of no truck, Louis. You stay with me. I'll take you home."

Louis said, "You're not my daddy."

Webber said, "And proud of it."

Hydro said, "Sometimes it seems like this ain't really my head. It seems like I'm carrying somebody else's head around on my shoulders."

Webber looked at him. He said, "I think we all feel that way sometimes, Hydro. Only it's my butt and my belly instead of my head. You could park a Chevrolet Bel Air in the shadow of my butt."

Mr. Raney said, "Say good night to the Prince of Darkness for us, won't you now. Tell him we said 'Much obliged.'"

Webber said, "Y'all try to get some rest."

Hydro looked at his daddy.

Hydro said, "Is it true he was brung back from the dead by a voodoo woman?"

Mr. Raney shrugged his shoulders. He said, "Yes. Yes, it is."

They stood around the truck for a while.

Hydro said, "Why does he have a name like the Prince of Darkness?"

Mr. Raney said, "His mama changed his name after he was brought back from the dead."

Hydro said, "I'm glad I've got me a nickname."

Mr. Raney said, "You don't like your real name?"

Hydro shook his head.

Mr. Raney said, "Sometimes in my dreams your mama is still alive, and we call you Ramon Fernandez."

Webber Chisholm said, "Louis, you stick around here with me. I'll take you home after a while."

WEBBER WENT back inside the funeral parlor. He knew the Prince of Darkness would want some help washing the bodies. Louis followed the marshal inside and stayed quiet so he wouldn't get run off.

Webber said, "Prince of Darkness, I'm going to run Louis home first, so his folks don't get worried about him."

Louis said, "They don't mind."

The Prince of Darkness said, "This won't take but a minute."

Webber said, "I ought to take Louis—"

Louis said, "I'm safer here with you."

Webber Chisholm looked at him. He said, "Well, you're probably right about that."

The Prince of Darkness said, "One minute, that's all it'll take."

The boy and girl were laid out on two slabs, stainless steel tables in a bright clean room. Louis stood over to one side, where he could see. The Prince of Darkness undressed the young man first and folded his clothes, bloody as they were, and laid them on a chair.

He said to Webber, "Here, hold this pan."

Webber said, "I'm going to have bad dreams, I just know I am."

Louis said, "I'll hold it."

Webber said, "Goddurn it, Louis." Louis didn't move.

Webber took the enameled, boomerang-shaped pan and slipped it up underneath the dead boy's neck. The Prince of Darkness smoothed back the boy's long greasy hair, out of his eyes. It was a little like watching your wife get her hair washed down at Maude's Beauty Shoppe.

Louis eased around next to the table so he could see better.

Webber said, "Louis, you run on out in the casket room and play. You ain't got no business in here."

Louis said, "Okay."

The Prince of Darkness said, "Take your shoes off if you play inside the caskets. Don't be getting mud on those satin cushions."

Louis said, "Yessir."

Louis didn't move.

The Prince of Darkness pulled a little rubber hose and nozzle up out of the sink and directed the stream onto the boy's head. The water in the pan turned pink as he cleaned the wound.

He said, "Hand me the Prell."

Webber only stood and watched. Louis handed him the bottle of shampoo.

The Prince of Darkness lathered the boy's hair and washed it with a little red rubber massager. He rinsed it with the rubber hose and toweled it dry with a rough, clean towel. He combed the boy's hair straight back with a hairbrush with a pink plastic handle.

The Prince of Darkness said, "I used to use Breck. I'm boycotting Breck now, though."

Webber said, "You don't say." He was about to faint, just from holding the pan.

The Prince of Darkness said, "It was Breck that sponsored the Shakespeare specials last fall. Lear, Hamlet, another one about a colored man, and some durn thing about a dream, fairies running every whichaway."

Webber said, "Well, that sounds pretty good."

The Prince of Darkness said, "It was good. It was the commercials I couldn't stand. The Breck commercials."

Louis said, "I watched the play about the colored man."

The Prince of Darkness said, "These commercials came popping up every time you turned around, right in the middle of the best parts—all these women washing their hair."

Webber said to Louis, "What was the colored man's name?"

The Prince of Darkness said, "Just when you was getting interested in the fairies or the fallen kingdoms, I'll be god-durned if somebody didn't have to bring up the subject of hair-washing. They couldn't let it alone."

Louis said, "It was a funny name."

The Prince of Darkness said, "A king had lost his daughters and his mind and his entire realm, and some big grinning ape comes in and starts talking to you about women washing their hair with Breck."

Webber said, "Well—"

The Prince of Darkness said, "Loss is important, magic

too. They're the most important things that ever happen to people. Breck shampoo made the whole idea of loss and magic seem trivial."

Webber said, "Don't get all worked up."

The Prince of Darkness said, "You don't see Cordelia washing her hair every five minutes of the livelong day, do you?"

Webber said, "Cordelia?"

The Prince of Darkness said, "You don't see Goneril—"

Webber said, "I'm acquainted with a Cordelia, out on Runnymede, takes in washing and ironing."

The Prince of Darkness said, "A big soap company has no business trivializing a king, I don't care how unpleasant he was to his family. Every family's got troubles. You name me one family that doesn't have some kind of trouble, sex or money, marriage or children. You can't do it. That doesn't mean you have to trivialize him."

Webber didn't say anything else. He didn't want to provoke the Prince of Darkness any more than he already had. One time the Prince of Darkness got all worked up and told him the entire plot of *The Mikado* and sang him two of the songs, every verse.

The Prince of Darkness finished bathing the boy in a tense silence. Webber helped him lift the boy off the table after his bath, and so then the Prince of Darkness cleaned up the girl in the same way. This time the marshal did the hair-washing. The two men rolled the dead boy and girl into the meat locker and closed the heavy door.

The Prince of Darkness said to the boy, "Louis, I hope I haven't kept you up past your bedtime."

Louis said, "I don't mind."

Webber said, "Well, maybe we better be moving on." He put his big hand on the child's shoulder.

Louis said, "Can I blow the siren?"

Webber said, "You want to wake up the dead?"

Louis said, "Can I?"

Webber said, "Wake up the dead?"

Louis said, "The siren."

Webber said, "Well, okay. But just this one time."

THIS LONG day was almost over for Mr. Raney. The sky was clear, and the moon was high. Mr. Raney parked his pickup down on Harper Road, next to the Roebuck bridge. The breeze off the lake smelled like willow branches and mimosa blossoms and weevil poison and fish.

Mr. Raney and Hydro clumped around in the dark for a while, getting settled in the boat, Hydro in the front end, and his daddy in the back. Mr. Raney unlashed the boat from the pilings and pushed it out into the water, underneath the starry-starry skies. He wrapped the little cotton pull-rope around the crank shaft on the Evinrude, and started it, again with the first pull. A fragrance of warm oil and gasoline soon filled their nostrils.

Mr. Raney turned the bow of the boat out into the bayou. They passed beneath the dark pilings of the Roebuck bridge, and smelled creosote on the breeze then. They passed among the tupelo gums and sweet gums and cypress and the wild pecan, where wild canaries slept, and jungle birds. In the deep water, the dolphins followed them, sliced the water and turned it silver, and left echoes of their voices in the swampy air, and then they swam away.

Through the starry night, the motorboat took Hydro and his daddy past the alligators in their nests, past beaver dams, where beavers as large as collies sliced through the stream, past a nest of water moccasins, far, far away from William Tell, and to their safe beds in their home, at the fishcamp on the island.

5

Desiree Chisholm, Webber's wife, was sleeping like a baby inside the little low-roofed house on Roebuck Road when Webber switched off the engine and let the patrol car drift into the driveway without any lights on. He had already dropped Louis off at the McNaughton house across from the Methodist church.

He eased to a stop, up under the porte cochère. He didn't want to wake her up. He still had some blood on his sleeves from hauling the head-ends of the bodies out to Mr. Raney's truck in the blanket.

He came into the house through the carport, into the little utility room, and slipped out of his shirt and dropped it in the washing machine. He felt around on the wall for the light switch and when he found it, he inspected himself all over, under the glow of the bulb.

There was blood on his shoes and on his pants cuffs, so he unhooked his gun belt — his scabbard, he called it — and slung it over a straight-back chair, and undressed down to his skivvies and dumped Oxydol into the machine and turned on the switch and started filling it up with water. It wasn't fair to make a woman wash a stranger's blood out of your shirt and pants. Two strangers, in this case.

He held his shoes up under the spigot in the laundry tub and watched the water turn pink and swirl around in the drain and run out. He took a brush with stiff bristles and loosened up the dried clots and knocked that off into the water, too.

He threw his socks and skivvies into the machine for good measure, just in case, although he couldn't see any blood on them. Nobody home but him and his wife, he could walk around naked if he wanted to, give his old belly a rest from that gun belt.

Webber had a grown-up daughter, lived in Memphis, name of Honoree, out in Whitehall. He hoped some big stranger like himself didn't go tromping his cowboy boots around in her sweet blood some day, and wondering if it got in his socks.

He turned off the light then. The house was small and built on a concrete slab, on one floor, so it was no trouble to find his way around in the dark.

He crept into the only bathroom in the house, just off the room where his wife was sleeping, and eased the door shut behind him, tick-a-lock, before he turned on the bathroom light. He still had hopes of not waking her up.

He couldn't go to bed, not yet, he couldn't lie beside her, and breathe her sweet breath, like clover, and smell Prell shampoo in her hair, like a field of green peas after a rain, not with all that death still on him, not with Prell from a dead boy and a dead girl still on his hands.

He turned on the water in the bathtub. There was more than just blood that Webber hoped to wash off of himself and his clothes. He would have liked to wash off the whole awful night, if he could. He put his hand up underneath the faucet and adjusted the temperature, hot and cold, until it felt about right. He squeezed a little bit of bubble bath into the water and swished his hand around until it foamed up.

Sometimes Webber could almost forget what a giant he was—six feet ten inches tall, three hundred fifty pounds, the last time he weighed himself on the cotton scales, down at the compress, probably more by now. He ate a dozen eggs and a pound of bacon for breakfast every morning. He was trying to cut back on his consumption of fig preserves, although he wasn't making much headway. He could eat a quart of fig preserves. That was what was putting the weight on him, probably. Fig preserves was loaded with calories.

Lord, he was big. How did he get so big? Forearms like fence posts, legs like bridge pilings, a gut like—well, a gut like nothing so much in this world as a big fat enormous tub of guts, a number ten washtub full of red-blood animal guts. Jesus Lord. What happens to our bodies? And what bodies are we given? And what lives to live in them?

The Prince of Darkness told Webber, right before he drove off, "Ain't no need to try to lose weight, Webber. It won't work. You'll always be fat. You'll be fat after you are dead and gone. You got fat bones. Your skeleton will weigh three hundred pounds, when ain't nothing else left of you. You one of them people that's got a real fat skeleton."

Webber said, "Well, I could of done without that ridiculous piece of information, Prince of Darkness, thank you so much."

The Prince of Darkness said, "You don't have to snap my head off."

In the car Louis had said, "I like the way you look. Your bones ain't fat."

Webber said, "They ain't?"

Louis said, "I'd be proud to have a daddy looked like you."

Webber said, "We better get you on home before somebody misses you."

Louis turned and faced straight ahead, out onto the roadway, and didn't bother to reply to that ridiculous notion.

The water filled up the bathtub, and Webber poured in some more of Desiree's bubble bath and swished his hand around in the water and stepped into the bubbles and submerged himself as well as he could. Wedged his big butt in, more like it.

His body dwarfed the tub. The bubbles disappeared beneath his massive hulk. His knees stuck up, in front of his face, like stanchions. His right elbow hung out into the bathroom, irrelevant as a two-by-four sticking out of a wall in a room. His left elbow banged up against the bathroom wall and he had to remember to hold it next to his body, inside the bathtub, there was no place else for it to fit. He couldn't slide the glass doors of the tub enclosure shut, his body was so big. His chest and belly filled up the shower stall. His butt sloshed water up over the sides of the tub.

Sometimes he could forget his size, especially when he made love to Desiree, his wife, and she told him he was her beautiful boy. But not when he was scrunched up in this modern little miniature bathtub, not when his whole enormous bulk was wedged into this narrow, white, clean, maybe even womanly space, foreign, himself the alien, the outsider, as big as a drowned cow, and more out of place, his flesh soft, pink, fragile, strange. If he looked between his big legs he could see a few bubbles, so he tried to focus on these and think of this as a relaxing bubble bath. A little later he dried off and didn't feel a whole lot better.

Desiree woke up and turned over when Webber climbed into bed. He was so heavy he like to spilled her off on his side of the bed, every time he put all his weight onto the springs.

Her voice was sleepy. She said, "Hey, Big'un."

He got up under the sheet with her, next to her, and arranged his head on his pillow. She cuddled up next to him and put her slender arm across his big chest.

Desiree Chisholm was tiny and beautiful. She had a body like a girl, narrow hips and shoulders and small breasts. She didn't have an ounce of flesh on her bones. She and Webber looked like the opposite of Jack Sprat.

He said, "Hey, Desiree."

She said, "What happened?"

He said, "Aw."

She said, "Baby, I'm sorry."

He said, "Sometimes the Prince of Darkness—"

She said, "Just don't think about it no more tonight."

He said, "A boy and a girl. Texas plates. Morgan shot them."

She said, "Tomorrow, baby-man. We'll talk about it tomorrow."

He said, "I hope I don't have no bad dreams."

She said, "Dream about me, Big'un."

They lay in the darkness for a while. A dog was barking somewhere down on the lake bank.

He said, "Hydro was looking after William Tell. In a way he's lucky, I guess. If Morgan hadn't been there, ain't no telling what would have happened."

She said, "That poor boy."

They were quiet again. The dog kept on barking.

He said, "I'm—I'm scared you'll be the one with footprints in your blood, some day. I couldn't live one minute without you."

She said, "I'll keep you safe, sweet thing."

He said, "They ain't no safety in all the land."

She said, "You're safe with me."

He said, "How am I going to be safe?"

She said, "Crawl up in my uterus, and let your sock feet hang out, Big'un."

He said, "I just hope I don't have no bad dreams."

She said, "We'll call Honoree in Memphis tomorrow."

He said, "Okay."

She said, "You just lay still, now, baby-man."

He said, "Prince of Darkness said my bones would weigh three hundred pounds when I died. Louis denied it, but that don't take away the fact that he said it."

She said, "Louis?"

He said, "Dr. and Miz McNaughton's strange little child. He was reading comic books with Hydro."

She said, "That child is ubiquitous."

He thought about that. He said, "He might be. Seem like half the young men in town are, these days."

She said, "Hush, now, hush up. Just relax. I'm right here. Here I am, baby-man. I'll never leave you. The Prince of Darkness is a madman, everybody knows that. You know he lost his mind when Miss Lily brought him back from the dead."

He said, "Don't look like nobody would ever want to hurt Hydro."

She said, "Hush up, now, baby-man."

He said, "Morgan, he's a different story. He's a mean motorscooter. Right between the eyes, both of them. He's pretty as a china doll, for somebody so mean."

She said, "Let me help you sleep."

He said, "Hydro ain't hardly got the sense of a billy goat, but I can't imagine nobody wanting to hurt him."

IT WAS pretty late by the time Louis got home. The porch light was on and the key was in the mailbox. Louis let himself in and found his daddy watching TV in the den, a dark room with a leather sofa and chair and ottoman. A deer head with glass eyes hung on one wall.

Louis said, "Hey, Daddy."

Dr. McNaughton didn't look in Louis's direction. Dr. McNaughton always wore a suit and tie, even at night, when he was home alone.

Louis said, "What you watching?" He closed the door behind him and stood in the dark room looking at the lighted screen. Dr. McNaughton just kept watching the television screen.

Louis looked at the screen too. It was an old movie. George Raft was dressed up in a double-breasted suit and a fedora. He was smoking a cigarette and holding a pistol in his hand.

Louis said, "Guess what happened out at William Tell tonight."

Dr. McNaughton leaned towards the TV a little, to hear it better.

Louis said, "Two robbers, all dressed up in black clothes came in and pulled out guns."

Dr. McNaughton said, "Watch this."

Louis looked at the TV screen again. All the men were wearing baggy suits and slouchy hats. There was one woman, blond-headed, wearing a tight dress. George Raft shot one of the men in a baggy suit, and he fell down on the floor. His hat didn't fall off. The woman held the fingertips of both hands over her mouth. The men backed away and looked scared.

Dr. McNaughton said, "What did I tell you?"

Louis said, "Where's all the blood?"

Dr. McNaughton looked at Louis for the first time. He said, "Blood?"

Louis said, "It looks like there would be some blood."

Dr. McNaughton said, "Are you being a know-it-all?"

Louis said, "I'm just asking."

Dr. McNaughton said, "I wish you wouldn't be so critical."

George Raft told the men the same thing was going to happen to them if they didn't watch out. He told them to put the dead guy in the car, so they picked him up and hauled him out the door and slung him in the trunk of a dark-colored, old-fashioned-looking car.

Louis said, "They could use a pickup. It would be a little more dignified."

George Raft and the blond-headed woman were still in the apartment talking about what they were going to do next.

Louis started making up dialogue. He said, "This place smells like a raccoon got loose in here."

Dr. McNaughton looked at him.

Louis said, "This guy has got fat bones. His skeleton will run three hundred pounds."

Dr. McNaughton said, "Louis, if you're going to make fun of the movie, just step out of the room."

"I sure do hate to call up the Prince of Darkness."

"I mean it, Louis. There is no point in spoiling the movie for everybody."

"We better call the hoodoo lady instead."

"Are you just trying to hurt me, son, is that what this is all about?"

"Miss Lily, we was just wondering, could you please bring this gentleman back from the dead?"

"Get out! Get out of here, Louis. I don't deserve this."

"I got a better idea. Call Dr. McNaughton. Get Dr. McNaughton to identify the body."

Dr. McNaughton jumped up out of his chair. He tried to grab Louis, but Louis got away from him.

Louis said, "Look!"

He pointed to the TV. The men in baggy suits were throwing the dead man off a pier, into dark water.

Dr. McNaughton was looking at the screen. He watched the body hit the water. He watched it sink beneath its dark surface. He went back to his chair and sat down, slumped there, his eyes fixed on the images on the screen.

Louis eased from the room and down the long dark hallway, into the depths of the house.

The TV music grew louder, so Louis was finished with his father-son talk. That was the end of that.

When Louis got back to the rear of the house, he saw his mama sitting at the kitchen table. His mama's name was Ruth. Ruth McNaughton was wearing a silk kimono, peach colored, which she had probably had on all day, maybe several days. The lights were on in the kitchen, bright as sunshine. Mrs. McNaughton was pouring a drink of bourbon into a glass from a bottle of Jack Daniels.

Louis said, "Hey, Mama."

Ruth McNaughton looked up. She smiled her bright, alcoholic smile at him and then screwed the cap back on the tall bottle. She said, "Well, hey there, Snerd, what are you doing up this time of night?" She called Louis Snerd after a character on "The Edgar Bergen and Charlie McCarthy Show." She was by far the most beautiful woman Louis McNaughton could imagine.

He said, "I been out at William Tell, reading comic books with Hydro."

She laughed a quiet laugh and shook her head. She said, "That shows you where my head is. I thought you were in bed asleep." She held the glass of amber fluid up to the light and then bared her teeth and took a dainty gulp from the glass. She said, "Yah."

Louis said, "Where's Katy?"

Ruth McNaughton said, "Katy?"

He said, "You know."

She said, "Well, of course I *know*, Snerd. I guess I haven't forgotten my own daughter's name. I just mean—"

He said, "Is she in bed?"

She said, "Well, sure. That's where she is. In bed. Must be. I remember now. She went to bed. Katy's a good little girl. She's her mama's girl. She puts herself to bed. I don't even have to remind her. You ought to try to be more like your sister. She's her mama's precious angel. You know that already, don't you? Katy's not going to run off. Katy's my precious angel." She said, "Well, come here, Snerd. Come on in the kitchen. Let me get a look at you. Looks like to me you're growing up and not even telling anybody about it."

Louis moved a couple more steps into the kitchen.

She reached out her slender arm and wiggled her fingers in the air. She was talking baby talk. She said, "Come to your mommy. Come to your mommy who loves you. Who wuvs you cho much. Are you shy? Did my handsome boy turn shy? Did he?" She puckered up her lips and made kissing motions in the air. She said, "Come to mommy. Give mommy a kiss. One weensie-beensie kiss. Mommy's going to teach you to kiss like a movie star. Kiss kiss kiss."

He said, "Mama, I'm going to check on Katy."

Mrs. McNaughton flushed with anger. She said, "Are you

ashamed of me? Is that why you won't kiss me? If that's it, just tell me. You might as well go on and break my heart. I gave birth to you. I'm not ashamed of you. Why should you be ashamed of me? Is it because of this?" She held up the glass of whiskey. "I'm having a cocktail, for God's sake. What's the great crime of having an evening cocktail? Where's the shame in that? Mamie Eisenhower has a cock-tail at night before bed, for Christ's sake."

Louis thought: Mamie Eisenhower?

Katy was eight years old, and her mother was right, she was sound asleep in her little bed, beneath its green com-forter with the print of tiny wildflowers. And her mother was right, too, about something else: Katy looked like an angel lying there, slender as a reed. She was the pretty child in the family, everybody said so. Louis agreed.

Louis crept into her room and sat beside her on the little bed. He pushed his glasses up on his nose and then pulled at the plastic earpieces, where they pinched the tops of his ears. Katy's hair had never been cut and was orange-colored red, all over her pillow, thick as a Shetland pony's mane.

Katy woke up when Louis sat down. She turned over on her back and looked up at him. A nightlight made the room bright enough for Louis to see her.

He said, "Goodnight, Katy."

She said, "Tell me a bedtime story."

He folded back her covers and smoothed them with his hand. He said, "Mama and Daddy are still awake."

She said, "You can whisper."

He took off his glasses, which had started to hurt his

ears, and rubbed his eyes. He said, "I saw some people get killed tonight."

She said, "Killed?"

He said, "Out at William Tell."

She said, "Oh."

For a while they sat without talking.

She said, "Is that the story?"

He put his glasses back on. He said, "No. What story do you want to hear?"

She said, "Little Lulu."

Louis told her the one where Alvin and the other boys in the club trick Little Lulu into walking on a leash and carrying a ball in her mouth like a dog. Little Lulu and Annie then steal the boys' clothes while they are swimming in a pond and leave them only diapers to wear home. Everybody in town sees them, and Little Lulu and Annie get the last laugh.

Katy said, "Was Little Lulu mean?"

Louis said, "No. It was a trick. It was funny. The boys got what they deserved."

She said, "It was funny. I know. I was smiling."

He said, "I saw you smiling."

She said, "Now tell me Plastic Man."

He said, "Tomorrow, okay?"

She said, "Did the people who got killed get what they deserved?"

He said, "I don't know."

She said, "You don't know?"

He stood up and said, "No."

She said, "Why not?"

He sat down beside her again. He said, "I'm too young. There's still stuff I don't know yet. Did you say your prayers?"

She said, "Yep."

He said, "Did you kneel down?"

She said, "Yep."

He said, "Well, that's good."

She said, "Like Timmy."

He looked at her. He said, "Timmy—right."

She said, "Can we get a dog like Lassie?"

He said, "It's late, Katy-did. I love you."

She said, "Please?"

Louis kissed her on the cheek. He said, "Now say it back."

She said, "No."

He said, "No?"

She said, "Okay, I love you too."

He said, "That's better. Good night, precious angel."

AFTER LOUIS had put himself to bed, his room lit up with the glare of headlights through his windows, from a pickup pulling into the driveway. Louis sat up in bed and listened. The room darkened again when the lights went off, and when he heard the sound of the pickup door slam, he knew it was Morgan, the sharpshooter, his mother's lover.

Morgan came clumping up the back steps, he didn't even bother to be quiet, even though he must have known Dr. McNaughton would be home. Louis heard him stop and stand outside the kitchen door.

Morgan said, "Ruth, can I come in?"

He had been driving around in his truck for a long time, out in the country, shining his headlights down country roads. He flushed out a deer. He saw a polecat. The reason he ran off to Texas in the first place was Ruthie. She said she didn't want to see him anymore.

Louis scrambled back down under his covers, where he had been reading *Wonder Woman*, with a flashlight.

Even beneath the covers he could hear the muffled sound of his mother's voice.

What are you doing here? she might have said.

I'm in love with you, I can't forget about you, Morgan might have answered.

Louis shined his flashlight onto the colored pages of his comic book. It was an old *Wonder Woman* he had picked up in a trade with Hydro. It told about the handsome Brad Spencer, who had black hair and wore a suit. Brad had a girlfriend named Carol. Sometimes the strap of Carol's dress would have fallen off her shoulder, and then a couple of frames later, it would have been pulled back up. Louis burned to see the undrawn panels.

You have to leave Louis's mother might have said, standing at the back door.

Please Morgan might have said.

Brad and Carol walked on breezy city streets together. They ate meals in restaurants. They went on a picnic. Once they even kissed. Louis checked Carol's shoulder strap and found that it had slipped a little. Louis thought of his mother speaking with Morgan in her peach-colored kimono. He thought of his mother's bare shoulder, then pushed the thought out of his mind.

One day Brad Spencer just happened to be walking past a secret atomic generator, all by himself, and he got hit with "a sizzling voltage of secret current." It was a completely unexpected malfunction, electrical and atomical. No one could have predicted it. Secret current. Sizzling voltage.

You have to leave Louis's mother might have said.

Please Morgan might have said.

The sizzling voltage of secret current turned Brad Spencer into a woman. Into Wonder Woman.

Louis could not concentrate on the comic book. The conversation at the kitchen door kept getting through. He put the book aside. He turned off his flashlight and sat in the darkness beneath his covers.

He listened to the faint sounds of his father's television set down the hall. He thought of the Prince of Darkness's anger at the Breck Shampoo company. Louis was angry too, but he was not sure at whom. His father? His mother? Morgan? Breck Shampoo? He really did not know.

Don't send me away

Don't ask me for what I can't give

One more time just once please

Louis switched on his flashlight and shined it on the comic book again. He read that the jolt from the atomic generator gave Brad Spencer access to powers that were already within him, including amazing will power. It made his body "a block of steel." Louis wished a sizzling voltage of secret current would hit his mother and give her amazing will power. She would stop drinking. She would forget about Morgan. She had powers within herself that she didn't even know about, he was sure of it.

He put the comic book aside. *A block of steel.*

Please

I can't

Louis heard the back door open and close. He heard fierce whispers. He heard a rustle of clothing.

Oh

Louis thought of Carol's errant dress strap. He thought of the kiss Brad had given her. He thought of his mother's peach-colored kimono. He heard a kitchen chair scrape on the floor. He heard something fall, truck keys maybe, onto the floor.

He's right down the hall he might come in

Louis snapped off his flashlight and sat beneath his tent of covers in the dark. He hoped Katy was asleep. He heard sounds from the kitchen he could not identify. He thought they were doing the same thing as the girl had made Hydro do, though he had not seen that either. He imagined his mother's kimono on the floor, his mother naked. He could not, he would not, imagine Morgan.

He snapped the flashlight back on. He shined it down onto his cotton underpants and saw his own aching little pecker poking at the cloth. He listened to his father's television set. He imagined George Raft on the flickering screen. He wished he had a gun to kill Morgan, as Hydro had killed the girl.

Much later, after Morgan's headlights had brightened his

room once more, and after the truck had pulled away, out of the driveway, he heard his father walk down the hall to the kitchen and help his mother up off the kitchen floor, where apparently she was still lying. He wondered if his mother was naked. He could not think of his father at all.

His father helped his mother to bed—set her on the edge of the bed, lifted her feet then and helped her stretch out, covered her with a light spread. Louis heard all this, imagined what he did not know. He heard his father walk back down the hall to the den, where the television was still playing. Louis knew that he would fall asleep there, on the leather couch. He would still be there in the morning, long after "The Star-Spangled Banner" had played and the flag had waved and a hillbilly preacher had said hillbilly prayers from Memphis.

6

Dr. McNaughton woke up on the leather sofa in his den and took a shower and put on a pair of khakis and a blue dress shirt with the collar open. It was Monday morning.

He said, "Louis, Katy, I want you to come with me in the car. We're going to Monday Music." Nobody could remember why morning coffee at the Arrow was referred to as Monday Music, it just always had been.

Katy said, "Why?"

Dr. McNaughton hesitated. He said, "Well—I don't know."

He really didn't. Last night he realized just how unhappy he had been, and for how long. How narrow and pathetic his life seemed. Renewal seemed possible at Monday Music, he was not sure why, or how—the proximity of male voices, male laughter, old stories.

Dr. McNaughton hustled the children out the door and into the Buick.

Louis said, "Daddy, something happened last night out at William Tell—"

Dr. McNaughton said, "Who's hot? Who wants the air conditioner?"

Katy said, "Turn on the air conditioner. I'm hot."

Dr. McNaughton started the engine.

He said, "All right, who wants to turn it on for me?"

Louis reached over and flipped the switch and adjusted the thermostat.

Dr. McNaughton said, "Ready?"

Louis said, "A shootout."

Dr. McNaughton said, "All right then! Monday Music, here we come!"

He was happy to be going to Monday Music, but the truth was, he was afraid, too. He had not been there since Morgan and Ruth—well, since they got together. There was bound to be gossip, jokes. He himself was probably the subject of all that male talk and laughter he had anticipated. Yet today for some reason, gossip didn't matter anymore. Not laughter either, even at his own expense. All that mattered was that he go and look for whatever he hoped to find there, redemption, maybe, transformation.

The old drug store was cool, on this hot summer day. The ceilings were high, the wood paneling was dark; the building was so deep that the cool was permanent, like a cave, or forest glen, umbrellas of live oaks and cypress, and long gray beards of Spanish moss. Shelves of patent medicines rose all the way to the high ceiling, S.O.S., Dr. Enough, Carter's Little Liver Pills, Hadacol, a million others. The soda fountain was made of marble, and a brass footrail ran along the bottom, flanked by two big bright brass spittoons that nobody was allowed to use. The mirror behind the fountain was huge, and reflected the whole store, and the big Crane cash register and racks of comic books. The high school boy jerking sodas behind the fountain, a kid named Claude, wore a paper hat and had bad acne and an odd, rare medical condition, a permanent erection, which caused the boy infinite embarrassment, but which had proved untreatable.

All the regulars were there, as Dr. McNaughton had remembered them, an eccentric group, frankly, when they were all lined up in one place. Wily Heard, the one-legged coach of the local arrow-catching team; Mr. Quong, the butcher, who carried his meat cleaver wherever he went; Hot McGee, an enormous man with a whip and a chair, like a lion tamer; Leonard Greer, who kept quails and cruised the Shell station; Cyrus Conroy, the grave digger; Shorty Grable, the barber; a few more. Monday Music was a man's world, like the rest of Arrow Catcher, Mississippi, like the rest of the world, maybe.

Somebody was saying, "Plugged two Texas desperados, killed them dead."

"You don't mean it."

"Bullets come right out the back of they heads into the vye-eena sausages, or poken beans one, I done heard both renditions."

"I wish I'd of been there to see it for myself."

"I throwed away my chance."

"Throwed it away?"

"I headed out there last night to have me a nip of potato whiskey, and I be goddurn if I didn't turn around and go back to prayer meeting instead."

"What you say!"

"Worst mistake of my life."

"You'll have other chances."

"I don't think so."

"He's got ice water in his veins."

"I always knowed he would do well in life. He didn't start

out with nothing. Found in a canebrake. Raised up by a hoodoo lady."

"The ones with humble beginnings, them's the ones rides with Destiny."

"Rides with Destiny?"

"It's an expression."

"It's a pitcher show. With Randolph Scott. I seen it one Saturday afternoon, down at the Arrow Theater. I forget who won the drawing."

"Randolph Scott's the one taught Morgan to sharpshoot that pistol. He worked on Randolph Scott's ranch down in Texas."

"Not Randolph Scott. Zachary Scott. Zachary Scott is the one taught him to sharpshoot the pistol."

"Zachary Scott?"

"Zachary Scott is the ugly one."

"I never claimed Zachary Scott was a thing of beauty."

"Morgan's a good-looking young man."

"Oo-la-la."

"I heard Morgan was a fairy."

"He's pretty enough. His lips are red as berries."

"If I was a fairy, Morgan'd be the first one of you ugly sons-of-bitches I'd ask out on a date."

"Zachary Scott ain't no fairy. Zachary Scott's too ugly. Zachary Scott never would get a date if he had to rely on men. How come you reckon a woman will go out on a date with anybody as ugly as most of you boys? Women ain't got no taste."

"Morgan can shoot, though. Morgan could join the Wild West Show. He could marry Annie Oakley."

"Or Buffalo Bill either one."

"Annie Oakley is still alive. Still makes public appearances."

"Annie Oakley?"

"Swear to God."

"Or do you mean Betty Hutton?"

"Why would I be telling you Betty Hutton was still alive?"

"Well, how old is she?"

"Betty Hutton?"

"Annie Oakley!"

"Oh, she's real old."

"Well, that clears up all my questions."

"Them two Texas desperadoes done drawed the winning number in the bullet lottery, when they met up with Morgan."

"Didn't they now?"

Katy said, "Can I get down?"

Dr. McNaughton shifted Katy on his hip, where he had been holding her. He said, "We're not going to stay long."

Just then a familiar voice said, "Morgan is a murderer."

The other voices in the Arrow stopped.

Dr. McNaughton looked at the person who had said this. It was Louis.

Everybody turned now and looked at the child.

Louis said, "I was there. I saw the whole thing."

Dr. McNaughton said, "Son?"

Katy was growing restless, wiggly.

Somebody said, "You was there, Louis? Out at William Tell?"

Louis reached into his pocket and took out a handful of spent cartridges. He dropped them on the floor in the midst of the men. They clattered and rolled and came to a stop.

He said, "These came from Morgan's gun."

The men looked at the cartridges. One or two men picked up a cartridge and held it in their hands. They looked at Louis.

Louis said, "They came into the store. Two lovely children."

Dr. McNaughton said, "Son—?"

Somebody said, "'Two lovely children,' them's the very words Webber used."

Louis said, "They didn't do a thing. They were nice. They wanted to buy a can of Dinty Moore."

Somebody said, "Dinty Moore—it's my favorite brand."

Somebody said, "It's extry tasty with fresh light bread."

Somebody else said, "And Morgan—he just drawed his gun and shot them down in cold blood?—is that the way it happened, Louis?"

Louis said, "Yessir."

Somebody said, "He just—"

Louis said, "Just like target practice."

The crowd fell back a step.

Dr. McNaughton said, "Son—?"

Somebody said, "Something just came over him, did it? Morgan just went into a fit of some kind?"

Somebody said, "Like a spell? Or a trance?"

Louis said, "Yessir."

Somebody said, "And drawed his pistol."

"Slow and easy."

"Like he was hypnotized."

Louis said, "Right before he did it—" He waited. The men fell quiet. He let the silence go on for a long time. He said, "Right before he pulled the trigger, Morgan looked like he got hit by *a sizzling voltage of secret current.*"

Somebody said, "My God."

Somebody else said, "A sizzling voltage."

"Secret current."

Dr. McNaughton looked at the spent bullets on the floor.

Somebody said, "For nothing. For a can of Dinty Moore stew."

Somebody said, "Target practice."

"My God."

Dr. McNaughton took a long breath and let it out slow. He looked at his children, as if he were seeing each of them for the first time.

All the men at Monday Music were looking at Dr. McNaughton.

He said, "Well—I guess we— I guess we better be going."

A long time passed and nobody moved.

Somebody said, "That cain't be Katy, can it?"

Dr. McNaughton looked at his daughter.

He said, "Actually—"

Somebody else said, "Come here, peaches." Speaking to Katy. He held out his hands for her, and she leaned towards him. She passed from her father's arms to his. He said, "You are heavy as a stump, punkin."

Somebody else said, "She favors her mama, don't she?"

There was a momentary silence, an embarrassment, after all the talk of Morgan.

Somebody said, "She's a beauty, all right."

Claude, the boy with the perpetual hard-on, said, "Pour you a cup, Dr. McNaughton?"

Dr. McNaughton said, "Oh—"

Claude held up the Pyrex coffee pot.

Dr. McNaughton said, "I guess I could have one cup."

The other men resumed their talking. They told about the death of Pap Mecklin, up in St. Louis, the blind daddy of Gilbert Mecklin the housepainter. Somebody said Pap's eyesight came back just hours before his death. They said the first words out of Pap's mouth were, "Gilbert, them false teeth don't fit."

Louis looked at his father and could see that something had happened, he was not sure what. He pulled away from his touch.

In a lull in conversation Louis spoke up again. He said, "Wonder Woman is really Brad Spencer."

All the men looked at him.

Louis said, "Brad Spencer got hit by a sizzling voltage of secret current and it turned him into Wonder Woman."

The silence went on. Dr. McNaughton held the cup of coffee to his lips and did not drink.

Somebody said, "Just like Morgan?"

Louis just shrugged his shoulders.

The man said, "Well, now, that's a coincidence."

There was some head-shaking, some chin-scratching.

Somebody said, "Are you sure?"

Louis shrugged again.

It was a long time before anybody said anything else.

Claude refilled some cups.

The next thing anybody knew, somebody said, "I see now that I've pretty much wasted my life."

It was Dr. McNaughton who had said this.

Everybody looked at him. Even Louis looked at him. Katy looked. Tobias McNaughton said he wasted his life.

Dr. McNaughton faced the little gathering of men. Nobody spoke.

Leonard Greer, the melancholy man who kept quails, said, "Uh, remember me, Dr. Toby?"

Dr. McNaughton looked at him. He said, "Leonard, hello—I didn't recognize you."

Leonard said, "I've put on some."

He said, "Uh, Dr. Toby, generally confession is heard out at William Tell."

The other men looked up now, allowed themselves to take a breath.

Leonard said, "Out on the highway, see? At William Tell. Never at Monday Music."

The air was cleared. The men began to drink their coffee again, talk among themselves.

Dr. McNaughton said, "I see—"

Leonard said, "You ought to try it. You could draw a pretty good crowd, I expect—with you wasting your life, and then Miss Ruthie and the sharpshooter carrying on like they do. I don't mean to speak in front of the children."

A couple of the men started to look at their watches. Monday Music was almost over.

Dr. McNaughton said, "Oh. Well—"

Everyone drank down the last of the coffee. They stretched. They scratched an itch if they had one. It was time to go to work. The pot was empty.

Claude gathered up the cups and put them in the little stainless steel sink of the soda fountain. He ran some warm water and squirted Joy in the sink and watched the water foam up. He adjusted his trousers and tried to keep the pained expression off his face. Dr. McNaughton eased over to the fountain, very discreet. He whispered, "Drop by the office sometime, Claude, I'll take another look, see if something can't be done." Claude said, "Much obliged." Claude scooped up the last of the nickels on the marble counter and dropped them in the change drawer of the cash register. Somebody bought a BC headache powder and he took the money for that too.

Somebody said, "I'm going to use your toilet, Claude, I won't be but a minute."

Claude said, "Don't wake up Mr. Shanker."

He said, "Mr. Shanker is sleeping in the toilet?"

Claude said, "He's got an army cot in there."

The man said, "Don't you worry none, Mr. Shanker won't hear nothing but the sound of a slowly draining lizard."

There were a few quiet, manly laughs.

Monday Music was over.

The men eased out in ones and twos.

7

Before the McNaughtons got home from the Arrow, a light rain had begun to fall. The sky had turned dark, almost a green color. The windshield wipers of the Buick were going zoop zoop zoop. Dr. McNaughton pulled the car into the circular drive and parked under the spreading trees. He picked up Katy, to carry her, and he told Louis, "Run for it." In this way, they came into the house together before they got wet.

Dr. McNaughton set Katy down in the front hall. He said to Louis, "Mama and I have got to have a talk."

Louis said, "Don't fight."

Dr. McNaughton said, "We won't fight, honey. I don't think your mama and I will ever fight again."

Louis said, "What are you going to talk about?"

Dr. McNaughton said, "Well, a lot of things." He said, "It'll be all right, don't worry. We're not going to fight."

Outside, the rain had started to fall in earnest now, making splattering sounds on the flagstone walks and patios and hissing sounds in the leaves of the cottonwoods and magnolias. Louis and Katy watched their father as he started walking up the stairs. He disappeared around a bend at the top of the staircase.

Katy said, "What happens to little birds when it rains?"

Louis looked at her. He said, "Birds are waterproof."

Katy said, "I know where some birds live."

Louis said, "Well, that's good."

She said, "Do you want to see them?"

Louis looked up the stairs, where his father had just walked. He looked back at Katy. He said, "I guess so. Okay."

She said, "I don't think these birds are waterproof."

He said, "We'll check on them."

Louis picked up an umbrella from the umbrella stand in the front hall, and they left by the front door. The rain had picked up a little. Fat drops made hollow sounds of tunk-tunk-tunk on the umbrella. Louis held Katy's hand so she wouldn't fall as they ran across the yard and across the street.

After a while they stopped running and just walked in the rain. The umbrella slowed them down too much, so Louis collapsed it and carried it in his hand.

Katy said, "It's kind of far."

Louis said, "Maybe we should have brought your raincoat."

Katy said, "And your raincoat too."

Louis said, "I'm waterproof."

Katy smiled.

It wasn't so far after all, about a mile. The rain kept falling. They walked under magnolia trees, their broad dark leaves, past the Methodist church. They cut through Curry Lumberyard and stood under a shed with a tin roof and listened to the rain. It sounded like distant drums. They smelled the fresh-cut lumber, sweet-scented sawdust and natural resins and turpentine in the wood. They cut across a lot that had an old yellow school bus sitting on it. The school bus had flat tires and busted-out windows and smelled of mildew. They got in the school bus and pretended to drive for a while. Katy sat in the driver's seat and twisted at the steering wheel. She said, "Sit down and shut up," pretending to be the driver, speaking to unruly schoolchildren.

Louis said, "Don't ever get in this school bus by yourself. Tramps sleep in here sometimes."

She said, "Okay."

They left the bus and walked across a broad field of grass, all the way to an inlet of Roebuck Lake. They were very wet now. Near the lake stood a spreading tree of some kind. It was not a large tree. A grownup could have reached the first limb. It would have been a good tree for climbing, on a drier day. Initials and a heart had been carved in the soft bark of the slender trunk.

Rain water was pouring off the children's faces. Katy's dress was stuck to her legs, and she had to keep pulling the cloth away from her skin. Louis's shoes went squelch squelch squelch when he walked. Katy's hair was slicked down on her head. They stood under the tree and listened to the rain fall through the leaves.

Katy pointed up into the boughs of the tree. She said, "See? I don't think they're waterproof."

Louis looked up into the branches. His eyes took a minute to adjust, the day was so gloomy, and the shade was deep.

Then he saw them, the little birds. They were wild canaries, with greenish yellow feathers, and a fringe of brown, like little skirts. They were soaking wet. They had their eyes shut and their little bird-shoulders hunched up against the weather. Louis had seen one or two of these beautiful, miniature creatures before, these wild canaries, with Hydro, in the shrubs near William Tell. But he had never seen so many. It was amazing how many birds were lined along the branches of this little tree. Thirty or forty of them together, sitting in a row like children in their desks at school.

They were living creatures, that was clear, pummeled and soaked by the weather, and yet they might as well have been made of china, they were so delicate, so small and beautiful. They did not move. They only sat in the sound of the falling rain.

Louis said, "Oh, Katy."

Katy said, "I don't think they like rain."

Louis said, "Well, maybe they do. We don't know for sure."

Katy said, "In sunshine they make noises. They say, 'chop chop,' they gargle their throats."

The two children stood under the tree and looked at the wild birds above them.

Louis said, "Maybe God takes care of them."

Katy looked at him. She said, "I doubt it."

The rain was falling harder now. The ditches were filling with muddy water. The rain fell almost as swiftly beneath the tree as beyond it. It poured through the branches. The limbs sagged with the water in the leaves. The little birds looked like they might topple off.

Louis said, "You look like a wet chicken."

Katy said, "What if they drown."

Louis said, "They won't drown, Katy."

She said, "I think they will. I found one on the ground before. It was—you know."

Louis said, "What, honey?"

She said, "Dead—you know?"

They started to walk back to the house.

Louis said, "We'll get some dry clothes."

Katy said, "Okay."

RUTHIE MCNAUGHTON was lying on the tiles of the bathroom floor, hugging the cool porcelain of the toilet bowl, when she heard her husband come in the front door. She was so comfortable. She hoped he would not come upstairs. Lying here, she felt almost at peace with herself, with the world. Even despite what she had done last night, she felt almost hopeful about her marriage. Hello, tub. Hello, shower stall. Hello, clothes hamper. Hello, rain, outside my casement window.

She lifted her head, testing, testing. She leaned over the toilet bowl and hawked and spit. She hauled a long strip of paper off the roll and blew her nose. The floral pattern of the toilet paper seemed friendly. The paper smelled of perfume that imitated the fragrance of fresh flowers. She wadded the paper up and wiped splatters off the rim of the bowl. She dropped the paper in and flushed.

She listened to the water going down the drain. She remembered the suck of a whirlpool beneath a woodland cascade where she had once bathed naked with her husband in a wilderness when they were young. She regretted that so much had happened since then. She regretted last night. The paper spun away, down the vortex, like forest flowers in a maelstrom. The toilet bowl was a spiritual thing.

She put her head down on the floor again. She felt no pain. She wrapped her arms around the bowl and pulled her knees up to her tummy. Her kimono was hiked up and her bare butt was sticking out. She breathed a deep breath. She smelled a hint of vomit in her long hair. She held the breath in her lungs as long as she could. She believed in life, in forgiveness, in transformation.

Coming up the stairs, Dr. McNaughton found himself filled with the same cool, clean, clear fragrance and quiet music of forgiveness and hope for the future as his wife had felt with her head in the toilet. Maybe it was Monday Music that had inspired it in Tobias McNaughton, this rush of feeling and hope and forgiveness, a residue of the manly laughter and gossip and absurdity at the drug store. Or maybe it was only a satiation of grief and regret, the moment when the bitter cup of unhappiness and loss was as full as it could get and so became, itself, a small hope, diamond bright. In any case, a fountain bubbling with cleansing waters might as well have been pouring gently over the sins of his past, and his wife's past as well, even last night. He felt transformed. He felt forgiving and forgiven. Love was the answer. Wasn't love always the answer?

When he got upstairs, he walked down the hall to their bedroom. He looked inside. Ruthie was not there. He noticed that the bathroom door was shut. He moved into the room.

He said, "Ruthie? Honey—are you in there?"

When Ruth McNaughton heard her husband outside the bathroom door, something ancient, like regret, crept into the serene space that her mind and heart had so recently occupied. She had wanted to see him, her husband. She had wanted to say so many things. And yet now, she wished she didn't have to leave this comfortable sanctuary of porcelain and tile and morning light from a green rain-sky. She wished she could just lie here a while longer. Hello, bathtub. Hello, clothes hamper. Hello, casement window, and distant thunder and hard rain on the tile roof. Don't disappear.

Her husband said, "Are you in the bathroom, Ruthie? Can we talk?"

There was no getting around it. He was out there. He had encroached upon her beatification. Why wasn't he at work? Wasn't there somewhere else he could go? She would have to get up now, rouse herself. From this hermitage, this pure privacy in the presence of God, or something like God.

A deep Arctic crystal blue wave of resentment rose up on the horizon of her transformation and made its way towards her serene heart. The man outside her bathroom door had frozen the waters of her miracle.

There were a hundred ways to say what she was feeling, there must have been, and yet when she tried to formulate words for her feelings, they came out in only one form: she did not want this spiritual moment disturbed by the spineless, yellow-bellied asshole outside her bathroom door, that he was less than a man for not knowing that she needed the spiritual nurturing of silent spaces and monastic cells. Especially when she had such a hangover. Especially now that her body had begun to ache so bad she was afraid she had rheumatoid arthritis. It might be cancer. Oh God, she felt so bad. Why had he done this to her? Miraculous transformations were really most valuable when you didn't have to get up off the bathroom floor and talk to your husband. He must have known this.

And yet it was true that they had things to talk about. She had thought of it herself. They did need to talk. She wanted to tell him she was quitting drinking. Had already quit, this morning. She had done it for him. Her beatification, the miracle, the memory of the mountain cascade and their youth and joy—she wanted him to know of these things. She wanted to tell him she had stopped seeing Morgan forever and that she would never see him again, except as a friend. She wanted to tell him she had found peace, that she wanted his forgiveness. She could go as far as that, to ask forgiveness.

And she wanted to tell him that she forgave *him*, for ignoring her affair, sanctioning it with silence, for sleeping on the couch every night and causing her to feel unclean, untouchable, unlovable and unloved.

She got up off the floor and sat on the toilet and leaned her head on her arm onto the lavatory in front of her. She was so sick.

Dr. McNaughton felt annoyed at the sight of the closed bathroom door. Well, who wouldn't? He didn't like closed doors. Not in his own house. Not even bathroom doors. It wasn't right. It especially wasn't right this morning. It was dispiriting to bound up the stairs with news that your son had witnessed a killing, that the murderer was your wife's lover, that all was forgiven, that you begged for forgiveness for yourself. You didn't want to have to say all that through a locked bathroom door. You didn't want to beg forgiveness for moral failure through locks and keys.

He said, "Can you come out, Ruthie? We need to talk, really. It's important."

She waited a few seconds. She wanted to say yes, she really did. She would have given anything to have said yes. What she said was, "I can't come out right now."

He thought about this.

He said, "Well—"

He waited for her to say something more.

There was only silence.

He sat down on the edge of the bed. He wondered whether Morgan had ever been in this bed. He believed he must have been—naked, or wearing the black vest. He thought how odd the boy must have looked here, small as a puppet, scarcely real, beside his wife.

He had to raise his voice to be heard through the door. He said, "Do you think you'll be much longer?"

There was a pause.

She said, "I don't know."

For a long time he only sat on the bed, looking at the closed door. He looked away from the door. He listened to the rain. He looked down at the bed. On the blue and white wedding ring quilt, he thought he saw a shadow. Or was it a stain? He touched the spot with his hand. He found himself looking for signs of Morgan.

He looked towards the bathroom again. The closed door seemed enormous between them.

He said, "Ruthie, are you avoiding me?"

He said, "Did you hear me?"

He said, "Ruthie, answer me."

If Ruth McNaughton could have chosen her words, she would have said, "I'm afraid." Instead, she lifted her head from the bathroom sink and said, "Is it too much to ask for a little privacy, please?" She put her head back down.

At just that moment, the children came back inside the house, Louis and Katy, wringing wet, speaking of the wild canaries. Dr. McNaughton heard them come in, though he could not make out what they were saying.

Katy said, "I wish I could bring them inside till it stops raining."

Louis took off his glasses and wiped the water off his face with his hand. He said, "The tree people used to tame wild canaries. That's what Hydro told me."

Katy said, "I could tame them. I could make them my pets."

Louis said, "The tree people could teach them how to talk. They would sit in the trees and talk with the wild canaries all the livelong day."

Katy said, "I could teach them to talk."

He put his glasses back on. He said, "I think you have to live in a tree, where they are more comfortable."

Katy said, "Really?"

Louis said, "Maybe."

"What did they talk about?"

"The canaries?"

"Uh-huh."

Louis smoothed his sister's wet hair. He said, "They talked about the meaning of good and evil and how to break into show business."

Katy said, "Oh."

They went to their rooms and dressed in dry clothes. Louis gathered up their wet things and put them in the dryer and touched the button and set it spinning. He started to tell Katy about watching the lovely children get their hair washed with Prell but decided not to.

Katy came out of her room.

He said, "Dry your hair."

She took the towel from him. She said, "The comforter on my bed looks like a meadow."

He said, "A meadow?"

"It was in my reading book at school. It's a big field."

"I know what a meadow is."

She dried her hair with the towel. She said, "See? It's all green like a meadow, and it has teeny tiny little flowers in it."

Louis said, "Primroses."

She said, "I wouldn't have to live in a tree."

They were standing in the doorway of Katy's room, looking at her neatly made-up bed.

Louis said, "The wild canaries?"

She said, "They would feel comfortable in a meadow. They could live here. They would think my bed is a meadow."

Louis took the towel from her and draped it over a chair-back to dry.

She said, "We could sit right here and talk all the livelong day."

Louis smiled. He said, "About the meaning of good and evil and how to break into show business?"

She said, "Right."

Louis said, "That would be pretty neat."

Upstairs, when Ruthie asked for a little privacy please, Dr. McNaughton said, under his breath, "Crazy bitch." He did not shout this, or even say it very loud, only mumbled it. But Ruth McNaughton heard it.

Through the closed door, she said, "What did you say?"

He said, "Nothing."

She said, "Why don't you call me a whore while you're at it?"

He said, "I don't have to. It's what the whole town is calling you."

She said, "What do they call you?"

They were screaming through the door now.

She said, "Do they call you liar? Quack? Cuckold?"

He said, "Are you aware that Louis and Katy heard you fucking that white-trash sharpshooter in the kitchen last night?"

Louis and Katy moved to the bottom of the stairs where they could hear better. Louis knew it would probably be better if he protected Katy from this fight, but he couldn't do it. He had to hear it himself. He didn't know why, he just had to. He couldn't protect her all the time.

They could hear their mother screaming now. Not words, only anguish and despair.

Their father said, "They heard the sounds you made, the words you said."

Ruth McNaughton was wailing with grief. She could not tell her stomach's sickness from the sickness in her soul. She said, "Please, please—"

Dr. McNaughton said, "I'm sorry. I'm sorry, Ruthie. I had no right to say that."

Downstairs, Katy said, "I'm scared."

Louis said, "Me too."

She said, "Is this our real life?"

He said, "No. I don't know. Maybe."

Ruth McNaughton's voice was full of tears, but she could still scream. Her voice came careening down the stairs like a runaway train. She said, "If you knew they were listening, why didn't you do something? Why didn't you kill us? That would have been better. How could you sit there and allow that to happen to them, no matter what you think of me? Why didn't you kill the two of us? Our children could have been proud of one of us, anyway."

He said, "Stop, Ruthie, stop, please, open the door, let me in, please just let me in—"

She screamed, "Oh, God, oh, God, let me die, I want to die—"

He said, "Open the door. Ruthie, right now, I mean it, open the door."

She cried and cried and cried.

He was frantic. He could not stop thinking about that

closed door. If the door were opened, things wouldn't be so bad, so awful. If she would only come to her senses and open the door. It was the door being closed that had caused all these problems in the first place. If she had just opened the door when he first asked her to—

He said, "Open the door."

She only wept and wept.

He said, "Open it, Ruthie. We can't talk with this door between us."

She screamed, "Go away, Toby. Please go away. I can't talk now. Leave me be alone for a while, please, Toby. We'll talk later, I promise, just go away, please, leave me alone."

He said, "This is the last time I'm going to say this. Open this door right now, or I'm going to break it down, I mean it."

Some part of his mind told him this was a bad idea. He knew the children were in the house; he was not sure how much they could hear. He rejected the nagging notion that he might be making a mistake. He told himself he had to break the door down. It was his duty. It was for her own good. She would thank him later. She had said, after all, that she wanted to die. She could kill herself in there. She might do it, too. There were razors and dangerous drugs. She had forced him into this position. Breaking the door down was the only safe thing to do. It was the only *sane* thing to do. It would be on his conscience forever, if he just walked away and did nothing to keep this family together and safe from harm.

He said, "All right, Ruthie, you asked for this. Is this

what you really want? Are you sure you know what you're doing, asking me to break this door down?"

She screamed, "I hate you, Toby, I hate you, I hate you!"

He did not count to three, or to any number at all. He rushed against the door with his shoulder. He crashed into it at full speed. It did not budge. He bounced foolishly backwards. His shoulder and upper arm smarted, where he had struck the wood.

He stepped back from the door and lifted his leg almost to his chest and kicked at the bottom panel of the door with his foot. Again, the door did not budge. He kicked it again and again. His footprints were all over the bottom of the door.

The children heard all this from the bottom of the stairs.

Katy said, "What is going to happen next?"

Louis said, "Let's go outside and play."

Katy said, "In the rain?"

Louis said, "Oh. Well—"

Ruthie McNaughton screamed through the door, "Don't kill me, Toby, please don't kill me!"

The children looked at one another. Louis held his sister close to him.

Dr. McNaughton turned and bolted from the room. He took the stairs two and three at a time. He passed the children on the landing. He kept on going. He went out the back door to the woodpile and yanked the axe out of the block of wood where it stood, then back through the house.

When he passed the children this time, carrying the axe, he called out, "I'm not going to kill her." He was bounding up the stairs.

Louis called out, "That's good, Dad."

Dr. McNaughton called back over his shoulder, "I'm sorry, Louis, Katy—"

He was going to break the door down with the axe. He was going to step over the splinters and drag her out of the bathroom by her hair. He was going to say, "No closed doors. In my house—"

When he burst into the bedroom, he found his wife standing there. She had already come out. He could see blue towels hanging on a rack behind her.

He dropped the axe onto the carpeting behind him.

He said, "I'm sorry."

She said, "I'm sorry."

They stood for a while. They stepped towards one another. They held each other, at first stiffly, then with more ease.

He said, "Do you love him?"

She said, "No."

"Really?"

She turned away. She said, "I don't know."

He said, "Did you tell him you loved him?"

Her back was still to him. She took a breath and let it out. She said, "Yes."

Now he took a breath. He said, "I just kept watching television."

She turned and faced him again. She said, "What we've done to those children."

They sat together on the edge of the bed. He touched the blue quilt with his fingers. The rain kept falling.

He said, "This stain. Is this Morgan?"

A dog was barking somewhere.

She said, "No. I don't know. It might be."

He said, "I had coffee at the Arrow this morning."

She said, "Monday Music? I'd forgotten about that."

He smoothed his hand across the quilt again. He touched the shadow, or stain, and then looked away.

He said, "I had the children with me."

The dog kept on barking.

He said, "That sounds like King, the Byrons' dog."

She said, "Shaboo must be in heat again."

He said, "I hope they're not out in this rain. I've never seen such rain."

They kept sitting. The dog finally stopped barking.

She said, "Are they all right, the children?"

He said, "Oh—actually, no. Louis witnessed a murder. Yesterday, out at William Tell."

She said, "Jesus." She put her face into his chest and held onto her husband, there on the edge of the bed. He smelled the vomit in her hair. She said, "Morgan."

He said, "I'm sorry, Ruthie."

She said, "Oh, oh, oh—"

He said, "It's nobody's fault. I don't know how things got—"

She said, "Those poor children."

He said, "Can I get anything for you? Anything?"

She looked up at him.

He said, "A drink? A Bloody Mary?"
She said, "Oh, Toby."
He rocked her slowly in his arms.

LATE THAT night the rain was still falling heavily. It was drumming on the roof and lashing at the trees. Katy was in her nightdress, propped up in bed against her pillows. She looked at her chest-of-drawers, and the mirror above her dresser. She looked at her Alice in Wonderland curtains and stuffed pillows. She looked at the green comforter with primroses. She said "meadow" a few times, just to see how it sounded. She looked out her window and could see heavy rain in the streetlights. She thought of the tree trunk with a heart and initials. She thought of the school bus. She said, "Sit down and shut up."

Katy couldn't sleep, although her parents had insisted about a hundred times what a good night for sleeping this would be, with the sound of rain on the house. Her mother and father were sleeping together for the first time in a long time. Before they went to bed they were smiling and cuddly and kissy. They talked baby talk to each other and laughed too loud and told dumb stories about when they first met. They came into Katy's room together to tuck her in and tell her good night and sleep tight and don't let the bedbugs bite. They told Katy I love you. Katy couldn't remember that ever happening before. She didn't know what they said to Louis. Maybe nothing.

After they closed their bedroom door, Katy listened for sounds. She wasn't sure if she heard anything.

The wild canaries were keeping Katy from sleeping. She kept thinking about them. They would never go chop chop or gargle in their throats in this rain. She wiggled her feet beneath the covers and saw the comforter move. The primroses rippled on the green background with the movement of her feet, like flowers in a field in a breeze. She wiggled her toes again. What if the wild canaries were drowning?

She pulled back the cover and got out of bed. She poked her head out the door and looked down the hall. Her parents' door was still shut, and the light was out, it didn't shine beneath the door. She looked the other way down the hall, towards Louis's room. His door was shut too, but she could see a light shining under it. She went down the hall and opened the door to Louis's room.

Louis said, "Hoo!" He was reading *Plastic Man*. He said, "You scared the donkey shit out of me."

Katy said, "Are canaries really waterproof?"

He put down his comic book.

He said, "Yes."

She said, "Are you sure?"

He said, "Pretty sure."

She said, "What if they're not?"

He said, "Come sit on the bed, Katy."

She came into the room and sat at the edge of Louis's bed. She smoothed her nightdress with her two hands in a prim little way.

Louis said, "Why aren't you asleep?"

She said, "I think the canaries are drowning. They don't like rain."

He said, "I think Mama and Daddy really do love each other."

She said, "Will you go with me, out to the tree?"

He said, "The tree?"

She said, "To check on them. To see if they're all right."

Louis said, "They're not bad people. I don't understand it, but somehow they're still good people."

She said, "Will you?"

He said, "Will I go with you to the canary tree?"

She said, "Yes."

He said, "Okay. I guess so. Go put on some shoes."

They left the house by the front door, and eased it shut behind them so that no one heard. They followed the same route they had taken before, past the church, through the lumberyard, beneath big trees, alongside the school bus. Louis had taken a flashlight out of the kitchen drawer, and he was carrying the umbrella in his other hand, so he couldn't hold on to Katy. She kept up, though, she stayed right beside him.

Louis swept the flashlight's yellow beam back and forth through the dark and the rain. The streets were like rivers, the ditches were filled with rushing water, the graveled roads were red as blood with clay beneath the streetlights. The trees sagged like old men in heavy overcoats. Louis and Katy didn't stop this time to get out of the rain. There was no shelter underneath the trees now, the lumberyard was too dark, the school bus might have had a tramp in it.

Louis said, "Are you scared?"

Katy said, "Yes."

Louis said, "Okay."

They walked through the field. The rain kept pouring. Katy had on her nightdress and shoes. Louis was wearing blue jeans and tennies. They were very wet now, even with the umbrella.

They came to the lake bank. Everything looked different in the dark. Louis shined the light, this way and that. They walked along the water. They looked for familiar landmarks. They finally found the tree.

Katy said, "There it is."

Louis said, "Are you sure?"

He shined his light but could not see much. They walked closer to the tree. They walked up under it.

Louis shined his light up into the branches. The two of them looked for the wild canaries. They could see nothing. Louis swept the light slowly along each branch. Nothing. The branches were empty.

Katy said, "They're gone."

Louis said, "Are you sure this is the right tree?" He turned the flashlight beam towards the tree trunk. The heart and initials carved into the soft bark shone in the light.

Louis turned the beam back into the branches again and looked up. He said, "They must have flown away. They must have gone to a drier place."

He let his arm fall to his side, with the flashlight beam pointing to the ground.

Katy said, "Look."

Louis shined the light onto the wet ground beside them, near their feet. What he saw, he could scarcely believe. The rain-drenched canaries, all of them, thirty or more birds, lay all around them on the ground in puddles of water. They had been washed out of the tree by the rain. Louis shined the light around him, frantic. He said, "I—I—" He saw their yellow little bodies, moving beaks, glassy eyes.

Katy said, "They weren't waterproof."

Louis said, "I—I—"

Katy said, "Put them in my nightdress." She lifted the long wet skirt of her gown, like an apron, and made a hollow in the cloth to receive the birds.

Louis made no protest. He knelt down, with the flashlight, and began to find the canaries, and to pick them up, one by one. Each canary felt like a tiny beating heart. It felt like a warm egg gathered from a nest. Louis kept at his work. The rain beat down on his back, where he bent over. He saw the muddy water wash up his sister's ankles almost to her bare knees. He kept on. He gathered up the birds with careful fingers. He cradled each for one second in his palm, feeling something, he was not sure what, a heartbeat, a sigh, the secret of life and death and how to break into show business, and then he set each little life into the hollow basket of Katy's up-raised gown.

Finally he was finished. He looked around for one he might have missed. He searched everywhere with the flashlight. He looked up in the branches again, in case one had not fallen. He had them. He had them all.

He looked at Katy holding the birds in her skirt, like an old woman with an apronful of eggs.

He said, "Are they heavy?"

She said, "No."

He said, "I'll help you."

Slow, very slow, they made their way home, along the lake, across the field, past the school bus and through the lumberyard, beneath the trees. Louis held the opened umbrella so the birds wouldn't get any wetter than they already were. The children took small steps, and so it took a long time. Louis helped Katy hold the birds safely in the bellow of her gown.

They eased into the front door. No one knew they had been gone. In Katy's room, quiet as they could be, Louis and Katy took the canaries from her skirt and placed them, one by one, onto the coverlet of her bed, the green field with primroses. As they did, Katy whispered, "Meadow, meadow," many times. The birds were wet little lumps of color. Their feet were yellow and small.

The birds were all over the bed, little ruffled bunches of feathers. Some of them were lying on their backs with their feet up. Katy eased into bed with them and got beneath the comforter. She stretched her legs out. Louis moved one or two birds out of her way, so they would not be jostled or disturbed. She could see her feet poking up. The birds lay still all around her.

Louis said, "Are you all right?"

She said, "I won't move my feet all night."

He said, "I'll turn off your light."

She said, "Leave it on."

He said, "Okay. Good night, Katy."
She said, "They might think it's a meadow."
He said, "They might."
She said, "They might be happy. They might get well."
He said, "Oh, Katy."

8

Esequeena Street was the rutted trail that ran through the Belgian Congo like a jungle stream, the Darktown section of Arrow Catcher, beneath the African-seeming moon. Poor cabins, some of them windowless, lined Esequeena, some on slabs, most on stilts, some shingled, some thatched with bundles of swamp grass or sheaves of purloined rice gathered from the flooded paddies. Every house was a shack, an unpainted cabin with a crumbling chimney, a cockeyed stoop, a cinder block or two for steps.

A few trees still stood, a cottonwood here or there for shade, but most were stunted shrubs, chinaberries, an occasional willow. No grass grew in the yards, which were swept clean each day with straw brooms.

Morgan woke up in one of those houses, his mama's house, the necromancer's cabin, thinking about Ruthie McNaughton.

It was breakfast-time, and Aunt Lily had mixed up some pan bread out of cornmeal and lard and water. She had built a fire beneath a tripod in the yard. Her hands smelled yellow and clean, with the meal and lard.

Morgan lay inside, on the pallet where he had spent the night, on the floor in a corner of his mama's house. Aunt Lily found Morgan in a canebrake when he was a baby, like Moses in the bulrushes, and raised him up as her own, although he was white.

Morgan wished he hadn't talked so mean to Hydro out at William Tell, wished he hadn't let the others shoot at the cantaloupe. He didn't know what got into himself sometimes. He tried to think about his real mama and daddy, carnival workers was what people said. A man who ran the merry-go-round and a woman who swallowed swords and fire. So that meant he had show business in his blood—that could explain a few things, he supposed. And that was why suicide had never seemed like much of an option to him, maybe. He came pretty close to it when he let Hydro shoot at the melon on top of his head, but he'd been pretty confident he'd be all right.

There was a breeze in the eaves this morning, and so the limbs of a chinaberry tree were scratching at the wall outside. The birds in the eaves kept up their evil racket, cowbirds. Morgan couldn't stand them.

Aunt Lily came in to get something. She was carrying a black skillet with hot grease in it, from the fire she'd built outside.

She was all worked up about something. She said, "Cain't eat no Mexican. Cain't eat no lovely children. Have to eat this sorry bread."

Morgan sat up on his pallet and leaned back against the bare wood wall. He had never claimed to kill anybody, just to steal a truck.

Still, he said, "You done got so hoity-toity you can't eat a Mexican?" He just meant to make a joke.

Aunt Lily flung the pan of hot grease in his face.

Morgan leaped straight up out of bed. His cheek and forehead were burning like fire. He said, "Goddamn, Mama!" He grabbed up the tattered quilt from the pallet and pressed his face into it.

She said, "Sass me again, why don't you."

He looked up at her out of the quilt. He said, "That was dangerous. It's going to blister. It might scar."

She said, "Now I got to heat up more grease."

She walked over to a five-gallon lard bucket and dipped out some grease.

He said, "What's got into you?" He looked into a sliver of mirror and saw water blisters forming on his forehead.

He got up and took a gourd dipper out of a bucket in a corner and poured the water over his face.

She calmed down some. She said, "I made some coffee."

He dried his face on the quilt.

He said, "You are going to hurt somebody, one of these days."

She said, "It's under the tripod, on a stone, outside. Use something to pick it up with."

He cut a look at her out of the corner of his eye. He said, "I wouldn't want to burn myself."

Aunt Lily fried up the pan bread, and they ate it together, and drank the black coffee with a little sugar, out on the front porch of the cabin. She sat in a high-backed rocking chair, and he just sat on the porch floor, leaned up against the wall, looking at her.

She said, "You blistering up a right smart." She was looking at his face, a man's face, and yet she saw the child in the basket, in the canebrake, where the carnies had left him.

She got up from her chair—it took her a while, she was so old—and went inside the cabin and made up a paste of some kind, a salve, from chimney soot and Vaseline and a few other things, and mixed it together with a cowbird wing. She smeared it on his burns, using the tip of the wing for a brush.

He said, "Watch out for my vest."

She said, "We used to use a bat wing, but it don't apparently make no difference."

They sat for a while, then, through the long hot morning. The breeze kept up, and fanned their sweaty faces and made them feel cool. The coarse bread and strong, sweet coffee felt good in Morgan's stomach. The fragrances of meal and hot lard and burnt coffee lingered in his nostrils.

When he was in his mama's house, the rage that sometimes boiled up out of him seemed to disperse a little, to thin out, almost to disappear—his immense anger at those faceless betrayers, his parents, who may or may not have been the persons they were rumored to have been, but in any case people who abandoned him in a swamp like a litter of kittens, his outrage at Ruthie for treating him the same way, as if he were disposable, his lost youth and broken heart of no cost to anyone. If he had not found sharpshooting in Texas, he believed he would have checked out of this life a long time ago, since what he lived was scarcely real life, anyway, but only endurance. For himself he wanted true love, its frank and amazing declarations. Hydro had it with his daddy. Morgan looked for it in Ruth McNaughton and was deceived—or maybe he only deceived himself, in despairing hope. But here, in his mama's house, he almost had it, he almost had life, not merely something like life, as sharpshooting was, show business, through which despair might be channeled until real life came along. Here he did know love, and it almost did not matter that his mama was not his real mama or that she showed her love by throwing hot grease in his face instead of with loving words. He thought he would like to buy Aunt Lily a little brick house, maybe down on Roebuck Lake, where the lake breeze was always cool, where there were still a few places on the lake that coloreds could live. A bungalow, with a kitchen-room, and a stove, and running water in the sink. His real mama may have swallowed swords and fire, but his grandmama, Aunt Lily's mama, Reena, when she was a little girl, had run behind the blue-uniformed soldiers on their horses when they rode through town after Lee had signed the Surrender. This was the depth of blood and despair that Morgan would have to plumb to find true love, real life, and this morning, in his mama's house, it actually seemed possible to find.

The Delta stretched out before him, flat as it could be, beneath the hot sun. The chinaberries, the willows, the bottle-trees, the tripods and cauldrons, the ditches and canebrakes and graveyards and railroad tracks, the rice paddies and cotton patches.

Morgan thought about Ruthie McNaughton, and last night, with Dr. McNaughton watching television down the hall. In this moment even this thought could not drag him into the slough of his ancient natural and adopted doom.

He said, "Mama?"

She was rocking with her eyes closed.

He said, "Did anybody ever write a book about this place?"

She kept on rocking, slow, slow. Eyes still closed.

He said, "The Delta, the Congo, all of it."

She was snoring.

He said, "Mama?"

She said, "Haw?" She smacked her lips, she licked them with her big red tongue. She still didn't open her eyes.

He said, "Is there any books about Miss'ippi."

She kept rocking. Her eyes were closed.

He said, "Is the Delta ugly?"

At this, Aunt Lily opened her eyes. She looked at him.

She said, "How come you to axe me a question like that?"

He said, "I don't know. I'm just asking."

She stretched herself in the chair.

She closed her eyes again. Morgan thought she had gone back to sleep.

He said, "Mama?"

She rocked a little in her chair, eyes still closed.

She said, "It's pretty goddamn ugly."

The morning moved along. The sun rose in the sky. The birds chattering in the eaves settled down in cool places and grew quiet and slept. Sheets flapped on a clothesline in a nearby yard. The ice wagon stopped for a delivery, blocks of ice for the iceboxes. An old man wearing wooden shoes slogged down the road.

Morgan walked down the street to the Ebenezer-Rides-into-Zion A.M.E. Church and swatted a few pigeons out of the rafters for supper, later on. Pigeon meat was a treat for Aunt Lily, and good for her too, old as she was. She was too old to climb up in the church rafters anymore and catch one for herself.

Morgan came back with the dead birds in a grocery bag from Jitney Jungle, their bodies as heavy and warm as loaves, and with their glassy, filmed-over eyes and metallic-colored heads shining, and put them under the house, in the cool dirt, in the shade, to keep until he could pluck and clean them and Aunt Lily could cook them later on. She would flour them and fry them and stew them in their own gravy until they were tender.

Morgan eased back up on the porch. He stepped light. Aunt Lily was snoring pretty good, real regular. She looked like a little black angel in her rocking chair. She was so sweaty she looked like she had been greased.

It was right then that he had a thought. He thought, "What did she mean about two lovely children?"

He said, "Mama?"

She said, "Haw?"

She smacked her lips and ran her big red tongue out and back in again.

That was when they heard that bacon-in-a-pan sound again, that hot-grease-sizzling sound of rubber tires on a gravel road. Morgan turned and looked out across the yard. A car had pulled up out in front of the cabin. The door was opening and a big man was getting out. It was the marshal's car, Webber Chisholm.

Aunt Lily was awake now. She and Morgan watched the

marshal make his way across the ditch. Morgan felt a trace of fear and anger rise up in him, and then he was all right. He took a couple of breaths.

Aunt Lily had a church fan on her lap, with a color picture of Jesus holding a lamb and suffering the little children to come unto Him.

Marshal Chisholm tipped his big hat. He said, "Mawning, Aunt Lily." He said, "Mawning, Morgan."

Aunt Lily started to rock in her chair again.

Morgan said, "What the hell do you want?"

In his voice, the anger would not be suppressed. Suddenly he found himself wanting to kill the marshal. He reached for his gun and realized it had fallen out of his belt onto his pallet while he slept. Would he really have killed this gentle man if the gun had been there?

Marshal Chisholm said, "It's about the killing you done out at William Tell—"

Morgan was shocked by the word killing. It was as if his mind had been read. And yet, what did it mean?

He said, "A killing?"

The marshal said, "Now, if they deserved it, well, now, that's one thing—"

Aunt Lily said, "They deserved every ounce of it. That Mexican with the truck wont no angel his ownself."

Morgan said, "Mama—?"

Marshal Chisholm said, "Well, see, that's the thing, right there. That's what I'm inclined to believe my ownself. Me— I washed their hair with Prell and had bad dreams, and I still tend to think they deserved it."

Even bitterness as old and unspecified as Morgan's was worthless in this confusion.

Morgan said, "Marshal—?"

He said, "Saving Hydro's life like you done, protecting Mr. William Tell's property—it was an admirable thing. I admire you, son."

Morgan didn't know what to say.

The marshal said, "So, you know, I hope it ain't true, what I'm hearing about that pore Mexican, and all—but anyway, as far as these two lovely children down at the Prince of Darkness with bullets between their eyes are concerned, well—"

Aunt Lily said, "The Mexican deserved it too."

Morgan said, "Mama—?"

She said, "I seen it in the crystal ball."

Morgan said, "That crystal ball don't half work. How many times has that ball picked up 'Your Hit Parade,' with Snooky Lansen?"

Marshal Chisholm said, "I see y'all been discussing this."

Morgan said, "Wait a minute, Marshal, Mama. Let me just say this. There ain't no such thing as the Mexican. I made up the Mexican."

Marshal Chisholm said, "To tell you the gospel truth, Morgan, it don't look like nobody really gives a French shit about the Mexican. You're never going to need an alibi for the Mexican. I do wish you hadn't of left the scene out at William Tell, though. If you hadn't never left the scene of the lovely children, I probably wouldn't have to be picking you up today."

Morgan said, "Marshal, who—I mean, who *are* the lovely children?"

Marshal Chisholm said, "Well, exactly! That's my point exactly, son. Who do they think they are, busting into William Tell, out of the clear blue sky and scaring the living daylights out of Hydro Raney—that pore boy ain't never going to be the same, he cain't hardly talk, ever since it happened—and demanding no telling what-all, just who in the blue blazes are they, doing such of a thing? It makes me mad just to think about it."

Morgan said, "Marshal, I truly don't know what you're talking about."

The marshal said, "But the thing is, see, not everybody in town holds my point of view. Do you see what I'm saying? There's another story going around too, a completely different one. It could be trouble. You might want to start thinking about what you're going to do, see. I don't have to pick you up right this minute, there ain't no big rush. I just dropped by to let you know I'll need to come out for you, later on today. You ain't exactly charged with no crime yet. We just need to bring you in to custody, to talk for a while, hear what you got to say. Okay, so I'll be seeing y'all later. Y'all stay cool. Bye now, Aunt Lily."

THE LITTLE cabin was empty, just the two of them. The sun made its way on across the wide sky.

Aunt Lily opened the front door and the back door to try to catch a breeze. The cowbirds were quiet in the eaves. She walked around fanning herself with the church fan. She sat down again.

She said, "I wish I had a good cat."

Morgan said, "I swatted some pigeons for supper."

Again they didn't talk for a long time.

He said, "I got gas in the truck. Half a case of oil in the bed."

She said, "You gone run for it, is you?"

They went back out on the front porch again. Aunt Lily took the rocker. Morgan sat on the porch floor and leaned up against the house.

She said, "How come you to kill the two lovely children?"

Morgan looked at her.

She said, "I reckon I can understand about the Mexican, nothing but a youthful mistake. And you did need a truck."

He said, "Mama, I ain't done what you think I done."

She said, "I won't love you no less if you's a coldblood killer. But I hopes you ain't, baby."

This was the first time Aunt Lily had ever told him she loved him. He was momentarily dumbstruck. He had always wanted her to say this, and yet now that she had, he found that he was furious at her. All he could think about was Ruthie McNaughton, when she said the same words, that liar. And he thought of his carny parents, dumping his young ass in a canebrake and probably saying the same words, "We love you, we are doing this for you, it's for the best," and then going on back to the sawdust lot of the carnival and cranking up the music on the floating horses of the merry-go-round, or swallowing their swords and torches and leaving him far behind.

He said, "What did you hear, Mama? What did the crystal say?" He knew that his voice was fierce, he could not help it.

She said, "I tried to understand about the Mexican—"

He said, "Mama, they ain't no such of a thing as the Mexican. I told you. He don't exist."

She said, "He still exists, chile. He's in God's heaven with the Baby Jesus."

He said, "I mean it, Mama! Stop blaming me for the Mexican. Hell with the Mexican, if you ask me. I gave that little son-of-bitch life. Me! Nobody else! Wouldn't nobody have ever heard of that little wetback, without me. Without me, he never would have had a truck in the first place. Wouldn't know how to drive. I can take away his truck if I want to. I can if I'm the one give him the truck. I can kill him too. I can do anything I want to do with that particular Mexican. That particular Mexican is mine, all mine, nobody else's but mine. Well, I don't know, Jesus! What am I saying? What am I talking about? I'm so mixed up. Why am I hollering at you about a Mexican? I got to go. I got to be going, Mama. I done had my heart broke, and they ain't nothing but miles and time that's going to cure it. I don't know why people are saying I killed somebody. I ain't killed nobody. Especially the lovely children. I ain't never heard of the lovely children. I got to go. The world's caving in on me, it looks like. I love you. I do. I got to be going, Mama. Goodbye, goodbye."

She said, "Don't go, Morgan."

He said, "I got to."

She said, "Ain't we gone eat them pigeons?"

He said, "Aw, Mama—"

She said, "Just stay long enough to help me eat them pigeons."

They were just sopping up the last of the gravy with pan bread when the marshal pulled up out front in his patrol car. They watched him from the porch.

Aunt Lily said, "I ought to of knowed better than pay attention to that crystal ball. Facts don't mean the first thing to that worthless crystal ball."

9

It was washday at the Prince of Darkness funeral parlor. The Prince of Darkness had stripped all the stretchers, parlor and car, and piled the sheets in the laundry room. He tossed in the dirty towels and washcloths and shrouds as well. He stripped the sheets off his own bed and threw them in with the rest. He dug down into the parlor hamper for the winding sheets, as he called them—plain hospital gowns that he used for prep work and state inspections and for indigents who had no one to dress them for the grave. He held each of these up critically to the light. A black splotch of blood here, some yellowing from urine or sweat there. He tossed each into the basket.

Out of his own personal basket he chose his white things—he only had two colors, white and black—and tossed them into the general pile of whites, his sleeveless, ribbed undershirts, his baggy BVD drawers, his two pairs of white socks from the time he caught athlete's foot. Where in the world did he catch athlete's foot in a funeral parlor? he often wondered. He tried to remember if there had been a coach.

So this is what the Prince of Darkness was doing this day, laundryman to the dead, not long after the shooting out at William Tell, with Morgan sitting in jail for questioning, when Webber Chisholm pulled up in the Arrow Catcher patrol car at the office entrance of the funeral parlor with some news.

The marshal eased down the hall and didn't look right or left. He didn't want to get surprised by whoever might be reposing in one of the viewing rooms.

The Prince of Darkness was dumping Oxydol into one of the machines by the time Webber got back to the laundry. It was never easy to know just what to say to the Prince of Darkness.

Webber said, "I just know I'm going to have bad dreams."

The Prince of Darkness said, "Did you go to the senior play?"

Webber said, "The which?"

The Prince of Darkness poured a cup of Clorox into the machine and waited for it to fill.

He said, "Doing this laundry reminded me of it. Down at the high school, *Summer and Smoke*. The senior play."

Webber said, "*Summer and Smoke*?"

The Prince of Darkness said, "It ain't much of a play, to tell you the truth. I seen better plays."

Webber Chisholm said, "Well—"

He said, "But do you know that part where the young doctor, John Buchanan, is trying to calm down Miss Alma?"

Webber said, "John Buchanan?"

He said, "It's the best scene in the play. I thought the part of John Buchanan was played real effective by the Bennett boy—Jeep, is that his name? Real large child, just got three fingers on one hand? Shot himself quail hunting, crossing a fence, dragged his Ithica across a strand of barbed wire. His big sister used to breathe refund gas fumes from the tank and knock herself out."

Webber said, "Remember that year Mr. Rant was the bride in the Womanless Wedding and got so drunk he fell off the stage in a floor-length gown? I like to died laughing."

He said, "Alma is hysterical. In *Summer and Smoke*, see. She has showed up in the middle of the night saying she's got palpitations. Do you remember what John Buchanan says to Alma? He says, 'Space has got a curve in it, Miss Alma. It turns back onto itself like a soap bubble, adrift in something that's even less than space.' Do you remember that part?"

The marshal said, "John Buchanan said that?"

The Prince of Darkness closed the lid of the machine. The first wash cycle had begun.

He said, "Those very words." There was portent in his voice.

Webber Chisholm was a foot and a half taller than the Prince of Darkness. The ceiling was not low, but suddenly it seemed close to Webber's head. The two of them stood for a while in silence in the narrow room, and listened to the sound of the machine. The comfortable, familiar fragrances of soap powder and bleach surrounded them.

Webber said, "Well—"

The Prince of Darkness went to the laundry tub and washed his hands with Lifebuoy soap, to take away the smell of chlorine. He took out a big white handkerchief and dried his hands.

Webber said, "Why do you reckon a doctor would ever

say such of a thing? Can you feature Dr. McNaughton ever starting to talk like that?"

The washing machine kicked into a new cycle.

The Prince of Darkness said, "It's loneliness. He's talking about loneliness."

Nothing else was said for a while.

In a minute, Webber said, "Was you, uh— Was you about through telling me about *Summer and Smoke*?"

The Prince of Darkness only looked at him. The Prince of Darkness's looks were black, black.

Webber said, "Because, you know, if you are, well, there's some folks—and, uh, they're waiting out in the car, in the patrol car. Needs to see you."

The Prince of Darkness said, "Someone with a loved one?"

Webber said, "No—"

He said, "Who would come to see me?"

Webber said, "They might can identify the two lovely children."

The Prince of Darkness turned back to the laundry.

He said, "Business guests."

Webber said, "Yes—"

The Prince of Darkness looked very tired. He lifted the lid of the washing machine and checked the load; then he closed it again. He adjusted the drain pipe in the laundry tub.

He said, "*Summer and Smoke* isn't much of a play, when you come right down to it."

Webber said, "It sounds pretty good. You make it sound right appealing."

The Prince of Darkness said, "He's slipping, Tennessee Williams is."

Webber said, "It still sounds all right to me."

They kept standing there in the fragrances of soap powder, and in the music of the machine and moving water.

Webber said, "I think I'd prefer the Womanless Wedding, if I had to choose." He waited a minute. He said, "You ought to come to try-outs some time."

The Prince of Darkness said, "Well, no."

Webber said, "You could start with just a small part, no lines. Flower girl, something like that. You wouldn't have to start off being the bride."

The Prince of Darkness said, "I'd be too stiff. I couldn't loosen up."

They stood there a moment longer, in the laundry room. The shrouds were sloshing behind them.

Out in Webber Chisholm's patrol car sat a married couple, the Barfoots, from Amarillo, Texas, Horace and Doris. They were starting to get restless, tired of waiting to be asked inside. It was hot in the car, even though the marshal had been kind enough to leave the windows open.

Horace said, "It's done got hot, ain't it?"

Horace was a big fat old man, near eighty. He was a preacher. An uglier man you never saw. He had a concave face, looked like he had been hit by a skillet. He killed a man when he was young, and for all these years afterwards had preached the Gospel of our Lord and Savior Jesus

Christ in hopes of being forgiven. He was wearing overalls and a straw hat.

He said, "Doris, I think they done forgot about us."

Doris was Horace's wife; she was only about thirty-five. She looked like a squaw, tall and skinny as an Indian, dark and hard as beef jerky.

She said, "What's gone make them any different from the rest of the universe?"

Horace opened the door of the patrol car and dragged his creaky old lard-ass out. He made his way around to the other side. Doris waited on him. He always insisted on opening doors for her.

He took her hand and helped her out of the car.

She said, "You know it's gone be them. You just know it is."

He said, "I know, darlin. I wish it wont."

She said, "I don't know how I'm gone stand it."

He said, "I know, darlin."

Horace and Doris were the mama and daddy of the two lovely children, brother and sister. They were here to make the identification of the bodies. The High Sheriff found them, somehow or another.

They walked into the Prince of Darkness funeral parlor and looked around. There was a desk, with papers all over it. A cup of cold coffee.

Horace said, "Anybody home?"

Doris trailed him down the hall. They poked their heads around corners. They looked into the viewing rooms.

Doris said, "I don't want to run up on them in a coffin."

Horace said, "Yoo hoo."

Doris looked at a corpse in one of the metal coffins. She said, "They do good work here, I'll grant you that much."

They stood for a while before the casket, looking at the dead stranger. Then they moved on.

They opened a closed door and stood looking into the laundry room.

Just then, the Prince of Darkness did the most amazing thing.

He stripped off his black suit coat and tied the arms around his waist and let the coat hang from his middle like a skirt.

Horace said, "Uh, Marshal—I hope you don't mind—"

Nobody paid him any attention.

The Prince of Darkness took off his tie and dropped it onto the floor behind him. He unbuttoned the first several buttons of his shirt.

He pulled his shirt down from one shoulder, almost seductively, like a brash young woman. His bare, bony shoulder shone as white as marble. The strap of his undershirt might have been a bra strap. His face changed, softened like a sexual woman's, and then, over that face, another formed, that of a bitter woman.

There was one window in the laundry room, and a shaft of light fell through it into a puddle on the floor. The Prince of Darkness stepped into the puddle of light.

He began to speak. His voice was a strange falsetto.

He said, "'Oh, how wise and superior you are!'"

Webber Chisholm looked around him, nervous.

The Prince of Darkness went on: "'John Buchanan, Junior, graduate of Johns Hopkins, *magna cum laude!*—'"

John Buchanan?

The Prince of Darkness said, "'Brilliant, yes, as the branches after the ice storm, and just as cold and inhuman! . . . You sat among us like a lord of the earth, the only handsome one there, the one superior one!'"

The marshal was starting to catch on.

The Prince of Darkness said, "'And oh, how we all devoured you with our eyes, you were like holy bread being broken among us—But snatched away! . . .'" Here the Prince of Darkness motioned with his hands, first this way and then that, out of the laundry and towards the viewing rooms, the embalming table, the autopsy room, the cooler. Then he went on: "'Oh, I suppose you're right to despise us—'"

Webber Chisholm said, "Uh—"

He said, "'—my little company of the faded and frightened and different and odd and lonely. You don't belong to that club, no. But I hold an office in it! . . . And when you marry, you'll marry some Northern beauty. She'll have no eccentricities but the eccentricities of beauty and perfect calm. Her hands will have such repose, so perfect repose when she speaks. They won't fly about her like wild birds . . . they won't reach above her when she cries out in the night! Suddenly, desperately—fly up, fly up in the night!—reaching for something—nothing!—clutching at—space.'"

The Prince of Darkness did not move, not yet. His hands

were reaching up, clutching at some invisibility, something more frail than the soap bubble, if he could only see it. His eyes were upturned, searching the hopeless skies.

The Prince of Darkness stood in this pose for a long time, thirty seconds, or more. Webber Chisholm said nothing. Horace and Doris said nothing. Doris moved near to Horace, and he encircled her scrawny body with his arm, which was as big-around and red as a ham.

At last the Prince of Darkness relinquished his pose. He dropped his arms to his side. He raised his eyes.

Marshal Chisholm clapped his big hands together, softly, slowly.

The Prince of Darkness bowed at the waist.

He looked up.

Webber looked at him, astounded. So did Horace and Doris, holding on to one another.

In the lengthy silence, something like awe hung between them in the incredible air.

The squawlike woman spoke, from her husband's capable arms. Her voice was nasal and apologetic and strange.

She said, "I heerd you might have my babies here."

The three men in the room looked at her. Her voice, even her presence, her substance, seemed less real than the voice and substance of Alma, in the Prince of Darkness's falsetto and literary words. *Heerd*? Nobody in Mississippi said *heerd* anymore. Who was this woman?

Now she stepped apart from her husband and stood between Horace and Webber Chisholm. She did this as if to prove her own reality. And yet it had the opposite effect. She seemed almost to disappear, she became a sliver by comparison to the bulk of these two men.

She projected her voice greatly, in order to be heard. She said, "Is my babies dead? Is they resting here?"

The Prince of Darkness seemed annoyed with her, fixed her in one of his black looks. It began to engulf her. She tottered a little on her feet.

Marshal Chisholm said, "Uh, this here's Horace and Doris."

Horace said, "We got a call, said they might be here."

The Prince of Darkness turned his black gaze on Horace.

Horace was an old man, accustomed to being reviled, but the black look was potent, and it staggered him.

Webber felt suddenly protective of the old man. He wished he knew what to do.

The Prince of Darkness's eyes were anchored to Horace, like leg irons on a prisoner.

He said, "They still got holes in their heads."

Horace said, "Well—"

He said, "I can't work cosmetic miracles." Suddenly, he grabbed hold of a drawer handle and pulled a big drawer out of the wall on rollers, it sounded like distant thunder.

Marshal Chisholm said, "They got clean hair. I can testify to that."

The girl came rolling out first, gray as ashes, no sheet on her, nothing, just a naked dead girl with tiny little breasts and a black hole in her forehead.

With his hand, the Prince of Darkness swept the girl's hair down over the bullet hole a little. Horace and Doris gave little simultaneous gasps.

Just then the Prince of Darkness jerked another drawer out of the wall and the dead boy rolled out, same condition.

Horace and Doris held on to each other as they looked at their children. They did not speak. They did not breathe.

The Prince of Darkness looked up with dangerous irony in his eyes. When he did, his eyes met the eyes of Webber Chisholm.

Nobody in Arrow Catcher, Mississippi, had ever matched the stare of the Prince of Darkness, but now Webber Chisholm had done so.

He received that stare like a blackness of the grave, like absence and worse than absence. When it struck him, it hurt, too. It laid him low. It swallowed him up. He almost gagged on its stench. He saw Desiree in winding sheets, his Honoree on a slab. Tombstones popped up out of every crevice of Webber Chisholm's memory and imagination.

Still he did not back down, for his own look, though unpracticed, was potent, too, born of habitual love, nourished on the impossible romance of a good and faithful partnership in marriage and lifelong friendships with other men —it carried a message for the Prince of Darkness. It said, "Have mercy, old friend, on these damaged souls from a distant land who have lost a child, two children, and who must live their days forever in the pain of regret and lost hope, do this if you value our friendship at all." That is what the look on Webber Chisholm's face said to the Prince of Darkness.

Doris said, in her dear, bladelike, sweet little voice, "Cheryl looks like she's put on a little."

Horace said, "She ran a little thin. It's good to know she's been taking care of herself."

The Prince of Darkness did not speak his ironic thoughts. He looked at Horace and Doris and no longer saw them as redneck intruders with comical names. He thought of his mother, dead, and of his own broken heart. He understood the triviality of his grief and loss, compared to that of these parents, these idealists who preached the Gospel from their home in a yellow school bus.

He said to Horace and Doris, "I'm sorry. I'm sorry you had to see. They were lovely children."

Horace and Doris looked at one another, and then at the Prince of Darkness.

Doris said, "I wouldn't go quite that far."

Horace said, "They was, you know, murderers. Rapists. Robbers. They been on the run a long time."

Horace and Doris held each other and cried. They said they didn't know where they went wrong, they tried so hard, they loved them so much. Horace said, "It's my fault." Doris said, "No, it ain't, dear, it truly ain't." He said, "I killed them. I give them the bad seed." Doris said, "I ain't been no angel my ownself." Horace said, "You're my angel. You're my onliest precious angel." She said, "I love you, Horace. We're going to get through this. We'll have other children. Something good will happen. You'll see."

Webber and the Prince of Darkness only stood and looked.

In a minute Horace and Doris sat down on a plastic couch and kept on holding one another. They cried and cried and cried. They spoke angry words. They said, "It served them right." They said, "They got what they deserved." They said, "Many a time I wanted to do it myself." They said, "It's for the best." They said, "I loved them so. I never stopped. Not once."

The Prince of Darkness walked over to the plastic couch and stood behind them.

He reached over the back of the couch and laid his hands on them, one on her shoulder, one on the old man's.

The Prince of Darkness said, "If love could bring them back, they would sit up right now."

Doris touched the back of his hand with her hard, bony fingers. She said, "Thank ye. You're a good man."

Webber Chisholm said, "I wouldn't go so far as to say that."

10

Morgan was sitting in the Arrow Catcher jail behind bars playing checkers with Webber Chisholm. City Hall was a big room with a couple of jail cells, with the iron doors standing open. The marshal's desk was on the far side of the room, along with the filing cabinets and a hat rack and gun case and small refrigerator that worked right about half the time. Webber kept a few cold drinks there, maybe a half a watermelon.

Morgan couldn't stand the game of checkers. Move and jump and king, lord, checkers is a game for morons. The checkerboard was faded and limber as a dishrag and had a round stain where a Nu-Grape bottle had been set.

Chinese checkers was a different thing, altogether different matter. Chinese checkers took some skill, some intelligence. All them marbles, all them players, it was some strategy to it. Couldn't just any idiot play Chinese checkers. It helped if you was a Chinaman, but it wasn't necessary. Mr. Quong, down at the meat market, could whip the shit out of a white man, or colored either, in a game of Chinese checkers. For some strange reason you don't meet a lot of colored folks who are skilled at Chinese checkers, nobody seems to know the reason why.

Webber said, "Can you jump over your own man?"

Morgan just looked at him.

Webber said, "I'm just asking."

Morgan said, "That's in Chinese checkers."

The marshal said, "Say which?"

Morgan said, "I don't want to play no more."

The marshal said, "You don't want to play no more?"

Morgan said, "You don't half know how to play."

The marshal said, "I'm a little rusty. You don't never learn nothing if you don't ask questions."

Morgan said, "I still don't want to play no more."

The marshal started to put up the checkers, fold up the checkerboard. He thought about telling Morgan about the floater, the dead man in Roebuck, to make conversation, something besides checkers. He had just taken the call and heard about it himself, didn't even have an i.d. yet. He hated to talk to the pore boy about any more dead folks, though.

The marshal said, "You ain't the first one to complain about my checker playing." He said, "You ought to seen how Mr. Quong acted when I played a game of Chinese with him one time down at the meat market."

Morgan got up off his chair and flopped down on his steel bunk.

The marshal said, "Such a quiet and peaceable people, generally. They do eat a lot of garlic, however."

Morgan said, "Throw me that pillow."

The marshal tossed him a feather pillow from a stool on the other side of the room. He said, "That's a clean pillow slip. Desiree puts on a fresh one every day, including weekends." He pushed open the cell door with his foot and carried the checkers and board out to his desk and put them in a drawer. He picked up a straw broom and walked back into the cell and swept the floor. He pushed aside the few sticks of furniture in the cell, so he could sweep better. As long as Morgan was propped up in his bunk, he swept under there too. He said, "I hope you ain't allergic." He was kicking up a fair amount of dust.

There was a gentleman in the other cell, a familiar face in town, Monsieur Dublieux. He pronounced his name W. Sometimes he signed it that way. Monsieur Dublieux was tall and thin and had a pencil-line moustache and wore a filthy tuxedo every day. He owned the Arrow Theater and described himself as being in show business.

The Arrow Theater showed a picture show every night and had a drawing at the Saturday matinee. One time a boy named Sugar Mecklin won a fishing rod and hooked a big red chicken in his daddy's chickenyard, like to scared his daddy and mama half to death. You never heard a sound like a chicken on a hook. It sounds like chicken all the way back to the beginning of chicken. Another time a boy name of Duncan won a motorsickle. Now that was an impressive first prize.

Sometimes Monsieur Dublieux brought in performers, a boomerang thrower, a classical piano player, a magician with steel rings and rabbits. Tex Ritter did a show one time, with a lariat and a big horse that took a great big, grassy-green dump on the little stage. All the children said, "Pee-yew." Hydro Raney said, "Pore thang." He felt sorry for the horse. Hydro said, "He's just got to be embarrassed." Another time Mr. William Tell himself got up on the stage and did his Red Skelton routines. He told jokes. He pretended like he was selling a brand of whiskey called Old Factory Whistle. Three blasts and you were out for the day. It was funny, even if didn't nobody know what a factory whistle was.

Webber said, "Monsieur, you need anything while I'm up?"

Monsieur Dublieux said, "Nothing for me, thank you."

To the sharpshooter, Monsieur said, "Ever think about breaking into show business?"

Morgan ignored him.

He said, "I've heard about that sharpshooter act of yours."

Morgan said, "I ain't really studying breaking into show business, Monsieur."

Monsieur Dublieux rolled back onto his steel bunk and covered his eyes with his arm. He said softly, "I could make you a star."

Morgan did the same thing on his bunk, lay back and covered up his eyes with his arm.

All them lies about killing a Mexican—why did Morgan tell those lies? And stealing a truck? He never stole no truck. He paid good money for that raggedy old truck, oil-burner like it was. They was coming back to haunt him now, the lies. And shell casings from his pistol, found right there on the scene. Why, that fact alone looked incriminating as all get-out, under the circumstances. He lay there thinking: how did I get myself in this mess? He thought, I've been working to this mess all my life.

Webber Chisholm was moving around the office with his broom, real slow, in his big old elephant way. Morgan just lay there on his bunk, propped up against his doubled-over feather pillow. He took his arm from over his eyes and watched Webber. Webber swept the floor of Monsieur Dublieux's cell, and then swept the floor of the main office. The pistol he carried on his hip was as big as an anvil. It flopped this way and that way on his hip as he swept. Morgan's own pistol was somewhere in this office. In a desk drawer, maybe. Morgan was trying to think how he could get his hands on that pistol, it would make him feel a little better.

Monsieur Dublieux said, "Did you-all hear that rain the other night?"

Webber said, "Woo-ee."

He said, "That was a rain and a half."

Webber said, "You said that right."

He said, "That kind of rain can wash the birds right out of the trees."

Webber said, "Boy howdy."

He said, "It can wash the graves right out of the ground."

Webber said, "Boy howdy."

Monsieur said, "One time up in St. Louis there was a big rain like that. Washed up a bunch of coffins out of a grave-yard."

Webber said, "Tell the truth."

Monsieur said, "No, it is the truth."

Webber said, "This sounds like one them stories the Prince of Darkness is all time telling."

Monsieur said, "Well, this one's the truth. A Western cowboy, all dressed up in chaps and spurs and six shooters and a ten-gallon hat—washed up out of a graveyard in St. Louis. Perfectly preserved. A bucktoothed cowboy."

Webber said, "Bucktoothed?"

Monsieur said, "That's it."

Webber said, "What's a bucktoothed Western cowboy doing in St. Louis?"

Monsieur Dublieux said, "You want to know where that cowboy is today? He's in show business. He's working out in California. I got him his first big break in show business."

Webber said, "You broke a dead cowboy into show business?"

Monsieur said, "He's with a traveling Wild West Show."

"A bucktoothed cowboy?"

"That's it."

Webber said, "Seem like his big break come a little late."

Monsieur said, "Perfectly preserved. Buckteeth. They set him up outside the tent in a leather saddle on a sawhorse. Tourists see it's the authentic, gen-you-wine item, and they pay top dollar. Solid gold."

Webber said, "I still can't help but think he would have enjoyed his celebrity a little more if he was alive."

Monsieur said, "They got him some new clothes, trimmed his fingernails and toenails, got him a shampoo and a haircut, put a coat of Shinola on them pointy-toed high-heeled boots, and he's good as new."

Webber said, "Well, I do say."

Monsieur said, "They ought to of put braces on them teeth. It was too expensive. It's a major capital outlay, I understand that. I can understand them wanting to economize."

Webber said, "Him being dead."

Monsieur said, "Still, you want to look your best."

Morgan lifted up on one elbow and looked into the next cell at Monsieur Dublieux. Then he just lay back down on his steel bunk. He said, "Lord God Baby Jesus in golden heaven."

After a while, Desiree Chisholm came in carrying three lunch boxes. She was bringing lunch to Webber and the prisoners. Webber brightened up when he saw her. He was scared he was going to dream about the dead cowboy. He wished Monsieur Dublieux hadn't gone on about them buckteeth. That's just the kind of detail that's all time showing up in a dream. He said, "Hey, Desiree."

She said, "Hey, Webber."

Monsieur Dublieux also perked up as soon as Desiree entered the jail.

Desiree had been a cheerleader at Arrow Catcher High, when she was a girl. She got Peppiest Cheerleader in the yearbook her senior year. She also got Most Sincere. She was a little less peppy now, but just as sincere and pretty Monsieur Dublieux had been trying to talk her into going into show business ever since she graduated from ACHS. He wanted to be her agent.

He said, "Desiree, how are you!"

She said, "Hey, Monsieur." Then to everyone, she said, "There's a chicken leg and some cold collards and a hunk of cornbread in these lunch boxes, if anybody's hungry. Oh, and a carton of sweetmilk and a Hostess cupcake."

Webber said, "You outdone yourself."

She said, "I had a little extra time."

She started to pass out lunch boxes.

Monsieur rubbed his hands together and waited for Webber to open up the cell and let her in with his lunch. He had a big smile for Desiree.

Morgan didn't move. Something about the appearance of Desiree Chisholm here, and the marshal's sappy love of her, and Monsieur's pathetic, alcoholic fascination, struck Morgan to the heart with the meaninglessness of all human existence. We are all truly alone in this world, just as he had told Hydro that day out at William Tell. Even a father who sung songs to you didn't change that one essential fact of life. Even a mama who all of a sudden one day said she loved you, even if you were a cold-blooded murderer. For the first time in his life, he believed he might be capable of testing Aunt Lily's bizarre declaration. He could escape from this place. He could leave a trail of hair and eyeballs behind him.

Webber was fumbling with the cell keys. Then he remembered the cell doors weren't even shut, let alone locked.

Webber said, "Well, I hope you boys are hungry." Desiree went into the sharpshooter's cell.

She said, "Hey, Morgan."

He didn't move, didn't answer.

She said, "I'll put your lunch box over here, in case you get hungry later on." Before she left his cell, she said, "I heard about the eyewitness, Morgan. I'm sorry as I can be." She turned then and walked out of the cell.

Morgan thought, Eyewitness?

Monsieur Dublieux said, "Did you bring a lunch for yourself, Desiree? Here, please, share some of mine, if you'd like." He brushed cornbread crumbs off the ruffled front of his shirt. He spread his napkin over the shiny material of his tuxedo pants.

Desiree said, "Naw, thanks, I ate before I came over. There's some pepper sauce for the greens in Webber's box. Y'all will have to share."

Morgan sat up on the bunk.

Webber and Monsieur opened up their lunch boxes and started to unwrap their chicken legs from waxed paper.

Desiree said, "Oh, and there's a hardboiled egg in there, too."

The jail began to smell wonderful with the fragrances of the food.

After a while Morgan opened his lunch too. He wished he could turn it down, not eat it, say "No thank you," but he was too hungry. That chicken smelled too good. Better than pigeon, that was for sure. He picked up a drumstick and took a little bite. Oh my God, it was so good, it was truly excellent. He sucked his fingers and closed his eyes. He thought of Ruthie. He hated himself for once imagining that they could be married, share a meal like this, a life.

The others talked for a while, about one thing and another. Morgan ate and kept quiet.

Somebody said, "Pass the pepper sauce."

Morgan thought, *I've got to get out of here.* And yet even as he held this thought, he did not really even care whether he got out, just so long as these voices stopped, for a little while anyway, just so long as love and magic, or what passed for them, even show business, in the desperation of the struggle against all the reasons for suicide, just so long as they shut up for a while, for now, and did not continue to remind him of what he lost, or never had, or was fool enough to believe was possible in a lifetime such as his own—he could be satisfied with that, as little as that. He could shut these voices up. He could if he had his pistol.

He said, "How do you mean 'eyewitness'?"

Desiree looked at him. She smiled her beautiful smile. She said, "Oh, you were able to eat a little something after all. Well, good. I'm glad to see you feeling better."

Monsieur Dublieux took a bite of cornbread out of the hunk in his lunch box and brushed crumbs out of his pencil-line moustache. He chewed for a minute. He said, "Desiree, I was just thinking about the old days."

Desiree was the cutest cheerleader on the squad, back in high school, and the tiniest, not even five feet tall. She was usually paired off with a girl named Barbara Ann, who was about Desiree's same size, maybe a little taller. They were cute as buttons. Barbara Ann had red hair and freckles and big green eyes. People came to arrow-catching matches just to see Desiree and Barbara Ann.

Desiree said, "Now, don't you get started on that again, Monsieur. I got me a career right here." She put her arm around her husband's big waist, as far as it would go, anyway.

Monsieur Dublieux said, "We could all be rich right now,

me and you and Barbara Ann, if you had followed my advice."

Desiree said, "Money can't buy what I've got."

Monsieur Dublieux looked at Webber Chisholm, big as a side of beef.

He said, "Well, I grant you that."

Webber was pleased as he could be. He said, "Y'all are embarrassing me."

Morgan said, "I was wondering about that eyewitness."

Monsieur Dublieux said, "I still know a few people out on the coast, if you ever change your mind." He said, "Same goes for you, Morgan. Don't let an opportunity slip through your fingers like Desiree did."

Morgan was thinking, That big pistol would slip right out. One second, and I'd be holding it in my hand.

Desiree said, "Stop now, Monsieur, I mean it." But she couldn't help being pleased.

They stopped talking for a while now. Morgan imagined a bullet hole in Webber Chisholm's big chest. These were new thoughts, he was not comfortable with them. He was no killer, never had been. Still, he thought them. He did not push them away.

For now, everybody concentrated on the food, even Morgan. They passed the pepper sauce back and forth.

Monsieur Dublieux said, "Them was the days, all right." He had finished eating his Hostess cupcake and was lying back on his bunk. He wasn't talking to anybody in particular. He said, "Nobody cared about the arrow-catching team. The team stunk. They were awful. We didn't have one white child in this town who could catch an arrow. The archers were almost as bad. They like to had to call an end to the sport before somebody got killed."

Webber said, "One time when I was a boy, I was eating a Hostess cupcake and heard a mawking bird up in a walnut tree, tra-la-la-tweedly-dee-dee, you know, this was in Pap Mecklin's backyard, that big old tree—and so I looked up in the tree, in the leaves, had my mouth wide open, looking for the bird, and you know what?—that durn mawking bird dropped a load of dooky right in my mouth."

Desiree said, "Webber!"

Webber said, "Sorry. I didn't mean to seem indelicate. I just thought about that mawking bird when I took a bite of this here Hostess cupcake."

Morgan said, "Tell me who the eyewitness was."

Monsieur Dublieux said, "That little four-eyed fat boy."

Morgan saw everything clearly now. Louis, the comic books, the revenge for falling in love with the boy's mama. For the first time in his life, Morgan felt truly and utterly hopeless.

Desiree said, "Webber, me and Monsieur was just reminiscing about the old days and breaking into show business, and you have got to get started on bird dooky."

Morgan felt giddy, light-headed, reckless. He got up off his bunk and walked over to the bars of his cell. He said, "That cream filling in the middle of a Hostess cupcake looks about like bird dooky."

Webber said, "Well, see, that's the way I figure it."

Morgan saw Webber Chisholm collapse onto the floor

and bust like a big watermelon. He saw him lying on the floor and puking up blood. He saw Desiree leaning over him. He saw her head explode like a cantaloupe. Anything was possible now.

He said, "Did you swallow it?"

Desiree cried, "You boys!"

Webber said, "Well, yeah—"

Morgan walked back over to his bunk.

He said, "Right."

He put his head back down on his pillow. He thought he could do it.

He said, "I've eaten my share of birdshit."

Webber said, "You know what I'm talking about, then. It ain't got that much taste, and a little bit once in a while never hurt nobody."

Monsieur Dublieux said, "Well, that's good to know."

Webber said, "Not if you chase it with a cupcake."

Monsieur Dublieux said, "More people ought to know about this, Marshal. They ought to put it on the TV."

Desiree said, "You don't have to get sarcastic, Monsieur."

Nobody talked for a while now.

Monsieur asked for a mirror and a basin of water. He needed to freshen up, he was getting out of jail later that afternoon.

Webber said, "Just use the facility, right down the hall there."

Monsieur Dublieux was gone a little while. The others could hear the water running. They could hear him singing show tunes. He changed the words of "My Fair Lady." He sang, "I've grown a costume on my face," and this made Desiree laugh.

She said, "Monsieur is just the most charming and witty creature."

Webber Chisholm gave his wife a look, like this.

Desiree gathered up the lunch boxes. She swept corn-bread crumbs into her hand. She threw the waxed paper and egg shells and milk cartons into the trash. She said, "Does anybody need an extra napkin?" Monsieur went back into his cell and pulled the door shut behind him.

He said, "Guess what they named the bucktoothed cowboy."

Morgan gave Monsieur an evil look, like this.

Webber said, "Anybody else need to use the facility before I lock up?" Speaking to Morgan.

Monsieur said, "Boy Howdy."

Morgan just looked at him.

Monsieur said, "The name was my idea, Boy Howdy. Where do you think Cary Grant would have ever got with a name like Archie Leach? It's the same with every actor and performer in the world. You got to have the right name."

Desiree said, "What stage name would you have given me, Monsieur? If I hadn't been so much in love?"

Morgan said, "You named a bucktoothed dead man Boy Howdy?"

Webber said, "Last chance—facility, anybody? Before I lock up the cells?"

Morgan said, "That ain't very respectful of the dead, it don't look like to me."

Webber went on and locked Morgan's cell door, too.

Monsieur Dublieux said, "That would have depended on many things, my dear." Speaking to Desiree.

Morgan got up off his bunk and walked to the cell door. He wrapped his fingers around the bars.

Webber struggled with the keys and finally got the lock to click. The big pistol was swinging this way and that.

Desiree said, "Like what kind of things?"

Morgan said, "I'd be more respectful of the dead if I was you."

Morgan eyed the gun butt. If he took it he would have to kill him. It would be an easy thing, taking it, snapping off a couple of quick shots.

Monsieur gave Desiree a big wink. He went back to an earlier subject. He spoke only to Desiree now. He said, "The crowds were big, anyway, at the arrow-catching events, remember? It didn't matter if the team stunk like *merde*. The crowds didn't care about the team. The crowds came to see the cheerleaders. They came to see you."

Desiree lowered her eyes in pleasure. Webber lumbered on over to his desk and started pulling out some papers and looking at them.

Monsieur said, "They called, *Desiree*, they called, *Barbara Ann*. You made them believe they were not all alone in the world. You made them whisper in the grandstands, in urgent voices, you made them debate the meaning of life and death."

Something about this conversation made Webber Chisholm uncomfortable. He put down his papers and paced the room. Desiree was remembering, too, the old days, the archers and the catchers, the green fields and the lights. Webber walked towards his wife and reached to touch her but she moved away. She said, "My stage name, Monsieur, what would it have been?"

Webber stood in front of Morgan's cell, watching his wife. He was backed up to the bars. He was afraid of losing her to Hollywood.

Morgan eyed the pistol, huge, chrome plating and ivory grips. It was as big as a lard bucket, as big as a pay phone, brilliant as sunlight. It was just asking to be lifted from the holster. Morgan loosened his fingers on the cell bars. He dropped his arms to his side, very slow. He eased his hand through the cell bars and touched the ivory pistol grip of Webber's big gun. Webber shifted his weight, and Morgan withdrew his hand.

Monsieur said, "Show us, Desiree."

Desiree was a child again. Barbara Ann was there beside her, also a child. They wore white sweaters with a big AC on the front. They wore black pleated skirts and saddle oxfords and bobby socks. Their hair was pulled back in identical ponytails. Desiree pretended to wrap her arms around her friend. She pretended to lean into Barbara Ann's embrace. She leaned and swayed. She sang, "I've got all my sisters with me." Her voice was so sweet it broke hearts.

Monsieur Dublieux cried out, "Who needs an arrow-catching team!"

She sang, *My guy's an arrow-catching guy, he goes to Arrow*

High. She clapped her hands and kicked her foot up over her head.

Monsieur Dublieux cried out, "You've still got it, Desiree! You could still be a star!"

Webber fought back tears at the sight of her beauty, at the fear of loss.

Monsieur Dublieux saw dollar signs, bright lights, big city, lunch with the stars. He wolfed down the last of his cornbread and collard greens. Hollywood, the Great White Way, the Catskills.

Monsieur Dublieux was in love with her. He always had been, since she was a child. And she would never be a star. She didn't have ambition. If she had ambition, Monsieur Dublieux could take her to the moon, to the Milky Way.

Morgan reached through the bars once more.

Desiree said, "Would you have given me your own name? Would I have become Desiree Dublieux?" She didn't pronounce the name W. She gave it all the French she knew. "Would my name now be Dez-ah-ray Doob-lee-uhh?"

Morgan lifted the big pistol from the marshal's holster.

Marshal Chisholm staggered away from the cellblock, gripped in pain and fear, though he did not even notice that his gun was gone from its place at his side. No one noticed.

Monsieur Dublieux leaped from his bunk. He grasped the bars of his cell. "Sacre Dieu!" he cried. "Dez-ah-ray Dub-lee-uhh! Toujours et toujours!"

Webber Chisholm collapsed backwards into the swivel chair at his desk. He let his head fall forward onto his ink blotter. He cried tears filled with heartbreak. He wept, "I ain't worthy! Oh life, oh death!"

Morgan cocked the hammer of the big pistol.

The marshal looked up from his desk. He dried his tears, checked his sobs. He saw the pistol, looked straight down its barrel and saw a deep tunnel of darkness that reminded him of what life would be like without his wife.

11

Late morning, Louis began to move beneath the light covers of his bed. The long, hard rain of yesterday was over. The breeze through his window was clean and new, a fragrance of wet trees, like big flowers. The sun filled up his room with yellow light. He rolled over in bed, onto his flashlight, which he had used the night before to read *Wonder Woman* beneath his covers, the bullet-deflecting bracelets, the magic lasso, the invisible airplane. What good did it do to have an invisible airplane if you weren't invisible yourself? He reached behind him and moved the flashlight. He had forgotten to turn it off before he fell asleep, so the batteries were dead.

It was late, he had slept hard. Outside his window he could hear the quiet noises of morning, children at play, calling out to one another, a power mower somewhere, far down the block, straining to cut the wet grass, a trundle of wagon wheels and the soft clop-clop of mules' hooves, a barely discernible peeping of waking birds. Louis came slowly awake.

And then he came very suddenly awake. He sat quickly up in bed. The birds outside his window reminded him. The dead canaries on Katy's bed. He had meant to wake up early enough to move them, to take them outside before Katy could find them.

He flung back the sheet and light spread and groped

around on his bedside table for his glasses. He fitted the little plastic hooks around his ears and pushed the glasses up on his nose. He swung his feet to the floor and rushed to his door. He looked down the hall and saw that his parents' bedroom door was still closed. It filled him with anger to look at that closed door. He knew why his father had wanted to break down the bathroom door with an axe. Louis believed he might break this one down with scorn alone.

Louis was wearing only his underwear, his Tex Ritter boxer shorts. He might order that Charles Atlas body-building course off the back of *Plastic Man* one of these days. He might knock that door down with his fist. He might tell them he was so angry he thought he would like to kill somebody. He didn't know why he was so angry. He'd like to kill that guy who kicked sand in Charles Atlas's face when Charles Atlas was a ninety-eight-pound weakling. Weaklings needed somebody to protect them. He wished he could do it. He wished he was a superhero. Or he could do like Hydro—pick up a gun and—Well, anyway—Hydro was lucky. Louis would just dearly love to put a couple of well-placed bullets between the eyes of somebody, he didn't much care who.

He walked to Katy's room and took a couple of deep breaths, and pushed open her door, and looked inside.

Katy was already awake. She seemed almost to be in a trance, looking down at her feet. She was sitting up in bed, straight as a little ramrod, propped against her white pillows with her feet stretched out beneath the covers. Her hair fell over her shoulders. She scarcely moved. She scarcely seemed to breathe.

The thirty or more birds that the two of them had brought home last night were still there, of course, the wild canaries, on the green comforter with tiny flowers. Sunlight fell over them, through the big windows, and warmed and brightened the room. In the sunshine, the canaries' feathers bore little trace of the green tinge or the brown, or of the rainwater that had soaked and darkened them the night before. In the night there had been a change. They might have been made of solid gold, their feathers' yellow shone so bright.

Katy moved her head slowly to the right, so that she might see Louis standing in her doorway. She neither spoke, nor smiled, nor cried, nor widened her eyes. Her face remained a blank. She turned her head again and faced the birds around her feet, the green expanse of her covers.

The birds had thought it was a meadow. They were alive. They were dried out now. They were up on their feet. They were hopping slowly about the bed. Now and then one or more stretched their wings, or ruffled their feathers. The tiny sounds of peep peep peep and chop chop chop came from this room, not from a tree outside his window, as Louis had first believed.

He whispered, "Katy! You were right."

When he spoke, the birds did not flush and fly, they were not frightened. They kept on about their business; they moved this way and that about the bed.

So Katy spoke then, too. She scarcely moved her lips. She said, "I didn't move my feet all night."

Louis said, "Katy, I told a lie. I said Morgan killed the lovely children, and he didn't."

Katy didn't say anything. She only kept watching the birds. The birds preened themselves and shrugged their shoulders and stretched their necks and scratched their little yellow heads with one foot, like a dog scratching fleas. They made a musical sound of gargling in their throats.

Louis closed the bedroom door behind him. He eased into the room, barefoot. He pushed his glasses up on his nose. He made no noise on the thick white carpet on Katy's floor. He moved silently around the foot of the bed, to the big casement window.

Louis said, "We'll have to see if we can get them to fly away."

Katy said, "Fly away?"

Louis said, "We can't keep them."

Katy said, "I want to keep them."

He opened the window, first one side and then the next. He pushed aside the Alice in Wonderland curtains, the Mad Hatter and the March Hare and the Queen of Hearts.

She said, "Don't let them go. Please?"

He said, "We have to. If we don't they'll—"

She said, "They'll what?"

He said, "You know."

She said, "Die?"

He had the windows wide open. Now he had to encourage them in that direction. He had to pray they wouldn't panic and fly into the walls and bloody their heads and flutter about and flounder and die, of hard blows or fright.

She said, "Can I keep just one?"

He said, "They're not pets, Katy." He said, "Jiggle your foot."

She said, "They'll think I don't love them."

He said, "Jiggle your foot."

She squinched up her toes a few times. The one or two or three birds nearest her feet hopped a little to one side.

He said, "More."

She bounced her left foot up and down a couple of times. Several birds leaped up, startled, but then settled back down on the bed, not far away from her foot.

But now all the birds were agitated. Their songs stopped. They looked this way and that, as if for direction. As if confused about where the movement came from, a few birds moved closer to Katy. One sat up on the cover on her leg.

Louis said, "Morgan could go to the electric chair on account of me, the lie I told."

Katy stretched out her hand to the canary nearest her, the one on her leg. She put her hand down on the cover right beside the bird. It hopped up on her hand.

She said, "Look."

Louis said, "Don't move."

He slid around the end of the bed to Katy's side. He held out his hand to her. She lifted her hand, the one with the wild canary perched on it. She stretched out her hand to her brother. Their hands touched. The canary hopped from her hand to his. He felt its tiny yellow feet, like small wires, on his flesh. He looked at his sister. For only one second, though.

Louis turned, slowly, slowly. He walked towards the open casement window. When he got there, he looked back at his sister.

Katy said, "Bye-bye."

Louis stuck his hand out the window and jiggled it. Suddenly, the bird's golden feathers rattled like crumpled paper, like dry leaves, like dry bones. The single bird, the wild canary, lifted off Louis's hand. It sailed away, out, out into the morning light, far out from the house, beating its wings as if for dear life, or a celebration of the dearness of life, and then finally it landed in the branches of a flowering crepe myrtle bush.

As if on a signal, then, all the other birds rose up, too, only thirty or forty of them but as if there were a million, sudden and loud, up off the meadowlike comforter of Katy's bed, filling the room with their warm bodies, their gold color, their beating wings, and then they, too, sailed away, out the same window, all in a flurry of strong hearts and dropping feathers, so close to Louis's face that he believed he could smell them, their bodies washed with rain.

Louis KNEW that Morgan was in the Arrow Catcher jail. He was not sure how he knew. No one had told him, that he could remember. In his mind's eye Louis could see Morgan there, the electrodes attached to his head and legs, the big chair, the big switch. Louis had gone to see the traveling exhibit of the Mississippi state electric chair when it came through town last year. He could see Morgan in that chair right now. He knew that he was there because Louis had put him there through the black magical force of anger alone, hatred had put him there. He had hated Morgan so much, had filled up so much space with pain and grief and rage, and all of it directed towards Morgan, that imprisonment and pain and even death were all that could have resulted, were the inevitable outcome of so much ill feeling, ill will, and nothing on earth, not the greatest of the superheros, not even Wonder Woman, with her gentle subtle gift of love and magic, could have prevented Morgan from being put in jail.

When the last wild bird had flown past his face and out the window, out far from the house, suddenly a great many things became clear to Louis McNaughton.

He had to go to the jailhouse and confess. To the marshal, of course, to try to save Morgan's life from electrocution—but mainly to Morgan. Louis would not ask to be forgiven, he would only pledge to forgive. He would love Morgan as much as he loved Katy. That was his promise to somebody, himself, God, the future of humankind. Hopeless, selfless, world without end. He thought of Morgan on the kitchen floor with Louis's mother, or chair, or wherever they did whatever they did. He knew where the axe was, where his father had left it. He thought of chopping off his own feet with it. He thought of breaking down his parents' bedroom door first—taking the axe and finishing what his father had had no need, finally, to do. He thought of murdering both his parents. He even thought of splitting *Katy's* head.

He said to Katy, "I've got to go."

She said, "Will you make me French toast?"

He said, "Not today."

She said, "With maple syrup?"

He said, "Okay."

She said, "I hope Morgan does go to the electric chair."

He said, "No, Katy. Not that. Don't say that."

She said, "I hope he does."

He said, "He didn't do anything."

She said, "He did so."

He said, "Love Morgan, Katy."

She said, "If I had a gun, I would kill him."

He said, "Oh, baby. I've got to run. I'll be back. I'll make French toast later. We'll talk more."

She said, "I would kill Mama and Daddy, too."

Louis ran out the door. He said, "I love you, Katy-did."

He ran down the steps and out the front door.

12

Louis McNaughton was walking fast, going to untell his lie.

At the sound of the gunshot, he stopped on the sidewalk, in front of Mr. Quong's meat market, a block away from City Hall. Mr. Quong saw him through the store window and waved his cleaver and gave him his usual big smile.

Usually Louis waved back. Not today.

He stood there. He cocked his head. He looked like a robin listening for worms. His lost childhood said, "So long, sucker." Louis said, "Goodbye."

He hurried his step, and felt a blister on his heel. His sock had bunched up in back and his shoe was rubbing. Louis said, "You ain't nobody, blister, compared to the rest of my life." He broke into a run. He felt a stitch in his side. He laughed. He said, "You ain't doodly-squat, stitch."

Louis entered City Hall and breathed the still cool air of the corridor. A candy and magazine stand, with no one in attendance, stood just inside the door and down the hall. A shoeshine chair, big as a throne, also unattended. The ceilings were tall, and the old building smelled of oiled floors and stale cigar smoke, a lifetime of grief, a long history of nothing but loss. Light came into the building from high windows, but failed to illuminate, dimmed by the ancient dark.

Louis looked at the doors that lined the hallway, the lower half-doors made of dark-stained wood, the top halves of opaque glass, with signs stencilled onto the panes—CITY AUDITOR, CITY MANAGER, JUSTICE OF THE PEACE, MARSHAL. He walked to the marshal's door and touched the doorknob with his fingers. He thought that behind this door lay the future. He thought that whatever he found there would be a creature of his own making. He knew, once and for all, that what a person does on earth matters. What a person does, in fear or envy or love or illness, reverberates forever through time, to eternity. He was not thinking of his father, or even his mother, he was thinking of himself.

Louis turned the knob. He pushed open the door. He stepped inside and saw what might have been a frieze, a tableau of frozen figures—Webber and Desiree, Morgan in his cell, behind the bars, holding the big chrome pistol, Monsieur Dublieux a shrunken creature on a corner of the artifice. He saw the marshal's desk, the marshal's big hat on a peg, the ancient, squatty old excuse for a refrigerator in a corner.

Louis had come here to confess his lie, he was ready to do so, was willing, but in the one second of his presence in this room, he understood what was almost unimaginable, that Morgan, the sharpshooter, whose aim was deadly, whose hand was swift, had just fired the pistol. Louis, too, froze, became part of the tableau.

He shifted his eyes, searched Webber Chisholm's big chest, the vast expanse of starched shirt, white as a snowfield in foreign lands where Louis now knew he would one day travel to cleanse himself of all that he had been, geographical and emotional. He searched each button on the marshal's shirt, the two pockets, right side, left side, looking, searching for the one small spot that would become the flowering blossom of let blood, to tell him the meaning of the gunshot he had heard, and that now he recognized.

He had not heard that Hydro was dead, no one had told him this—but now suddenly he knew that it was true. As true as anything else he might have meant to say.

Louis said, "Hydro Raney is dead."

The marshal looked at Louis. Everybody in the room did.

Louis remembered the night that Hydro blew out the brains of the two robbers—how different he had looked in that instant after the shots were fired, when Louis had peeked out of the cupboard. In Louis's memory, Hydro's head had not been enlarged, Hydro was not simple-minded, only brave and vengeful as a strange angel. His skin had seemed to glow. That had been the moment of Hydro's death, not later, not however people would tell it when the facts came out. It seemed to Louis almost as if someone had told him this, whispered it to him, just as he entered the room.

The tableau started to break up.

Desiree said, "Hydro is dead?"

Everybody just stood there for a while and didn't know what to say.

The marshal said, "Hydro was the floater I got the call about? Oh, Lord."

Morgan looked at Louis as if he were a creature from a distant planet.

Desiree said, "I can't believe it. Hydro? Dead? I can't

believe we were just sitting around here talking, playing checkers, like nothing had happened. Eating greens and cornbread and shooting the refrigerator. Webber, you knew about this?"

Webber said, "Not that it was Hydro, Lord no—I wouldn't have been standing around here—"

Louis said, "Shooting the refrigerator?"

He looked over in the corner. There was a bullet hole in the refrigerator door.

There had been a moment of tension, of course, when Morgan lifted the pistol from the holster, more than tension, astonishment and fear, maybe outrage, and even genuine rage, anger. It was a dangerous thing to do, a completely dumb-ass damn thing to do, not a bit smart, irresponsible and foolish and melodramatic, even in a moment of despair; it might have had serious consequences, tragic consequences, as almost all actions do; it was serious, a serious violation and lapse of good sense. A lead bullet, especially one the size of the ammunition in that incredible handgun, flying around a room, a ricochet, could split apart, bust into little pinhead-sized fragments, and then if it hit somebody, even the smallest sliver, well, lives could be changed forever, it could put somebody's eye out. Not to mention scaring the living daylights out of everybody. The sound alone, in a closed-up room, could have busted somebody's eardrum.

Still, no harm was done in the long run, not really; what happened, bad as it was, was understandable, excusable in its way, they all finally would agree, much later, when the story was told for the one-millionth time at Monday Music, or confessed to at William Tell, by people who were not even in City Hall on this day, an act perhaps excusable in one so young as Morgan, and underprivileged, but dangerous in any case, criminal even, if anyone wanted to press the matter to its limit.

Webber had looked down the barrel and had seen life without Desiree. It was a life marked for a long time only by emptiness and regret, and then, with work and good health and luck, which were necessary to diffuse bitterness, a lifetime of love's reapplication inward, regeneration, grown deeper and richer and stranger each year, burnished and reburnished by pain and loss and the weird work of the spirit and the passage of days. Monsieur Dublieux had collapsed in a corner of his cell. Lord only knows what he saw.

They all looked at Morgan, saw him holding the marshal's gun. He looked like a child in a cowboy suit.

Webber looked down at his empty holster. He said, "I thought I felt a little light on this side."

Morgan thought for one moment. If he was going to shoot anybody, it would have to be himself. He said, "I ain't going to shoot nobody."

Desiree said, "Well, I should think not, Morgan, for heaven's sake."

Morgan held the gun out, flat in his palm, for somebody to take from him. He said, "I thought I could, but I can't."

That's when he noticed the refrigerator. Before even he knew what was happening, he flipped the pistol to his other hand.

Forget about how the gunshot sounded and smelled, it was awful. What was impressive was the way the bullet hit the refrigerator. The bullet hit the refrigerator so hard, so solidly, that the appliance seemed to tilt backwards, and the door flew open and the light came on.

The marshal said, "Goddamn, man! Excuse my French." Desiree said, "Morgan, I have to tell you, I don't appreciate that little display one little bit. My ears are ringing. Did you see that little light come on, Webber?"

Monsieur Dublieux only groaned.

The marshal walked over to Morgan's cell and jerked the pistol angrily out of Morgan's hand and shoved it back into its scabbard.

He said, "Honest to God, Morgan! If you're so dead set on shooting a refrigerator, I wish you would give a body some warning. And use a smaller-caliber pistol, for crying out loud."

Desiree was mad too. She said, "That refrigerator could have been worth something, you don't know."

Webber said, gently, "Not that refrigerator, honey."

Desiree was still angry. She said, "In theory, I mean. It could have, for all he knew."

Webber said, "Okay, okay."

Monsieur Dublieux got up off the cell floor, where he had slumped down when the pistol went off. He had recovered himself a good deal.

He said, "Brilliant. Simply brilliant."

It was then that Louis came in and made his surprising announcement about Hydro. They spoke with him for a minute.

Then Desiree said, "Monsieur, are you all right?"

Monsieur Dublieux was no longer interested in Desiree. He said, "The Great Blackwell could not have lifted that pistol more deftly, Morgan. Houdini could not have. I can get you into Actors Equity by the end of next week. You can be working by the end of the month. "

Louis then did what he came here to do. He said, "I lied about the sharpshooter." He cast an apologetic glance in Morgan's direction. He said, "Morgan never killed anybody."

Desiree had gotten over the worst of her anger at the sharpshooter. She was interested in Monsieur Dublieux's offer to the young man. She said, "You're young, Morgan, you're talented. Don't let your opportunities slip away. Show business can work, at least until, you know—" She meant to say, At least until true love comes along, or at least real life, a cessation of despair.

Webber Chisholm lowered his eyes.

Louis said, "Hydro killed the two lovely children, not Morgan. I saw him do it. He looked like a Mexican bandito, he was so handsome and brave."

Monsieur Dublieux said, "Exactly! That's how we'll bill you—The Mexican Bandito! What do you think, Morgan, how does that sound to you?"

Morgan looked at him. He said, "I ain't really Mexican. I wouldn't want to tell no more lies."

That was what he said, and it was true enough. He was through with lies. What he was really thinking, though, was that for all the trouble he might have caused, for all the danger he had put people in today, there was something to be proud of here as well, a good thing he had done, if you looked at it in just the right way. Morgan looked over at the child, poor bewildered hopeful Louis, standing there at the door, in the confusion and cordite, trying to undo his lie, untell his tale, and Morgan thought of what Louis would never know—that by Morgan's choice of life over death— not drilling the big white slow-moving target of Webber Chisholm's innocent chest, and not putting the pistol barrel into his own mouth and tasting the gun oil and the fire—he had given Louis, and maybe the whole world, the rare gift of effective moral damage control, a lie without consequences, or at least not the consequence of the rules of contagious despair, as they are usually practiced on this earth. By this choice of life, Louis had been set free.

There were details to iron out. Firing the gun was a crime, of course. Taking it from the marshal was a crime, maybe even attempted escape. Other decisions would have to be made, choices with their own meaning, their own consequences. For now, these could wait. Everyone was only glad to be alive, to hear words of truth, sad at the thought of Hydro's passing out of this life.

Desiree had another sad thought as well—that she would never know what her stage name might have been.

13

Out on the island, the big rain the night before had filled up all the boats with water, even those anchored under the shed, and so Mr. Raney had gone out early in the morning and started pulling them up onto the worn boards of the dock. There were only a dozen boats altogether, most of them rentals, and his own boat, of course.

Mr. Raney hadn't slept too good, so he was huffing and puffing a right smart by the time he was halfway through getting the rentals pulled up on dry land. He wasn't getting no younger neither. He dreamed last night somebody stole all his boats. He thought he heard his daddy's little Evinrude start up in the middle of the night. At first he thought his daddy might be coming back from the other side for a visit, and then he knew he was dreaming.

Them was some heavy sapsuckers, his boats, all full of water like they was. He ought to invest in a few aluminum boats, is what he ought to do. Modernize his operation a little bit. He was getting too old for this kind of exertion. He might just leave the rest of them sitting in the water, until Hydro woke up and could give him a hand. A little physical exercise might perk Hydro up some, might bring him out of his doldrums.

That's when he noticed that his own big boat, with the nets and poles and little motor, was missing, gone. Well, that was odd. It must have broken loose from its mooring during the night, during the storm. He had tied it up good, too, he thought. Well, that was all right. It don't matter. He would find it. It was out there somewhere, up among the gum stumps, or pushed back in a canebrake, or hung up in a drift of brush or laying up alongside a beaver dam. That boat was like Bo Peep's sheep. Sooner or later it would come home, always had.

Anyway—No need to wake up Hydro, he reckoned. He'd got so he hated to ask Hydro for any favors. Hydro hadn't been hisself since Morgan saved his life. He was real touchy, if he spoke to you at all. Let the boy sleep. They could go out looking for it later. Lash it to one of the rentals and tow it in, full of water, like towing a dead whale. It could wait.

Mr. Raney stretched himself and then squatted and took a good hold on a gunwale of one of the rentals he had just pulled up on the dock. He turned the boat up on its side and held it there while the water drained out. Then he eased the boat on over and let it rest on the dock upside down to dry out. These durn boats was about half waterlogged to begin with. All he needed was this rain to finish off the job.

After a while Mr. Raney heard a motor coming, far up the lake, towards town. He shaded his eyes with his hand and looked out across the wide water, into the glare of the morning sun on the lake, and the boat he saw coming, heading towards the island, was Mr. Roy's launch, the mailman. Well, wont that nice. Maybe Mr. Roy had a fresh batch of wanted posters for Hydro. Hydro could use a few good wanted posters, blue as he'd been.

The last batch was full of mail fraud folks. Mail fraud? Who cared about mail fraud, when you come right down to it? Mr. Raney hoped Mr. Roy wont condescending to his boy's limited intelligence, bringing him another batch of mail frauds. It don't require Mr. Einstein to figure out that a mail fraud poster is a low-rent form of educational materials, or entertainment either one. One of them durn posters didn't even have a picture on it. How is a body supposed to catch a desperate criminal without no picture of him, is what Mr. Raney wished he knowed. It wont logical.

Mr. Raney squinted and kept holding his hand up over his eyes and looking across the sun-reflecting surface of Roebuck Lake. The porpoises were rolling like wheels, leaping and showing their blue bellies. White birds were circling Mr. Roy's launch, as it made its way towards the island, with black water lapping against its bow. It was Mr. Roy all right, and something else too, something different, he wasn't sure what.

Mr. Raney kept his eyes shaded, looking. He listened to the island forest as he looked. The trees were suddenly alive with chatter, the monkeys and the bright-plumed birds. Mr. Roy was towing something behind his launch, that's what he hadn't been able to make out before. Well, now, what in the world—

It was Mr. Raney's boat, the one that had broken loose during the night, in the storm. The little Evinrude was still attached to the stern. Mr. Roy had found Mr. Raney's boat, and he was towing it back out to the island for him. Well, wont that nice? Wonder where he found it? It was riding low in the water, filled with rain probably. It's got to weigh a ton.

He hoped Mr. Roy could stay for breakfast. Mr. Raney would fry him up a mess of fish to say thank you.

Then Mr. Raney noticed something else, somebody else. It looked like there was another man in the launch with Mr. Roy, somebody coming out to the island for a visit, nobody Mr. Raney recognized at all. A man. A shimmery-looking stranger, like heat rising from a highway. Well, that was all right. It was fine. He just wished Mr. Roy would give him a little more notice if he was going to be bringing strangers to breakfast.

He might better go wake up Hydro. That's what he better do. He believed he would. It might cheer the boy up some, to have some company out here for a change. Almost like a party. Anyway, he'd been feeling a little uneasy about Hydro. Mr. Raney didn't know what to make of this strange silence of his, this hard sleep. Look like to Mr. Raney it was time for him to snap out of it by now, maybe go down to the jail and tell Morgan thank you, show a little gratitude. Hydro wasn't interested in peach pies or none of his other hobbies, he wasn't interested in nothing, it don't seem like.

Mr. Raney turned away from the sight of Mr. Roy and the stranger coming up the lake in the launch, and walked off the dock, up into the fishhouse. He blinked his eyes as he entered the dark interior of the house. He tried to let his eyes adjust. The furnishings were vague outlines, like ghosts.

Hydro had been sleeping on a bed on the sleeping porch, a divan he called it, where the breeze was cool through the window screens. The sleeping porch was always shaded by the cypress limbs that hung over that end of the house, draped in long gray beards of Spanish moss.

The thing was, Hydro wasn't on the sleeping porch. Mr. Raney stood in his room by the trapdoor. He kept looking at the bunk, trying to make Hydro's form appear there. It wouldn't appear. No matter how hard Mr. Raney looked, Hydro wasn't there. The rumpled covers were there, the pillow, with Hydro's head-print still in it, even his clothes. His bunk was empty.

Mr. Raney said, "Hydro?"

He kept on looking at the little bunk, like he might not be seeing it right. Like his eyes just hadn't adjusted yet. He turned and looked at the empty hammock on the other end of the sleeping porch.

He said, "Peaches?"

He scratched his armpits. He could hear the motor of Mr. Roy's launch getting closer. He walked through the little fishshack, looking in each room. Hydro was not there.

He walked out of the fishhouse, back out onto the dock. It wasn't like Hydro to run off. He thought about the dream he had, the sound of the little Evinrude in the night. He wasn't sure it was a dream, after all.

He looked out at the mail launch, which was much closer now. Mr. Raney could hear Mr. Roy cut back the engine. He saw the launch slump down in the water when the power was cut back and the boat slowed. Water washed up over the hull. He could hear the voices of Mr. Roy and the stranger in the boat with him. Who was that handsome stranger in the launch with Mr. Roy?

Mr. Raney stood by the spar and waved the launch in. When it was close enough, he hollered, "Chunk me your painter," and Mr. Roy stooped down and hauled out the heavy hemp rope from the bottom of the launch and looped it into big circles and threw it out from the boat to the dock. The stranger only sat there on the boat seat and did not help. He looked familiar to Mr. Raney.

Mr. Raney caught the heavy rope in the air and got control of it and lashed it to the spar on the side of the dock. Mr. Roy cut the motor off, and the launch turned sideways and glided up alongside the wharf. Water was sloshing up on the boards as the boat slid into the berth. Mr. Raney stuck out his foot and slowed the boat down some, and then the handsome stranger bestirred himself.

He stood up in the boat and reached back for a second rope. He threw this line out from the stern, and Mr. Raney caught this, too, and lashed it to a second spar, and so then in about a minute, the launch was secure. The handsome stranger was wearing clothes like Mr. Raney had never seen before—tight black pants and a white frilly shirt and a black vest and shiny leather boots. He had his long hair slicked back and tied in a ponytail in the back, like a Mexican. His eyes were black as death, and his face, pale as marble, he was handsome as a movie star. He was more handsome than Mr. Roy. For one second Mr. Raney believed that, somehow, this was the Mexican Morgan had killed for his pickup. Mr. Raney blinked his eyes to stop the shimmering, the mirage, in the figure of the stranger.

Mr. Roy said, "Hey, Mr. Raney."

Mr. Raney said, "What you doing out here so early in the morning?"

Mr. Raney's boat, the one being pulled behind the launch, came banging in behind the first. Mr. Raney got hold of it and secured it as well as he could. Mr. Roy steadied himself in the boat as the second boat was banging around and being hauled over to the dock.

Mr. Roy said, "Well, I didn't know what to do. I hope I ain't done the wrong thing, coming out here."

Mr. Raney cut his eye over at the Mexican apparition. Lord, he looked familiar. He wished Mr. Roy would introduce them, let up on some of this durn tension.

Mr. Raney said, "The wrong thing?"

Mr. Roy said, "Coming out here like this."

Mr. Raney looked directly at the handsome stranger. He said, "Howdy, stranger. Do I know you from somewheres?"

The stranger was still standing in the rear end of the boat. He looked at Mr. Raney but did not speak, not a word. His body seemed to separate into watery particles, and then to reform.

Mr. Raney said, "That's a fine outfit you're wearing. I wish I could get my own boy more interested in fashion."

The stranger still said nothing. He was younger than Mr. Raney had first thought.

Mr. Raney looked back at Mr. Roy. He figured maybe the

man don't speak the American language. He hoped he ain't offended nobody, talking American to him. Mexicans are a moody people, it looked like to Mr. Raney.

Mr. Roy said, "I probably should have motored back to the mainland. Spared you this a while longer."

Mr. Raney said, "Did you bring wanted posters with you?"

Mr. Roy said, "Wanted posters?"

Mr. Raney said, "I hope it ain't mail fraud. Who cares about mail fraud?"

Mr. Roy said, "Raney, this ain't no time to be complaining about mail fraud."

Mr. Raney said, "I don't guess it was your intention to insult me and my boy with them mail frauds."

Mr. Roy said, "You done complained enough about them mail frauds."

Mr. Raney said, "Maybe it wont your deliberate intention, but it was a slap in the face to both of us."

"Mail fraud was the best I could do at the time."

"One of them didn't even have a picture on it. What kind of wanted poster is it that don't even have a picture on it?"

Mr. Roy said, "Listen to me, Mr. Raney. I'm sorry about the goddurn wanted posters. This ain't no time to be talking about wanted posters, but if you insist on talking about them, all right, I'll talk. I'm sick of hearing about you and Hydro not liking them wanted posters. I just brung them to you. It was just a gift. I'm sorry you didn't like it. I don't tell nobody what crimes to commit, and don't nobody consult me on the layout and printing of wanted posters. When

they's more interesting criminals committing more interesting crimes, well then, I'll bring you more better wanted
posters. That's the best I can do, Raney. I can't do no better
than that. I ain't the one letting all the dullest criminals on
earth escape out of jail. Maybe some murderers will break
out of jail pretty soon. I hope so. I hope they do. For your
sake, I truly hope they do. But until then, you are just going
to have to get by on mail fraud."

Mr. Raney looked at the handsome stranger in the back
of Mr. Roy's boat. The man was shiny, you might say. He was
more solid now, but still he glowed. His pale skin, his black
clothes. He almost looked wet.

Then Mr. Raney recognized him. It was odd he didn't
notice before. Maybe it was the clothes, his brilliant skin.
The handsome stranger was Hydro. His head was no longer
enlarged. It was a normal size. Hydro was handsome and
smart. He was a man of mystery. He was Ramon Fernandez.

Mr. Raney said, "Ramon Fernandez?"

Ramon Fernandez said, "Buenos días, Padre."

He said, "What happened to your head? Where did you
get them nice clothes? You ain't been abducted by space
aliens, is you?"

Ramon Fernandez looked away. Ramon Fernandez had a
mother who loved him.

LATE IN the night, last night, when the storm sky was apple
green and the rain fell in tons across dark waters and lashed
the fish nests and the carved-wood net floats and the weath-
ered boards of the fishshack and rocked the rental boats like

strange cradles and filled them up with rainwater, Hydro had lain awake on the sleeping porch, breathing the perfumed air of the swamp, the swamp flowers and big wet trees and the fish and the rot, and thinking of the tree people, a safety of heights and tree limbs with their stiff leaves and Spanish moss. He imagined their good lives among the parrots and the monkeys, their constant chatter about happy things, above the sweet swamp waters where porpoises smiled all day. He lay in the dim light of the sleeping porch. He heard his father's snores in a farther room. He kicked back his light covers and lay naked on the sheets of his small bed.

He thought that he would have been happier if he had been a tree person. He would have climbed rope ladders. He would have lived among the leaves. The monkeys would have been his friends, the parrots and the cockatoos. He would have poached electricity. He would have swarmed the looseherds, and the wild buffalo. He would not have been odd, then. He would not have been disfigured, or had a big head, he would have had a mama to hold him when he cried, he would never have heard the phrase "atrophy of the brain," he would have married and knocked off a piece of tail in the afternoon just for fun and loved his wife more than ever afterwards, he would have had a child, he would have baked that child peach pies, he would have been called Ramon Fernandez, he would have grown old and cried at his daddy's funeral and completed his grief and gotten on with his life and made the best of a bad thing and contemplated the meaning of life and death and thought about how to break into show business, like anybody else in this world.

He got up off his bunk. The sleeping porch was dark. He could see almost nothing. He turned on a tiny lamp on a table beside his bed. He went to his comic book closet and picked up *Two Fisted Comics*, a war comic. He sat on the side of his bed again; he opened the comic book to a story he had read a hundred times.

A Korean War soldier stood on the banks of the Imjin River. The soldier watched many things float past on the Imjin, driftwood, ammunition boxes, ration cases, shell tubes, then a floating corpse, a man in the uniform of a Korean soldier. The American soldier imagined the death of the Korean soldier. He imagined that an American soldier fought with him, with fists, with sticks, lost his weapon, his bayonet, struggled, fell into the river with him, pressed him down under the water, held him there, felt him struggle, felt the Korean soldier's body, as small as a girl's beneath his hand, remembered swimming back home in the city pool, remembered playing dunk with friends, dunking his girl-friend for laughs, felt the Korean soldier relax beneath his violent weight, the small hands stop clawing, the feet stop thrashing, the end, the bubbles coming to the surface.

Hydro turned the page. He looked at the panel in which the dead man lay face-down in the river. He looked at the next panel. He saw a breath of Korean wind stir the hair on the back of the dead man's head. He looked at the next panel. He saw the water ripple, lap at the shore, rock the body side to side.

Hydro was a little afraid the man might be Mr. Quong. He said, aloud, "I'm sorry, dead Korea man."

He looked at the next panel. The body turned this way and that in the current. He looked at the next panel. The body drifted towards the ocean.

Hydro said, "I'm sorry."

Lightning flashed in the Korean hills, and on the rain-swollen Imjim.

Lightning flashed, too, across the Delta sky, over the flatscape and bearcats and loblollies. It flashed across Bear Creek and Berclair and Phillipston and Scratch Ankle and Victim and Runnymede.

Hydro got up from the side of his bed. He turned off the bedside lamp. He listened to the regular, comfortable sound of his father's breathing, snoring. He listened to the falling tons of rain, a tropical rain, a jungle rain.

He said, "I'm sorry, Daddy."

He forgot to put on his clothes. He walked naked out of the sleeping porch. He went down the ladder, through the trapdoor, out through the kitchen and onto the dock. The rain was falling with such force, it almost washed him off the pier. He was as slick as an otter.

He climbed down into his daddy's boat. He unlashed the painters from the spars. He wound the soaking-wet stiff little pull-rope around the crankshaft. He switched the gas tank switch to On, he pulled out the choke, he set the throttle at Start. The little Evinrude started on the first pull. The rattle-rattle-rattle of the engine and the sound of the impossible rain were like a music of the swamp. Rain was pouring off his head, and he breathed warm oil and gasoline into his nostrils like a fragrance of swamp perfume.

He pushed the throttle forward and turned the nose of the boat out into the deep water. The rain was lashing at the surface of the lake and filling up the boat. The porpoises were hidden deep beneath the dark water. The white birds were somewhere safe. The motor pushed the boat forward, down, down the lake.

Before he got to the place where he would drown, Hydro remembered Cheryl, her body as bony as a skeleton, her almost nonexistent breasts somehow managing to droop like the breasts of a very old man, her skin covered with pathetic bruises, her youthful butt sagging, the patch of hair between her legs dark and thick-furred and wide, hip to hip, like that of a person twice as large and twice as old. She was both beautiful and ugly, she was a child and she was ancient.

She said to him, "Do you like my red lips?"

Hydro said, "No."

She said, "Let my red lips kiss your blues away."

He said, "No."

She said, "It's a tattoo. My lips are tattooed this color."

She held the pistol to his head.

She said, "Fuck me, waterhead."

He said, "Don't make me. It will ruin my life."

She said, "I don't care nothing about your life."

He said, "I don't know how."

He thought of his mama and daddy, he wondered how tail was different for them. How could you do this just for fun?

How could you love anybody afterwards? Cheryl was ugly to him, her body was monstrous and sad. He shrank at her touch. And yet she was an angel, she was so beautiful. He was hard. Filled with fear and disgust and yet hard. She got on top of him, straddled him on the narrow cot at William Tell. She put him inside herself for one minute, less than a minute, before it was over. She wiped herself off on his bedspread. She said, "I want to throw up, I'm so disgusted." He thought of her skull and hair blowing backwards into the Vienna sausages. He said, "I love you." He said, "I'm sorry."

WHEN THE boat had taken him far out into the lake, when he could see, far off in the impossible rainy distance, dim shimmery yellow ghosts that might have been Casper, or might have been a car's headlights crossing the Roebuck bridge, when in fact he had already slipped over the side of his daddy's boat and beneath the black water, his hands no longer clawing, his feet no longer thrashing, his lungs no longer straining, when he was already almost a suicide, he remembered the Imjin River in *Two Fisted Comics*, he thought of his mother, dying for him, of his father, who would die for him now every day for the rest of his life for what he was doing, had to do, had no choice but to do—when all these things were true, Hydro became Ramon Fernandez and passed peacefully over to the other side, and died a happy man.

MR. ROY said, "Let's go inside for a few minutes, Mr. Raney. I'll tell you what I know." He stepped forward in the launch.

He stuck out his hand to Mr. Raney, asking to be helped up onto the dock.

Mr. Raney didn't see Mr. Roy's hand. He was watching Ramon Fernandez.

Ramon Fernandez turned and left the boat, and began to walk away, across the water.

Mr. Raney called out, "Ramon Fernandez, don't go, don't leave me."

Ramon Fernandez stopped. He looked back, but he did not speak.

Mr. Raney said, "I done the best I could."

Ramon Fernandez only stood there, with skin like white light and eyes as black as death.

Mr. Raney said, "Tell your mama I said 'Hey.'"

Ramon Fernandez turned again and walked across the water, slow, slow.

Mr. Raney called, "I ain't never stopped loving her. Tell her that, will you? Be sure she knows I never stopped loving her."

Ramon Fernandez was far out across the water now, walking away.

Mr. Raney called, very loud, "I'll never stop loving you, neither, son."

The sound carried far across the wide water of Roebuck Lake.

Mr. Raney shouted, "What does that sign out at the spillway mean?—where we one time saw deer drinking?— NO WALKING ON THE WATER. What do you reckon that sign means, Ramon Fernandez? Tell me if you know!"

Mr. Roy grabbed hold of Mr. Raney's outstretched hand. The hand was reaching for Ramon Fernandez, but Mr. Roy took it as if it had been extended to him. Mr. Raney looked at him as if he were seeing him for the first time. He gripped Mr. Roy's hand tight and hauled him up out of the boat and onto the dock.

Mr. Roy said, "I'm sorry I snapped at you about them wanted posters, Mr. Raney."

Mr. Raney looked once more out onto the water. Ramon Fernandez was gone.

Mr. Raney turned back to Mr. Roy. He said, "I guess I know why you're here."

Mr. Roy said, "I found him way down the lake, almost to the Injun Mound."

Mr. Raney said, "As far as the Injun Mound."

Mr. Roy said, "I guess you figured out he took your boat."

Mr. Raney said, "It took me a while. I didn't even know it was gone. I never heard the outboard start up."

Mr. Roy said, "What he done, it looks like, was go just as far as the gas in the tank would carry him. And then—"

Mr. Raney said, "Come on in the house. Set down for a while."

The two men walked on up to the house. They went in by the trapdoor.

Mr. Raney avoided going onto the sleeping porch or Hydro's regular room. He guided Mr. Roy into the kitchen.

He said, "He's—I don't guess he's alive, is he?"

Mr. Roy shook his head. He said, "No, Raney. I'm sorry, he ain't."

Mr. Raney said, "I got a jar of white whiskey here. Mr. William Tell sent it out with Hydro a while back. Could you have a taste, or are you still on duty?"

Mr. Roy said, "I could use a taste, sho could."

Mr. Raney reached up in the dry sink and took down a Mason jar with a screw-on lid. He took down a couple of glasses that Peter Pan peanut butter had come in and poured a couple of good shots for the two of them and eyed the cartoon figures on the sides of the glasses. He started to hand one of the glasses to Mr. Roy.

He said, "Do you want Peter Pan or Tinkerbell?"

Mr. Roy said, "It don't matter."

Mr. Raney looked up in the dry sink. He said, "I got Captain Hook."

Mr. Roy said, "Tinkerbell is fine."

He said, "Take that rocker there by the Chambers. I'll set on this here stool."

Mr. Roy waited until Mr. Raney put his glass to his lips, and then they sipped white whiskey at the same time.

Mr. Roy said, "Jesus wept!" Talking about the whiskey. It was strong, and it tasted like kerosene.

Mr. Raney said, "It grows on you. It's some of that potato whiskey."

Mr. Roy said, "Potato whiskey?"

Mr. Raney said, "The Russian Communists drink it all the time."

Mr. Roy said, "How do you reckon they get it to taste like coal oil?"

The two men laughed a little, a soft chuckle between them.

Mr. Raney was quiet now. Mr. Roy was quiet, too. They only sat and sipped from their Peter Pan glasses. Peter Pan didn't never want to grow up. Mr. Roy didn't rock in his chair. He leaned back, sat still. Mr. Raney leaned forward on his stool. They just both looked down at the diamond pattern in the yellow linoleum on the floor.

Mr. Roy said, "He was floating face down when I come up on him."

Mr. Raney said, "Face down. Out almost to the Injun Mound."

Mr. Roy said, "I seen the boat first, before I ever seen Hydro in the water. I was scared there might be some kind of trouble."

Mr. Raney said, "Where is the boy now?"

Mr. Roy said, "He's okay now. He's with the Prince of Darkness."

Mr. Raney said, "Okay. All right."

Mr. Roy said, "He'll be well took care of."

They sat for a minute. They finished their drinks.

Mr. Raney gave a little smile. He said, "He might even learn a little something about the dramatic arts."

The two men laughed at this. Not a chuckle, they got a pretty good laugh out of the Prince of Darkness.

Mr. Raney said, "He one time told me the whole plot of Congreve's *The Way of the World*."

Mr. Roy said, "Remember old Witwoud: 'Pray, Madame, do you pin up your hair with all your letters?'"

Mr. Raney said, "'Only with those in verse, Mr. Witwoud. I never pin up my hair with prose.'"

The two men laughed together again, this time softly, sadly.

Mr. Raney began to cry now.

Mr. Roy said, "Aw, Raney, I'm sorry. You know how much I loved the boy."

He got up and went over and knelt beside Mr. Raney's stool and held Mr. Raney in his arms. Mr. Raney put his head on Mr. Roy's shoulder and allowed himself to be held. He cried hard now, from some deep place.

Mr. Roy held him. He rocked him gently back and forth. He sang "Money Honey." He kissed Mr. Raney on his unshaven cheek.

Mr. Raney said, "I done this to him. I'm the one killed that boy."

Mr. Roy said, "Hush now, Mr. Raney. You ain't killed nobody. You truly ain't."

Mr. Raney said, "Ain't nobody done it but me."

Mr. Roy said, "Hush now."

Mr. Raney said, "I didn't listen to him. He tried to tell me."

Mr. Roy said, "I know. You hush now, hush up. You go on and cry from your broken heart."

Mr. Raney cried and cried and cried. He got snot all over everything. Somebody was going to have to hose down Mr. Roy.

Mr. Raney said, "I cain't live without him."

Mr. Roy said, "All right, all right, you go on and cry now."

Mr. Raney said, "I cain't even believe it's true."

Mr. Roy said, "You go on and cry."

Mr. Raney cried himself out. He stopped crying. He cried so hard he had the hiccups. Mr. Roy started to say Boo, but he decided not to. They wont no need. The hiccups went away by theirself.

Mr. Raney blew his nose real hard on a red bandanna.

He sat back from Mr. Roy. Mr. Roy let loose of the hold he had on Mr. Raney's hand and just knelt there beside the low stool.

Mr. Raney said, "Why do you reckon everybody in the state of Miss'ippi wants to break into show business?"

Mr. Roy stood up now. It was time they left the island. They needed to go into Arrow Catcher and talk to the Prince of Darkness. Arrangements needed to be made.

He said, "So the rest of us don't do the same thing Hydro done, I reckon. You go wash your face. I'll take you in in the launch."

Mr. Raney said, "Much obliged."

A little later they motored up the lake towards the Roebuck bridge. When they passed under it, in the shadow of the creosoted pilings, Mr. Raney stretched his neck to try to see around the next bend, far up the lake. He was looking in the direction of the Indian Mound. He could see nothing. It was too far away. Mr. Roy turned the launch towards Arrow Catcher.

14

Down at the Prince of Darkness Funeral Parlor, Hydro was lying on a slab in Receiving, blue as an Andalusian rooster. He stayed in the water all night, in this warm weather, so he was swole up some, but not bad, mostly just blue.

The Prince of Darkness was wearing his black suit, like always. He did what he had to do, the minimum. He bathed the poor boy, washed his hair with Prell, set up the drain tubes, let the trocar do its terrible work, upper body cavity, lower body cavity, Lord what a sound that instrument made. He used a hand pump for the embalming fluid, left arm, right arm, you can imagine the rest. The blue color went away. Hydro's eyes bulged beneath the closed lids. His cheeks got plump as a baby's with new fluid. The Prince of Darkness put in a few quick stitches, one two three, to keep his lips and eyes shut.

All right. He was done. That was enough science and technology for one day. No more for now. The rest could wait. He put his instruments aside. He washed his hands. He covered up Hydro's body with a sheet. He sat in a straight-back chair across the room.

The Prince of Darkness did what he always did when no one was around, when there was a body in the house. He put his face in his hands and cried for his mama. He wouldn't never get over that good woman's death, it didn't look like. He understood that Elvis took Gladys's death real hard. That was another thing the two men shared in common, aside from being in show business.

When the Prince of Darkness was just a little tyke and had to stay home sick from school with a fever, his mama would cut off the lights in his room and get a table lamp with a bright bulb and make shadow shows on a bedsheet she hung up on the wall. She would say, "Looky at this one. This here's a zombie, been brung back from the dead, just like you." They would laugh together. She would play the pipe organ. She would sing "Blood on the Saddle." She would read him Longfellow. She would make her voice real scary. She would read, "Little Orphant Annie's come to our house to stay." The Prince of Darkness would say, "What's an orphant, Mama?" She would say, "It's what you will be when I die and go to my grave. Won't you be a sad little boy then?" He would say, "Don't never leave me, Mama." Then she would read, "And the goblins will git *you*, ef you don't watch out."

His mama held contests for children in the Prince of Darkness's elementary school. She was the judge. Who could hold their breath the longest? Who could play dead the best?—you have to lay real still, you can't move your eyeballs. Who could hold a handful of ice the longest? These were wonderful moments for the Prince of Darkness. He always won the ice contest. He could hold ice until his lower arm was blue, until his wrist ached. She would say, "You've got formaldehyde in your veins, sweetness." He loved his mama. The other children soon drifted away. She and the Prince of Darkness played the games and held the contests with only the two of them.

He couldn't look at Hydro's body without weeping for her again. He never wanted to stop crying for her, even if she had lied to him about being brought back from the dead. That was probably only a game, too, and he had been too young to understand. It didn't matter. It was a good game. It made him love her more. His love for his mama was the reason he stayed in show business.

HYDRO WAS indifferent to the Prince of Darkness's tears, of course. To anybody's tears. To almost everything. He was dead. He'd done gave up the ghost, shucked off the mortal coil, crossed to the farther shore. His butt was already as flat as a sat-on hat. His butt looked like a sandbar after a flood, a few wavy lines at sea level, brother, that was about it. It didn't have no snap left in it, that was for sure. Some folks might get brung back from the dead, but not this one, not Hydro, he was gone, goodbye, ain't coming back, so long, it's been good to know you.

Hydro was too dead to consider what kind of pain his daddy was in. Didn't give it a thought, never crossed his mind. Self-centered don't hardly describe being dead, what you don't care about no more, don't matter how important it might seem to somebody else.

Hydro was just too durn dead to figure out that his daddy wouldn't never pull a fish out of Roebuck Lake again without wondering if that fish, or one of that fish's relatives, didn't nibble at a little rag of loose flesh on Hydro's body when it was laying out in swamp water for all them hours. His daddy couldn't look a pet-shop turtle in the face, you bank on it, for the rest of his days, without thinking of Hydro and the swamp and the food chain. You can't hardly blame the turtle.

You didn't have to be as dead as Hydro to fail to know certain things, simple as they might seem to a person who is still alive. Like, Hydro's daddy wouldn't never see a dog with a bone again that he didn't think of Hydro's bones. He wouldn't never cut himself shaving and put a little piece of toilet paper on his face and watch a red dot appear in the mirror that he didn't think of Hydro's blood in a pan in the Prince of Darkness's back room. He wouldn't never sniff the leftover chicken he forgot about in the refrigerator for a few days, that he didn't think of Hydro pulled out of a swamp in summertime, what Mr. Roy must have smelled when he hauled him up to the side of the mail launch, too slick and heavy to bring aboard, and motored in with Hydro still in the lake, his face breaking through the water. It was an evil thing to have your heart break for the rest of your life every time you looked at a peach pie, every time you washed a spoon, every time you looked at the sky's blue and thought of your child's eyes' blue, to wake up in the night all alone and think, "I wonder does Hydro need another blanket, and then to remember, "He's dead, died in unhappiness, wanted to die, and I'm the one done it to him."

But Hydro don't care, not in the least. Hydro don't give a tinker's damn, self-centered as a dead man is. How's Hydro gone consider for one minute the suffering the living is left to endure? Cain't. It cain't be done. Not no more. Hydro is dead.

RAMON FERNANDEZ is a different story altogether. Or so Mr. Raney imagined, looking across the wide water at the vision of his miragelike son pacing away from him in the distance. He ain't dead, but he's about as gone as Hydro. One or two quick visits to the planet Earth, like at the boat dock, and he's done forgot about his old friends, he's having too good a time to concern hisself with the living. Adiós, mother-fuckers. I'm gone make like a library and book. I'm outta here. Ramon Fernandez is high-stepping on the other side.

First thing Ramon Fernandez did was look up his mama. Took him a while, but he found her. She was standing in a blues bar with a slender young man with pale hair and a British accent, drinking scotch and smoking Picayunes. There was a Miller High Life sign turning real slow over the dance floor. His mama was wearing a low-cut red dress and listening to Robert Johnson tunes. In fact, she was listening to Robert Johnson hisself, up on a little stage, picking and grinning.

Ramon Fernandez said, "Hey, Mama."

She looked around. At first she didn't recognize him. Another new boy from the other side.

She said, "Hey," and turned back and went on drinking scotch with the good-looking man with pale hair, the British accent. They went back to their conversation. She had on red lipstick.

The man with pale hair said to her, "So I says to this chap, 'Don't get bloody hinkety with me, pal, y'unnerstand?'"

Ramon Fernandez said, "It's me—Ramon Fernandez."

She looked again. She like to of jumped out of her skin

when she finally did figure out who he was, if she'd had any skin.

She said, "Jesus Christ!"

Her date looked up and smiled. Both of them looked at Ramon Fernandez.

She said, "What are you doing here? Like to of scared the dogshit out of me. Hoo. Don't never sneak up on me like that again."

The man with pale hair wore an ironic smile. He said, "Can I order you a drink, old bean?"

Ramon Fernandez said, "Well, I might have a tequila sunrise, now that you mention it. I ain't sure why. Pass me that basket of pretzels."

The man with pale hair ordered a fresh round of drinks.

To his mama Ramon Fernandez said, "I kilt myself. I slipped over the side of Daddy's boat and drowned myself in the swamp."

His mama said, "Oh, excuse my manners, punkin, this here's my friend, Jesus Christ. Jesus Christ—my boy, Ramon Fernandez." She said, "Ramon, me and Jesus here, we's just friends, that's all. Jesus owns this here bar. That's how come we can get Robert Johnson."

Jesus Christ held up his glass and rattled the ice.

The two men shook hands. Ramon Fernandez bowed smartly and clicked his heels as he did.

Ramon Fernandez said, "Señor Christus. Buenos días."

Jesus Christ said, "You'll do swell here, old chap, splendid! I mean that sincerely. Simply splendid." He said, "It's always Happy Hour in Chez Jesus."

15

After Hydro's ashes had come back from the crematorium in Jackson, on the night before the funeral, Mr. Raney didn't feel like spending the night alone, out on the island, so he slept in a spare room in the home of his old friend the Prince of Darkness, up on the third floor of the mansion.

Mr. Raney sat on the edge of the tall four-poster bed and pulled off his boots and then his socks. The bed was tall, so his feet didn't touch the floor. He massaged his hard-as-nails feet, right foot, left foot, and stuffed his socks down in the bottom of his boots and dropped them down under the bed. He got up and pulled off his pants and shirt and folded them and laid them on a little love seat and then hitched himself up onto the bed and sat back down again, just wearing his drawers.

The Prince of Darkness stuck his head in the door of the guest bedroom. He was still dressed in a black suit and tie. He said, "I hung your suit in the closet, for the memorial service tomorrow."

Mr. Raney said, "Thank you."

He said, "Clean shirt, good shoes, everything. You're all set."

Mr. Raney said, "Thanks. You're a friend."

The Prince of Darkness said, "Do you need anything? I put you a clean towel and washcloth on the back of the commode."

Mr. Raney said, "Thank you, I saw them there."

He said, "Plenty of toilet paper, soap—"

Mr. Raney said, "All right."

The Prince of Darkness said, "Well—" He kept on standing in the doorway.

Mr. Raney said, "You wouldn't happen to have a little drink of something laying around, would you?"

The Prince of Darkness shook his head, slow, side to side. He said, "No, nothing but a bottle of bonded whiskey. That was thoughtless of me. I've about quit drinking the real stuff. I just didn't think—"

Mr. Raney said, "You've got a bottle of whiskey?"

The Prince of Darkness said, "Nothing but a fifth of Old Grand-Dad."

Mr. Raney said, "Well, that sounds all right. Where is it?"

The Prince of Darkness said, "Don't drink it just to be nice."

Mr. Raney said, "No, really, I like legal whiskey. I wouldn't drink it just to be nice."

The Prince of Darkness said, "You mean it?"

Mr. Raney said, "Well, yeah."

The Prince of Darkness left the doorway and came back from the kitchen with a new bottle of bourbon.

He held up the dark bottle apologetically. He said, "Twelve years old, it may not be no good anymore—it's all I've got." He held two water glasses by the rim in the other hand.

Mr. Raney said, "No apologies required, it'll be fine. You just pour us a stiff one."

The Prince of Darkness poured two dark-amber drinks

and put the bottle on the chifforobe. He sat down on the bed beside Mr. Raney. They didn't look at one another. They drank from their glasses.

Some time passed.

The Prince of Darkness said, "This used to be my mama's room."

Mr. Raney looked around, the curtains and valences, the Persian rug, the little pipe organ and heavy furniture.

He said, "You don't say."

The Prince of Darkness said, "You're the first houseguest I ever had."

Mr. Raney stared into the bourbon in his glass. He saw Ramon Fernandez in there. Ramon Fernandez waved to him. He said, "Habla habla, Señor Daddy." Mr. Raney finished off the whiskey and then stared into the empty glass.

The Prince of Darkness said, "The first one who lived to tell about it, anyway."

He finished his glass of whiskey.

The two men looked at one another.

Mr. Raney smiled. They laughed a quiet laugh together, and the Prince of Darkness poured them another drink.

Mr. Raney said, "Hydro's real name was Ramon Fernandez. His mama got it out of a poem. She was bad to read poetry."

The Prince of Darkness said, "I could get used to this bonded whiskey."

Mr. Raney said he had to agree, it tasted just fine.

Some more time passed. They just sat there on the edge of the bed, with their feet hanging down.

Finally Mr. Raney said, "I got to be truthful. It's hard for me to be here."

The Prince of Darkness said, "Well, I can imagine. It's got to be hard. Just to go on living."

Mr. Raney said, "No, I mean, it's hard to be *here*. With *you*."

The Prince of Darkness said, "It's that durn bonded whiskey, ain't it? I knew it was going to come between us."

Mr. Raney said, "No—"

The Prince of Darkness said, "I wish you hadn't never drank it just to be nice."

Mr. Raney said, "No, really—"

The Prince of Darkness said, "I should have poured it down the sink and drove straight out to Mr. William Tell's store, got us a quart of that potato whiskey everybody's been raving about."

Mr. Raney said, "This is fine—"

The Prince of Darkness said, "Clear as water and tastes just like coal oil, ain't more than a week old."

Mr. Raney said, "It ain't the whiskey, Prince of Darkness, I swear it ain't."

The Prince of Darkness said, "How do you reckon they get it to taste like coal oil?" He sipped on his second glass of Old Grand-Dad.

Mr. Raney said, "It's *you*."

The Prince of Darkness looked at Mr. Raney. He said, "Me?"

Mr. Raney said, "I'm sorry, old friend."

The Prince of Darkness said, "It's what I said to Hydro

that night, ain't it? I said he would live forever with the blood of them lovely children on his conscience. I wish I hadn't never said that."

Mr. Raney said, "Aw naw, that ain't it. Turns out you was the onliest one who understood what the boy was going through. I blame myself for not seeing it."

The Prince of Darkness said, "It's because I've got a defective personality, ain't it?"

Mr. Raney said, "Prince of Darkness, would you just hush up for a minute."

The Prince of Darkness said, "I never claimed to have no good personality."

Mr. Raney said, "Your personality is fine."

He said, "I've got a morbid personality, I know it, you don't have to pretend around me. And all this old furniture—"

Mr. Raney said, "I admire your furniture. Your pipe organ is especially fine."

He said, "Well, it belonged to my mama." He said, "I just want you to know one thing, set the record straight, you know. I just want to assure you, once and for all—I wasn't never brung back from the dead."

Mr. Raney said, "I figured as much."

The Prince of Darkness said, "It cain't be done."

Mr. Raney said, "I know that."

He said, "The dead cain't be brung back."

Mr. Raney said, "I wish they could."

He said, "Don't you think I'd bring Hydro back if it could be done?"

Mr. Raney said, "That's awfully kind of you."

He said, "I was in a coma for a few days, a couple of weeks, encephalitis, when I was a boy. That's it. That's all it amounted to, nothing more. I had started to stink, I don't understand that part. My flesh had started to decay a little. Just in patches, you know, not all over. That part does sound a little suspicious, I grant you, the decaying part. That part never was too durn satisfactorily explained, if you ask me. They didn't have no fine-tuned instruments to find a heart-beat, or to see was I breathing. Somebody said, 'He's dead.' Some ignoramus. Old Hot McGee, ain't got the sense of a baboon, he happened to be there, at my bedside, you know. Hot McGee, he's diagnosing time of death, see, that fool, he's the one put words to it, and him all time carrying a whip and a pistol and a straight-back chair with him, everywhere he went, like a lion tamer, and that's who they are going to believe about a child's life and death, that's who they got diagnosing me. What a system they had back then."

Mr. Raney said, "I'd still love you, even if you had been brung back from the dead."

The Prince of Darkness shut up for a minute. He said, "You would?"

Mr. Raney said, "You know I would."

The Prince of Darkness sipped on his whiskey. He said, "I know, old brother. I know."

After a while, Mr. Raney said, "It's because you seen my boy at his worst."

The Prince of Darkness said, "Aw, Raney—"

He said, "You seen him bloated and blue. You seen what

the fish and the turtles done to him. You seen him nekkid and pitiful. You split him open and autopsied him."

The Prince of Darkness got down off the bed. He walked over to the chifforobe and put the cap back on the bottle of Old Grand-Dad. He said, "I never done the autopsy."

Mr. Raney said, "You didn't?"

He said, "The autopsy was in Jackson. The state of Mississippi does the autopsy."

Mr. Raney said, "The state?"

He said, "It's the law. I ain't allowed to do no autopsy."

Mr. Raney said, "You ain't?"

The Prince of Darkness said, "All I done was wash your boy's hair with Prell, Raney. I gave him a bath. He was a beautiful boy. I never seen such a beautiful boy. I hope you know what a beautiful child he was. I hope you know I will wish to the day I die that I had one just like him."

Mr. Raney sat there, staring at his hands. Wearing only his BVDs, and with his feet dangling over the side of the tall bed, he looked like a child himself.

After a while, they sang a few songs together. They sang, *Full fathoms five my father lies.* They sang, *Where the bee sucks there suck I.* They sang part of an aria from *Tosca: And the stars would be shining, and the earth smelling sweet, my dream of love has vanished forever.*

Mr. Raney said, "That Puccini was a song-writing motherfucker, wont he?"

HYDRO'S ASHES—fragments of bone, not ashes, the remains after the big heat in Jackson—sat in a plastic container, on a shelf, out on the island, in the fishshack, alone in the silence. The big lake, old Roebuck, was vast and black. Porpoises slid among the cypress knees. The Mississippi sky was amazing and clear, a million stars, a peach-basket-sized moon. The Doric columns of the house where the two men sat, or stood, one grieving, one only plunged in deep sorrow, were tall, silent, white as bone.

From far away, another world, a distant music. Somewhere, God alone knows where, marimbas, guitars, the bongo, the mariachi, the flamenco, castanets, dancers dancing, spurs jangling, sombreros flying, black eyes bright, glances quick, the crack of a black bullwhip, loud shouts, tequila, tortillas, and laughter, laughter, laughter. "*Ramon!*" came the cry. "*Ramon Fernandez, tell me, if you know!*"

AFTER THE long night was over, and the moon was only a ghost in the new sky, and the early morning sun was just starting to burn the dew off the Johnsongrass and the lespedeza, and after those who were awake had begun to hear the first sounds of quails, partridges they were sometimes called, whistling to one another out back behind the chickenyard fence, the melancholy bug-eyed organist, Leonard, woke up in his trailer on the day of Hydro's funeral, on the outskirts of Arrow Catcher.

Leonard was not a small man. Naked he seemed even bigger. He rubbed his eyes and felt the eyeballs click in their sockets. He came awake uncertainly. He felt the great mass of himself all around. He felt surrounded by his own melancholy. And in the efficient, cramped little trailer-house bedroom, he might as well have been a walrus, he felt so enormous, so sad and blue.

He was not sleeping alone either, and so this made his melancholy more immense, and the trailer bedroom even smaller. Leonard was sweating. The morning sun pounded down on the little Airstream. The tiny window was open, but it didn't let much air in.

The man asleep beside him was a broad-shouldered, muscular white man with several homemade tattoos scattered around his body. His name was Kevin. On four knuckles of his left hand were tattooed the letters I-R-O-N; on the five knuckles of the other hand, S-T-E-E-L. On his left forearm, a crude dagger with black blood dripping from the point, and just above that the slogan BORN TO LOSE. On his other arm his name was misspelled, KEVINE. Somebody else must have done that one. Kevin was snoring, and his teeth were bad. He was so tall he had to bend his knees to sleep in the little bed.

Leonard met Kevin out at the Shell station near Fort Pemberton. He invited him to spend the night in the trailer, leave his rig out in the Shell parking lot, Leonard would drive him back out in the morning.

The sooner the better, as far as Leonard was concerned. He was filled with remorse. And anyway, Hydro's funeral was today.

Leonard said, "Kevin, wake up."

Kevin snorted. He said, "Huh?"

Leonard said, "Wake up. You've got to go."

Kevin sat up and rubbed his eyes with the backs of his fists. He looked like an enormous baby.

He said, "I've got to go? What time is it?"

Leonard said, "It don't matter what time it is. Get up. I'll take you back to your rig. Come on." He swung his big legs off the bed, like hauling a deer carcass out the back end of a pickup truck, and started to pull on his pants.

Kevin said, "I guess I'm smart enough to figure out when I ain't welcome."

Leonard was cramped for space. He lifted up one side of his big butt and tried to pull his pants up over one cheek at a time. He couldn't do it. He was huffing and puffing. He couldn't see his dick for his belly. He put his elbows on his knees and his face in his hands.

Kevin said, "Is something wrong? Was it something I said, or done?"

Leonard didn't answer him.

He said, "It's because I went to sleep so fast, ain't it? I'm sorry, Leonard. I didn't mean no disrespect. I was tired. I been on the road since Albuquerque."

Leonard still didn't take his face out of his hands. He said, "It's okay. It's not you."

Kevin laid IRON lightly on Leonard's shoulder. He said, "What is it? It's best to talk about your feelings or else you'll end up whipping the monkeyshit out of yourself."

Leonard felt the manly calluses of IRON on the soft flesh of his back. He said, "Mm, that feels nice."

Kevin put STEEL on Leonard's other shoulder and began to massage lightly with his thumbs.

Leonard said, "Mm."

They stayed this way for a while without speaking.

Kevin's skillful thumbs loosened a knot of tension in Leonard's neck.

Kevin said, "Go on, give it a try. Tell me what you're feeling."

Leonard said, "Well, I feel like you are disgusted. I feel like you think I'm repulsive to look at."

Kevin said, "Well now, see—there's your problem. That's where you're going wrong right there, right off the bat. That ain't really a feeling, what you're talking about. What you are talking about is a *belief*. Altogether different sort of thing. My ex-wife used to make the same mistake, refused to change. I'd say, 'Tell me what you're feeling, Dierdre,' and she'd say, "I'm feeling like you're a fucking queer.' Well, she had a point, I suppose, can't take that away from her. Maybe that's a bad example."

Leonard said, "I get the idea."

Kevin massaged Leonard's shoulders a while longer.

Leonard said, "Do you have any children?" Looking back over his shoulder a little.

Kevin said, "They won't have nothing to do with me. I'm always on the road, and then so is their mama. We done our best. I guess it wasn't all that good."

Leonard said, "How many children do you have?"

He said, "Just the two—Pierre and Emile. Two boys. We wanted a girl."

Leonard said, "Pierre and Emile?"

He said, "They were sweet when they were little, but they are bitter now."

Leonard said, "Your wife must have been French."

Kevin stopped massaging and looked at Leonard. He said, "French?" He had a quizzical look on his face. He laughed a little snort of a laugh, and shook his head. He started massaging again. He said, "What are you going to come up with next, Leonard? You act about half-crazy, boy, you know that? French! That crazy-ass country gal?"

Leonard said, "I want to show you something. Come here."

He heaved himself up off the bed and squeezed out towards the kitchen area. Kevin followed along behind. He had to duck to keep from splitting his head on the ceiling supports.

Leonard opened the little refrigerator door and the light came on. A stick of oleo sat on a saucer, and there was a bottle of buttermilk, almost empty, a hunk of cheddar cheese. The two men stood at the open door and stared.

Kevin said, "What is it?"

It was quail eggs. Hundreds of them, like white irregular-shaped marbles, in refrigerator bowls. Bowl after bowl, on every shelf in the refrigerator.

Leonard said, "Quail eggs. I started raising quails for the meat, but then I couldn't kill them. I just couldn't do it. They say, *bobwhite bobwhite*. You heard them this morning. I gather the eggs so they won't hatch, so I won't be overrun with quails. The hens lay ten or twenty eggs at a time. I cain't keep up with them."

Kevin said, "Quail eggs."

Leonard said, "I've got all these eggs, running over with them, and a henhouse full of quails I cain't bring myself to eat, and yet I fired a pistol at a cantaloupe sitting up on top of a friend's head, can you believe I done that?—shot so close to him he could hear the bullet, could have drilled him right in the head, and now he's dead anyway, killed hisself by drowning, maybe because I shot at him, nobody knows, maybe because I was so careless, so disrespectful of his life he didn't see no need to respect it neither. I'm probably the one who killed him, gave him the final reason, the green light, and I don't hardly know how I'm gone live without him, and I'm fat and popeyed and all time bringing drunk truck drivers home from the Shell station and ain't never even looked for the sunk Confederate battleship out at Fort Pemberton. Oh Kevin, I don't know, I don't know, what's going to come of me, what does my worthless life amount to, why don't I just do what Hydro done—?"

Kevin said, "Just for the record, Leonard, I ain't drunk."

Leonard just looked at him.

He said, "I ain't had nothing to drink in twelve years."

Leonard said, "You wont drunk last night?"

Kevin said, "Not for twelve years."

Leonard said, "Twelve?"

Kevin said, "I go to them meetings. Them Don't Drink meetings."

Leonard said, "How come you to stay with me last night?"

He said, "Because you're beautiful. Because I seen something spiritual in you."

Leonard said, "Spiritual?"

Kevin said, "I don't have to be in Boston with that load of zippers until day after tomorrow."

Leonard said, "You go to Don't Drink meetings?"

Kevin raked his fingers through his hair. He said, "I tell you what—I could go to that funeral with you today, if you wanted me to, if you needed the support."

Leonard said, "You could?"

Kevin said, "We could go to the funeral, and then maybe I could pick up a meeting before I haul them zippers to Boston. I'd be there in plenty of time."

Leonard said, "Well—"

Kevin said, "Reach out, Leonard. It's what they teach us in the Don't Drink Club."

Kevin and Leonard made love one more time that morning, in the tiny Airstream bedroom. They like to kicked out all the windows. Then Leonard shredded some cheese and melted some oleo in a skillet, and cracked a couple of hundred quail eggs and made the strangest omelet Kevin or anybody else in the world had ever tasted.

Kevin said, "You never know when you start out in the morning what the day is going to bring."

Leonard said, "I miss Hydro. I'll probably cry at the funeral, really blubber, you know."

Kevin said, "You just lean on me." He wiped his mouth on a paper napkin. He said, "Did you ever think about leaving Miss'ippi? Living somewheres else for a while?"

Leonard said, "I don't hardly think about nothing else."

BEYOND THE water tank and the fire truck and the light plant, out beyond the apple orchards, fragrant as flowers, out past the railroad tracks and cross ties and ballast and spikes, beyond the ditches and the buzzard roosts and the colored barber shop, where men with voices gravelly from cigarettes and stong coffee with whiskey sang Robert Johnson tunes, deep in the Belgian Congo, Morgan was saying goodbye to his mama, old Aunt Lily, the hoodoo lady. They weren't going to the funeral.

Morgan was out of jail, of course. There had been no indictment, no arraignment even, only apologies. Most people in Arrow Catcher never really got it straight that Morgan wasn't a hero, let alone that he might be guilty of anything. Nobody at Monday Music connected the gossip that passed among them with anything that happened or had consequences in the real world—everything was just a story, at Monday Music—so it never quite occurred to them, even when the sharpshooter was in jail for that short time, that he had ever really done anything wrong. To Monday Music, it was just a detail in a story. Leonard himself had said, "I loved the part about the sizzling voltage of secret current. I hope the fact that it happened to Wonder Woman and not Morgan won't keep it from being told again." Even Webber Chisholm finally said, "Except for my refrigerator, I never did see what all the fuss was about. That refrigerator still had some miles on it."

Soon there would be another story, one about Morgan shooting his way out of jail, and yet another about him shooting the refrigerator in memory of Hydro, or in honor of Hydro's daddy. As long as there was a story, that's all that really mattered. It didn't have to be true, or to make much sense.

Morgan had packed a few things in a cardboard suitcase. He didn't have much to pack, owned almost nothing, white shirts, his vest, those few threads. He had a pair of high-heeled boots he bought at an Episcopal church thrift shop in El Paso.

Aunt Lily was poking at the ashes in the fireplace. There was no good reason for her to be doing this, she wasn't going to light a fire. A few wild dogs were chasing a chicken through the yard and underneath the house.

Morgan said, "Mama, I'm going to leave these here boots with you. I don't like filling up another man's shoes no more."

She leaned the poker up against the brick fireplace. She said, "Have you got another pair of shoes?"

He said, "There's some tennies around here somewhere, ain't they? Didn't I leave a pair of tennies here last time I come through?"

She said, "They make your feet stink so bad."

He said, "I ain't trying to impress nobody."

She said, "You can look up under my bed. Ain't no telling what's up under there."

Morgan went on packing—a few shreds of jockey underwear, a shirt or two he bought with his own money down in Texas. Aunt Lily picked up the broom and swept the hearth, though it didn't need sweeping. She took a clean rag and draped it over the straw of the broom and reached up into the corners of the room, sweeping away invisible spider webs.

The finches were chattering in the eaves, and the cowbirds complaining in harsh voices. A stray mule ambled through the yard. A car slid past on the road. A man wearing blue plastic shoes clogged on a bridge. A barebreasted woman carrying a big bundle of laundry balanced up on her head passed by in the street outside. Bottle-trees clanked in the summer breeze and frightened evil spirits away from the house.

Morgan said, "I feel like I ruined a lot of lives."

Aunt Lily said, "Pshaw."

He said, "Hydro might still be alive, if I hadn't showed up back here in town."

Aunt Lily said, "Horseshit."

He said, "Well, anyway—"

Aunt Lily took a raggedy patchwork quilt off her bed and took it out on the front porch and shook it out, though it was clean. She spread it over the bed again.

She said, "It matters what you do, the lies you tell, the way you act. I won't deny that. It matters, all the way down the line, for a long time."

He said, "Did you say them tennies was up under the bed?"

She said, "You can look. Ain't no telling what you'll find."

He said, "I hate what I done to Ruth's folks. To her husband and them children."

Morgan got down on his hands and knees and looked way back into the darkness up under his mama's bed.

She said, "You was in love, sugar."

In the dimness beneath the bed, Ramon Fernandez was sitting by a campfire, with his knees pulled up to his chest. He was wearing a sombrero and crossed ammunition belts across his chest, a big pistola at his hip. He had a Mexican blanket folded and draped across one shoulder. A coyote howled at the Mexican moon in the underbed distance. Yellow sand stretched for many miles, out into the dark hills.

Morgan said, "I'm sorry."

Aunt Lily said, "Don't be too hard on yourself, dumpling."

Ramon Fernandez said, "Habla, habla."

Morgan pulled out the pair of old tennis shoes and a couple of pairs of clean socks. He stood up and walked back over and put one pair of socks in the cardboard suitcase and pulled the other pair onto his feet.

He said, "There's clean socks under here, too."

Aunt Lily said, "They ain't no telling what you'll find underneath that bed."

Morgan said, "One time down in Texas I went into a little streetcar diner, you know? Two little booths jammed up in a corner, a waitress with a long scar down one side of her face standing in back of the counter, a cigarette with a long ash dangling out of the side of her mouth.

"I had drove my truck into El Paso for the day. Nothing special, just wanted to get off the ranch for a while, go to a picture show, something another. I was happy, working, learning stuff, taking pistol lessons, had a few dollars in my pocket, slept in the bunkhouse, ate two good meals a day at the commissary, or off the chuck wagon, kept rock candy under my pillow at the bunkhouse, so I could suck on peppermint, or lemon drops, or horehound, anytime I felt like it, day or night."

Aunt Lily said, "Sounds like you found happiness."

"But I was all time lonesome, lonely, you know. I was thinking about Ruthie. I was so young when I fell in love with her. Just a kid. I'm still just a kid. Anyway, I was filled up with longing, of all kinds.

"So, see, I went in this little streetcar diner in El Paso, in the middle of the night, and I seen this young couple, a boy and a girl. They was eating flour tortillas, had a big stack of them, you never saw anything that looked so tasty."

Aunt Lily said, "Tortillas."

Morgan said, "I just stood there looking at them. I couldn't pull my eyes away. They was dressed up all in black, black suit for him, with broad padded-out shoulders and big lapels, and black sweater, black tights for her, black beret hats on, both of them.

"I felt like I was wading into strange water and not caring if I drowned. My head turned dizzy, my heart was swimming with feeling like I never felt before. I looked at them and saw *me*, what my life might could someday look like, if I just knew the secret that they knew, the meaning of life. It wasn't true, it turns out, I was wrong, but in those few seconds, believing that I was just like them, that I belong in this world, was better than hearing Ruthie tell me she loved me, better than being a sharpshooter."

Aunt Lily said, "I remember when I found you in the canebrake—"

Morgan said, "Then they noticed me, staring at them, the boy did. He stopped eating. He said, 'Look what we've got here.' The girl stopped eating then, too, and looked at me."

Aunt Lily said, "The polite thing would be to introduce yourself."

Morgan said, "I didn't know what to say. I said the first thing that popped into my head. I said, 'I'm a sharpshooter with a pistol.'

"The boy put his tortilla down on his plate and wiped his hands on a paper napkin.

"He said, 'Well, ain't that a coincidence. So are we. Same thing. Me and my sister here.'

"I said, 'You are? Really?'

"The girl said, 'Come on over here and sit down beside me, pretty boy.'

"But the boy held up his hand at me, stopped me, so I didn't move. He said, 'We don't have time for that, I'm afraid. I'm sorry, truly I am. I would love to have you stay for a while, if we had more time. But just for comparison's sake, I was wondering, what kind of automobile is a trick-shot sharpshooter driving these days? Just for comparison's sake, you know.'

"I said, 'Just that old truck setting out there. It's good transportation. Burns a little oil.'

"The girl said, 'We don't want that piece of shit.' Her voice was a whisper, but fierce.

"That's when I first made up the story about the Mexican. I said, 'I robbed a Mexican for that truck.' I don't know why I said that. I had to say something, that's what came out.

"The boy said, 'You ain't from around here, are you. You ain't from Texas originally, am I right? You talk a little bit like a nigger. My guess is, you're from Arkansas. Is that where you're from, Arkansas?'

"I said, 'Miss'ippi.'

"The boy said, 'Wonderful state, Miss'ippi.'"

Aunt Lily said, "You should have knowed he was lying, right there."

Morgan said, "He said, 'The state bird of Miss'ippi, that would be the—'

"I said, 'Mawkin bird.'

"He said, 'Right, the mocking bird, exactly right, just testing, hope you don't mind, just checking you out, see are you lying to us. We want to trust you, of course, but you can't never be too careful, not in this modern day and age of ours. Even the preachers are corrupt.'

"The girl just snorted.

"The boy said, 'Where do you come from, in Mississippi? What is your hometown?'

"I said, 'Arrow Catcher.'

"The boy's eyes got narrow. He said, 'Arrow Catcher. I remember Arrow Catcher. You go past it on Highway 49, south of Memphis.'

"I said, 'That's it! That's right!'

"The boy said, 'Mississippi—the last dry state in the whole country. All them bootleggers still doing a cash business, all that money, thousands of dollars, untaxed, unaccounted-for money, thousands and thousands, just laying around like manna in Moses' desert.'

"I said, 'Like the William Tell Grocery.'

"The boy picked up his paper napkin now, real slow, and wiped his mouth again, although it didn't need it. He looked at his sister. He said, 'Well, exactly, just like the William Tell Grocery. William Tell, Arrow Catcher. I think I can remember that. Can you remember William Tell, in Arrow Catcher, Mississippi, little sister?'

"I said, 'Right at the junction of Highway 49 and Highway 82.'

"The girl said, 'Get rid of him.'

"The boy looked straight at me. I couldn't see his white teeth no more.

"He said, 'Beat it, asshole.'

"I didn't listen to what I didn't want to hear. I still wanted to believe that this boy and girl held the answers to all my questions, to the meaning of my life, by their beauty and their youth. I said to the girl, 'How come your lipstick don't rub off when you eat them tortillas?'

"She said, 'Listen to me, pretty boy—'

"The boy interrupted, her brother. He said, 'It's a tattoo. Question asked, question answered. End of interview, goodbye.'"

Aunt Lily said, "I wish I could have gived you a better life, son. I wish I could of taught you the meaning of love."

He said, "Come with me, Mama, to Texas. I'm gone get me some self-respect. I'm gone put the past behind me. I'm gone study for the GED. I'm gone throw this pistol in the Rio Grande."

She said, "Go with you? To Texas?"

He said, "I'm scared I won't never see you again, if you don't come with me now."

She said, "To Texas? I ain't never been no where. I ain't hardly been outside the Belgian Congo."

He said, "What about astral flight, to distant galaxies, and the lost city of Atlantis?"

She said, "Oh, well, that—but Texas?"

He said, "The ranch will take me back any time, they told me they would. I told them all about you, they want to meet you. I told Mr. Scott hisself. He said, "Hell, bring your mama, too. Y'all'll have to use one of the efficiencies for a while, until we can work out something better. It wouldn't do to put your mama in the bunkhouse."

She said, "Mr. Scott?"

He said, "He owns the ranch, the movie star, Mr. Zachary Scott."

She said, "Real ugly motherfucker?"

He said, "That's him."

Aunt Lily thought about this.

She said, "I wouldn't be hasty, if I was you. I wouldn't advise you to act on impulse right now."

He said, "How do you mean?"

She said, "You might want to hold onto your gun."

He said, "Mama, I'm through with violence. I'm changing my life. I never want to hold a gun on nobody again for the rest of my life. I never want to think of tasting gun oil on my tongue."

She said, "I don't mean violence, honey."

He looked at her.

She said, "Show business. You ever heard of Annie Oakley? Ignorant white-trash girl? She done well."

He said, "Let's go, Mama. Let's do it. Let's go all the way to Texas in this raggedy-ass old truck."

She snatched up a bunch of washed-out dresses and torn underpants and stuffed them in a pillow slip. She picked up the velvet bag with the crystal ball in it. She said, "I seen you shoot a short stout white man in this ball."

He said, "It was a refrigerator."

She looked at the bag in her hand. She said, "You think I ought to take this worthless thing along with us? Do you think it's worth the space it's gone take up?"

He said, "Bring it along. Throw it back in the bed of the truck. It ain't never too late to break into show business."

16

Mr. Raney was widely known throughout the Delta for his fishcamp on the island, so Hydro's funeral at St. George by the Lake was filled with mourners.

A great many cars were already there when Dr. Mc-Naughton pulled his Buick into the graveled area that served as a parking lot. The Prince of Darkness himself was there, of course, wearing his black suit as usual. He stood out in the gravel, waving a white handkerchief, this way, this way, park right over here, that's right, directing traffic. It was a clear bright day, very hot. The Prince of Darkness took special care today to see that things operated smoothly.

Louis McNaughton was with his father. Louis was dressed up in a blue suit and white shirt and a bow tie. His shoes glistened with Shinola, and his hair was slicked down with water.

Louis pushed his glasses up on his nose. The two of them, father and son, had not spoken since they left the house, or longer.

Finally Louis asked the question that had been on his mind lately. He said, "Daddy, do I look like a geek?"

Dr. McNaughton turned the steering wheel and aimed the big car towards an empty space and followed the Prince of Darkness's waving handkerchief to a parking place. When he had put the car in Park, he looked at Louis.

He said, "What kind of question is that?"

Louis said, "I don't know."

They sat in the car for a few minutes without speaking. With the air conditioner turned off, the car became hot very quickly. Both of them were sweating, even Louis. Dr. McNaughton rolled his window down, and so Louis rolled his down as well.

Dr. McNaughton said, "We'd better go on in. See if we can find us a seat."

Louis said, "Because I would like some better clothes."

Dr. McNaughton looked at him. He said, "Well, we'll see."

Louis said, "And different glasses."

Dr. McNaughton said, "Well—"

Louis said, "I'm tired of being a geek."

Dr. McNaughton said, "It's hot in this car, let's go on inside the church."

Louis said, "Because when I look at myself, all I can see is a geek."

Dr. McNaughton opened his door but didn't get out yet. Louis didn't move. It was a face-off.

Dr. McNaughton said, "Do you know what a geek is?"

Louis bit his lip in thought. He said, "Sort of a sissy?"

Dr. McNaughton said, "No."

Louis said, "Sort of a person that nobody likes because they look different, like a midget?"

Dr. McNaughton said, "No."

Louis said, "Okay, what is it?"

Dr. McNaughton said, "A geek is a person who eats live chickens at a carnival."

Louis looked at his father. He said, "No way."

Dr. McNaughton said, "Absolutely."

Louis said, "At a carnival?"

Dr. McNaughton said, "That's it."

Louis said, "Yikes."

He chewed at his lower lip some more. He tugged at his collar with his finger and made his bow tie go crooked.

Louis said, "Have you ever seen one?"

Dr. McNaughton said, "I think I hear the organ."

Louis said, "Have you? Have you ever seen a geek?"

Dr. McNaughton said, "I've never known a geek personally, if that's what you mean."

Louis said, "But you have seen one?"

Dr. McNaughton said, "Well, yes."

Louis said, "You *have*?"

Dr. McNaughton said, "Just one. I saw one."

Louis said, "Yikes."

They sat in the sweltering car a while longer.

Louis said, "There ought to be a comic book about geeks."

Dr. McNaughton said, "There are books about geeks."

He said, "There are?"

Dr. McNaughton said, "I'll read you some Faulkner sometime. I'll read you some Eudora Welty, some Flannery O'Connor. Geeks, midgets, anything your heart desires. Better than comic books."

Louis looked at his father. He said, "You'll read to me? Really?"

The organ was playing "Sixty Minute Man." The deep bass notes rolled down Roebuck like summer thunder.

Dr. McNaughton said, "We'll never get a seat now." He put his left foot out of the car, onto the ground.

Louis said, "Don't go, Daddy. Not yet."

Dr. McNaughton looked at Louis. He said, "Don't go?"

Louis said, "Not yet."

Dr. McNaughton said, "What is it, Louis? What's got into you? We're already late."

Louis said, "You never talked to me before."

Dr. McNaughton looked at him.

He said, "I haven't?"

Louis said, "Not that I remember."

Dr. McNaughton said, "I must have talked to you—"

Louis said, "I like it."

Dr. McNaughton pulled his foot back into the car.

He said, "They're usually painted up to look like some kind of savage, war paint, you know? They might be wearing a leopard-skin loincloth. Maybe a spear, or a club. Some feathers."

Louis said, "Geeks."

Dr. McNaughton said, "Right."

Louis said, "Yeah?"

Dr. McNaughton said, "Well, they grab up the chicken, you know—it's in a cage, maybe, or maybe just in a croaker sack."

Louis said, "Do you feel sorry for the chicken?"

Dr. McNaughton said, "A little—but then you sort of forget to. You get used to it. It's so exciting."

Louis said, "Like when Hydro shot the lovely children."

Dr. McNaughton said, "Right. A little like that."

Louis said, "Like Mama and—"

Dr. McNaughton said, "Right, you feel bad about it later on, but right then it's the excitement you're interested in. You don't think about anything else. You don't think about how you're going to feel about yourself, or how the world is going to change."

Louis said, "Right."

Dr. McNaughton said, "They growl and snarl and dance around at first."

Louis said, "Geeks."

Dr. McNaughton said, "Right."

Louis said, "Yikes."

Dr. McNaughton said, "It's all part of the act, see. It's real but it's an act."

Louis said, "Like show business."

Dr. McNaugton said, "Well, exactly."

Louis said, "Monsieur Dublieux could be the geek's agent."

Dr. McNaughton said, "Now you're getting it. Right. In fact, I think Monsieur Dublieux did handle that geek, the one I saw that time. I think that particular geek did happen to be one of Monsieur's clients."

Louis said, "Uh huh."

Dr. McNaughton said, "So he grabs up the chicken, see, out of the cage, or crate, or whatever, out of the burlap bag, and dances around with it, holding it up in the air, baring his teeth, you know, in a savage sort of way—"

Louis said, "Yeah—"

Dr. McNaughton said, "And then, well, he just, you know, goes for the throat."

Louis said, "Goes for the throat?"

Dr. McNaughton said, "Bites into the chicken's throat. Chomps its head off, if he can."

Louis said, "Yikes."

Dr. McNaughton said, "It's pretty quick. I don't think the chicken suffers."

Louis said, "Well, that's good."

The organ was playing "Money Honey" and then it played "Ruby Baby."

Dr. McNaughton said, "There's a lot of blood, though, of course."

Louis said, "Right. Of course."

Dr. McNaughton said, "The chicken is hard to hold onto. It starts flopping, slinging blood everywhere. That's normal, chicken with its head cut off, you can understand that."

Louis said, "Right."

Dr. McNaughton said, "There's not much more to it. The geek drinks some of the blood. Takes a bite or two out of the breast, feathers and all. Swallows as much as he can. That's about it. The curtain falls, lights come up, end of show."

Louis said, "Does it make him sick?"

Dr. McNaughton said, "I'm not sure about that. It could. Eating raw meat's not good for you, especially chicken."

Louis said, "Will you take me sometime?"

Dr. McNaughton put his hand on Louis's head and patted his slicked-down hair. He said, "Maybe we better start with the new clothes and eyeglasses first."

Louis said, "So I won't look like a geek?"

Dr. McNaughton smiled. He said, "Right."

Louis said, "Did your daddy ever talk to you?"

Dr. McNaughton said, "No."

Louis said, "He didn't?"

Dr. McNaughton said, "No, he never did. He took me fishing one time, though. One time only."

Louis said, "He did? Fishing?"

Dr. McNaughton said, "He got so drunk he fell out of the boat and drowned. I had to paddle back into the fishcamp without him. I was just eight years old."

Louis said, "Your daddy got drowned? That's why I never got to meet him? That's why I never had a granddaddy?"

Dr. McNaughton said, "Yep."

They sat for a long time now without talking. They only sweated. The organ was playing "I Just Want to Make Love to You."

Louis said, "Do we live like the rest of the people in the world?"

Dr. McNaughton said, "Who?"

Louis said, "Us. People in Arrow Catcher."

Dr. McNaughton said, "I'd say so. Pretty much the same."

Louis looked towards the church. He said, "Do I have to wear this bow tie?"

Dr. McNaughton said, "No."

Louis unhooked it from his collar and threw it out the window, into the gravel. He took off the suit coat, too, and unbuttoned his collar button. He said, "I miss Hydro."

Dr. McNaughton said, "I know."

Louis said, "I can't believe he drowned. Drowned himself."

Dr. McNaughton pulled Louis over on the car seat next to him and sat with his arm around the child in the terrible heat.

He said, "He was your good friend."

Louis said, "He was almost like a daddy."

Dr. McNaughton paused. He said, "I know."

They sat for a minute.

Dr. McNaughton said, "He talked to you. He read comic books with you."

Louis said, "Right."

Dr. McNaughton said, "I'm grateful to him for that."

Louis said, "Did your daddy kill himself?"

Dr. McNaughton thought about that. He said, "In a way, yes."

Louis said, "Do you miss him?"

He said, "Yes, I do."

Louis leaned into his father's body. The two of them sat and cried together for a while, as the organ played. Louis's glasses got all fogged up. He took them off and pulled out the tail of his shirt and wiped them off.

He said, "You said you would read to me?"

Dr. McNaughton said, "Right."

"And take me to the geek show?"

"I don't know about the geek show."

"And buy me some new clothes? And glasses?"

Dr. McNaughton said, "It's a start, anyway. It's a step in the right direction."

Louis said, "Thanks."

Dr. McNaughton said, "Well, we haven't bought them yet."

Louis said, "I mean for talking to me."

Dr. McNaughton said, "Oh—"

Louis said, "We ought to try it again sometime."

Dr. McNaughton said, "Do you think so?"

Louis said, "I wish we would."

Dr. McNaughton said, "Something besides geeks next time, maybe."

Louis said, "All right, okay."

Dr. McNaughton said, "Let's go into the funeral. Let's say goodbye to Hydro."

Louis said, "Geeks are okay, too. Geeks are fine. We could talk about geeks."

Dr. McNaughton said, "We'll think of something."

Louis said, "I'm glad you didn't take me fishing and drown."

Dr. McNaughton said, "I'll tell you all about your granddaddy, maybe."

Louis said, "That would be good. That would be even better than geeks."

LITTLE ST. George by the Lake had once been the old Colony Town depot, before it was reclaimed and moved to lakeside. It still looked a little like a Delta depot, with its silvery cypress boards and slate-shingled steep roof. Inside, the first rows of pews were old depot benches, fitted out with needlepointed kneelers.

Preacher Roe was saying, "We brought nothing into this world, and it is certain we can carry nothing out." Candles were guttering in the candelabras, and Preacher Roe was wearing his vestments, purple and white. One acolyte sat sleepily in a low chair to one side. He had already drunk a good deal of the wine.

Mr. Raney and a few others were seated off to one side of the altar in a special couple of rows of pews, normally used by the choir—family and close friends. He could look out at the whole congregation from where he sat.

The church door opened, and Louis and Dr. McNaughton squeezed inside and found a spot along the back wall to stand. Others were standing as well, husbands and wives and children. Everybody knew Hydro. Mr. Raney was proud.

Preacher Roe said, "Oh, spare me a little, that I may recover my strength, before I go hence and be no more seen." He was reading from Corinthians, out of the Book of Common Prayer. He would go from there into Psalms. Mr. Raney watched Louis, Hydro's friend. Louis picked up a prayer book and found the Burial of the Dead.

Louis looked up and saw Mr. Raney looking at him. Mr. Raney looked a hundred years old, pale and drawn. There were others on the pew with him, people Louis didn't recognize, family from out of town, he supposed. Louis and Mr. Raney smiled at one another; then Mr. Raney looked around at the rest of the congregation.

All the old crowd was there: Gilbert, the housepainter; Runt, the gravedigger; Mr. Quong, the butcher; Red, who owned the Goodlooking Bar and Gro., competitor to William Tell; Wily Heard, the one-legged arrow-catching coach; Leonard, of course, at the organ; and Leonard's new friend Kevin, with IRON and STEEL tattooed on his fists; families Dr.

McNaughton had known all his life. Even Mr. William Tell was there, whom nobody ever saw, who didn't show his face around town, or even around his own store, for months at a time, years sometimes. Mr. William Tell was a tall, goofy-looking man who did Red Skelton impressions. He could make you fall out of your chair with his Heathcliff and Gertrude impressions, the pigeons. He would tuck his arms up under like wings and get that goofy look and make that funny yuk-yuk voice of his, and boy you would bust out laughing, you couldn't help it. Mr. William Tell could make you laugh at a funeral.

Preacher Roe said, "Now Christ is risen from the dead, and become the first fruits of them that slept."

Sweat was pouring off Mr. Raney's face, drenching his back and underarms. Fans were flapping throughout the congregation, but none of the air seemed to reach him. He looked out at Louis to be sure the child was all right. He saw the boy's father whisper something to him. Louis looked up at his father and smiled.

Preacher Roe said, "But some will say, How are the dead raised up? And with what body do they come?"

Louis looked around the crowded little sanctuary. Pap Mecklin, wearing green aviator sunglasses, was at the funeral, the housepainter's blind father who had died in St. Louis. He was sitting beside Mr. Raney on the depot bench. Could this be true? Louis blinked his eyes and they stung with salty sweat. He heard the words, "You look like a fool in them false teeth, Gilbert."

Louis said, "Daddy?"

Preacher Roe said, "Men, beasts, fishes, birds—"

Louis said, "Daddy, look—"

Preacher Roe said, "Terrestrial and celestial, the sun, the moon, the stars, and every star a different glory—so also is the resurrection of the dead."

Also on the depot bench sat the two lovely children, zoot suit and red lips and berets. And beside them, Louis's grandfather who had drowned long ago while Toby McNaughton sat with a fishing pole in his hands. And Mrs. Raney, dead for so long now, at her own son's funeral. And Ramon Fernandez, in a bolero, and many more. Louis's head was reeling and rocking, he tottered, he almost fell over.

Dr. McNaughton whispered, "Is the heat too much for you, honey? Do you need to step outside for a minute?"

Louis said, "No."

Preacher Roe said, "Behold I show you a mystery. We shall not sleep, but we shall all be changed, in a moment, in the twinkling of an eye, the dead shall be raised incorruptible, and we shall all be changed—"

In his head Louis heard a great rushing, as of waters, rivers and rains and spillways, even oceans sucking sand off the beaches and carrying them far away. In the sound, which was also the sound of Preacher Roe's voice, he heard that there is a great river, the streams and pools whereof make glad the city of God, and the lake where his grandfather drowned, and where Hydro took his own life, and the Delta rains, like a monsoon, that could wash the birds right out of the trees, and even the blood that blew backwards out of the heads of the two lovely children into the groceries on the shelves of William Tell, and the swelling in Hydro's head that caused the atrophy of his brain, and the cancer that clouded the eyes and finally killed Pap Mecklin were all the same water—they were the multitudinous streams of the great river whereof the City of God is made glad, no one knows how.

And the roaring in his head, this rushing of elements older than life, older than death, as old in fact as God, went on, increased, swelled as music swells, sighed as storms sigh. The room turned. It tilted.

He heard Preacher Roe say, "The Lord be with you."

All around him he heard voices say, "And with thy spirit."

Louis called out, "Mr. Raney!"

The noise in his head was unbearable. It was like a passing train, it was like the Dixie Flyer, sucking up Colony Town, its cotton gin and dogs and people in the vacuum it left as it blew through the station, back in the old days, back when there was a station, and a depot, at Colony Town and no St. George by the Lake, diesel smoke and steam valves and whistles and wheels and couplings and cross ties dancing and ballast flying and alarm and dangerous discord, wild bison and looseherds of wild horses swarming out of the path of the locomotive, and him too close to the tracks. It shook him as if he were weightless, without substance, a fluttering broken heart in the aftermath of lost love, lost self.

He heard a voice from heaven say, "Write this—"

He looked up into the rafters, as if into heaven. He said, "Who me?" He cried this out: *Who me?* He said, "Write what?"

The voice from heaven said, "Write this: all who die are blessed, for they rest from their labors."

Dr. McNaughton said, "Son—?"

Just then Louis saw the train outside the smoky-glass window of St. George by the Lake. The Dixie Flyer, the jingle and the roar, and no rails at all, only Roebuck Lake— whistle screeching, wheels weighing a ton each, the caboose tilting, passengers reading newspapers in cars flashing past with overhead lights flickering, a skim of ice coating the cowcatcher, smoke and steam. It came to a stop on the lake, just outside the little church. Trash and newspapers were sucked up in the vacuum and whirled away in little tornadoes.

Louis looked around. No one else seemed to notice.

Dr. McNaughton said, "Come on, son, let's get some air."

Louis shouted, "No!"

A few people looked in Louis's direction. Some whispered, "They were so close."

The conductor leaned out from a platform near the rear of the train. He said, "Board!" The conductor was a black man with a blue uniform and billed cap. He said, "All aboard!"

Passengers left the little depot and boarded the train, all the dead, and Ramon Fernandez among them. They waved goodbye, goodbye. The train was headed to the other side.

When the train pulled away, the front pew, the depot seat, was empty except for Mr. Raney.

Dr. McNaughton led Louis out the door, into the cooler air.

Preacher Roe said, "The Lord make his light to shine upon you, and be gracious unto you. The Lord lift up his countenance upon you and give you peace."

The congregation said, "Amen."

17

This was the morning of Ruth McNaughton's third day without a drink. She had decided not to go to Hydro's funeral. She couldn't take a funeral, not today. She hadn't been feeling very well.

She was in the bathroom sitting on the toilet, with her head leaned into her arms on the lavatory. She had stomach cramps, diarrhea. She was sweating like a field hand. She hadn't slept well for two nights. In fact, she had slept almost none at all.

At least she wasn't nauseated. At least she didn't have a hangover. That was the one positive thing about today. She could live with insomnia and a dose of the flu, or whatever this was, a lot better than not remembering going to bed. But no funeral for her.

She wouldn't have gone to the funeral in any case, even if she hadn't been feeling so shaky for the last couple of days. She didn't really know Hydro all that well. She just saw him around town. He used to chase cars and howl at the fire whistle when he was younger. He ate all those peach pies, everybody knew about that. She had plenty of good laughs at Hydro's expense, but she couldn't say she knew him all that well. With his outlandish head and odd ways and funny name, Hydro had been more of a cartoon character to her than a real person, if she admitted the truth. Hydro could have been a character in one of those comic books he was so famous for reading. And living with his daddy, a man who liked to shoot refrigerators out on the island—well, it was a little hard for Ruth to take such people seriously, or to think of them as being truly broken up, grieved by death. Weren't they just comical rednecks?

She lifted her head off her arms and said, "Katy."

She had to try to keep remembering that Katy was in the house. That child was quiet as a mouse, it was easy to forget about her. Anyway, the last thing Toby had said to her before he left for the funeral was, "Take good care of Katy while we're gone." Toby hadn't wanted to take her to the funeral with him and Louis. He thought she was too young. When did Dr. Tobias McNaughton become Father of the Year? When did he start thinking he knew more about taking care of her own daughter than she did?

She called again: "Katy!" She could hear the impatience, a shrillness, in her own voice. Well, that's what she intended. Where was that child? She called, "Katy!"

Katy didn't answer.

Goddamn it.

Toby told her before he left, "I think Katy leads some kind of secret life. She's alone so much. I'm not sure, you know, what she does, where she goes. Maybe we'd better watch her more closely." He said he had found bird feathers all over her bed.

Ruth stripped a long stretch of toilet paper off the roll and cleaned herself up as well as she could. She flushed the toilet and pulled up her underpants. She was never wearing that girdle again, she didn't care how big her stomach got.

She hollered, "Katy, answer me this minute. I mean it."

What kind of secret life could a child have? Dr. Tobias McNaughton was nothing if not dramatic. Bird feathers?

Still—where was she? Why wasn't she answering?

Ruth came out of the bathroom and looked around the house. Her hands had a slight tremor that bothered her. She thought if she had a drink, just a beer, the shaking would stop. She went into the kitchen and opened the refrigerator. There was a beer in there all right. Two of them, in fact, way back in the back, cold as ice.

She kept standing at the refrigerator with the door open, staring at the two beers.

She closed the refrigerator door. She opened it again. She stood there staring. Just one of them, maybe. If she drank just one beer, it might be just the thing to calm her down a little. It would help her think where Katy might have gone off to. It would give her more patience to deal with Katy when she did turn up. She closed the refrigerator again.

She screamed, "Katherine Ann! Goddamn it!"

She opened the refrigerator and stared at the two beers. She closed the refrigerator.

She walked out on the front porch and looked up the street, towards Scott Butane, and then down the street, in the direction of the schoolhouse. Pecan trees and oaks, wide lawns. A chalk drawing on the sidewalk where Katy had played hopscotch.

She looked across the street at the Methodist church, at the tall steps where kids liked to play with Slinkys. She couldn't see her. It wouldn't have killed Toby to take Katy with him to the funeral, would it? Toby knew Ruth wasn't feeling well. He could have done that small favor for her. And he called himself a doctor.

She walked down the steps, off the porch, and stood out on the sidewalk, looking this way and that.

She called, "Katy, honey?" Trying to keep the shrillness out of her voice so the neighbors wouldn't notice.

Then—she could not have said why this happened at just this moment—a thought came into her head that she had never entertained before. Maybe she had, maybe she hadn't. It seemed like a new thought. She thought how dangerous the world is, how many dangers lurk here.

That was all. Not much more to it than that.

And yet suddenly it was so clear, so incredibly clear, the danger. Not just a danger of marrying a man who turned out to be a person you did not expect or want, not just weakness of character and an unhappy marriage. Those were dangers enough, and real, but those were not what she was thinking about. Not even just alcoholism, and loss of self-respect, and not just that you were a person you had never expected to become, with experiences you had thought belonged only to others, lesser creatures than yourself. And not just becoming a bad parent, or a bad person—or even a child molester, as she supposed she had been when she first let Morgan see her naked, when he was still a mere child, and stripped him of whatever childhood he might have been able to salvage of his hard life. Not just looking back on a lifetime and thinking, This is not what I wanted, these were not the choices I meant to make, this is not what I counted on.

But real danger, life and death dangers, the kind that happen quickly and are no one's fault, or maybe they are. A small quirk, a twist at birth, or before birth, and then so fast you didn't even know what was happening, hydrocephalus, maybe, or mental illness, or suicide—even that might be genetic, or congenital, or caused by an unkind word at just the wrong moment, or both, or all these, or worse. You could lose everything, just as easily as that, before you even had it, or had anything, it could all be gone. For no good reason, you could, in one second, become a laughable figure, a cartoon character to the rest of the world, abandoned to a life of loneliness and oddity in the flicker of an eyelash. You could become pathetic. You could suddenly become a parent whose child died. Whose child committed suicide. You never knew. There was too much danger in the world to predict it all.

And there were other dangers, plenty of them. There were rapists, child molesters more treacherous than herself, murderers, lurking in church basements, on playgrounds, in friends' homes, in abandoned school buses, or walking randomly off the street and into country stores or people's homes, capable of unimaginable crimes—who on earth knew where they were, or even what all the dangers were.

And then, in that same instant, she thought how little she knew of her own daughter's movements in this world, Katy's, and of how foreign those imminent dangers had always seemed before now. For the first time Ruth McNaughton understood the concept of neglect, and secret lives, and her own responsibility in all this, and of doom, and fate, and chance.

Something like panic swept through her, standing there on the sidewalk in the pecan shade. Was it panic—or was it despair? They seemed to be the same.

Her first thought was to run down the street screaming Katy's name. She took one step this way and then one step the other way. She looked right and left. She wrung her hands. She was frantic, and yet she was rooted to the sidewalk. She became breathless. She turned and turned in circles, she didn't know which way to go.

Her second thought was to run inside the house and drink the two beers. She didn't know how that would help; it just would. Just the thought of those two cold beers going down was enough to stop her from turning in circles.

She stopped turning. She stopped wringing her hands. She collected herself for a minute. She crossed her arms over her chest and held herself. The shortness of breath improved some; she was able to take a couple of deep breaths. She even smiled—put on a smile. She patted her hair with her hand, still smiling.

She looked up and down the street to see if anyone had seen her turning in circles. Still smiling. Nobody. Nobody saw her. No one was in sight. All right, fine. Good. Shit. Fuck. Excellent. She felt better already. And Katy was fine. Well, of course she was. She had panicked. Just like a mother. She felt silly. Katy was just fine.

There might still be a part of a bottle of vodka in the house as well. Wasn't there? Didn't she remember that? She thought so. Okay, well, that was good. Just in case she needed it. She might not need it. If she felt all right after she drank the beers, she wouldn't have to touch the vodka. She probably wouldn't need to touch it.

It was good to have it as a backup, though, of course—to know it was there, in an emergency—but she probably wouldn't need the vodka at all. She would just drink the two beers, and see how she felt. Maybe just one beer would be enough. Then, if she still felt shaky, or panicky, she could mix a shot of vodka with a little orange juice, or just pour herself a shot, or two, or just drink a little out of the bottle, something like that. She would be fine. No problem, no problem at all.

Except that there was no vodka in the house. Oh, God. She remembered now. The other day, after that awful fight with Toby, when they had made up and he offered to make her a drink, a Bloody Mary, she had thrown a fit. She had been indignant. How dare you, she had said. How dare you offer me a drink when I've all but admitted to you that I'm an—well, she couldn't quite say the word "alcoholic," but he knew what she meant. She told him he must like to keep her drunk. It was in his best interest for her to be out of her mind. She said he was the reason she drank so much in the first place, his weakness, his lack of self-respect, and now she found out he had a stake in keeping her hooked.

He had looked at her in a kind of shock. At himself as well. Was it possible that what she was saying was true?—that he actually—These were thoughts that had never entered his mind. He told her this. He said, "I'm not fully convinced, but maybe—" Good Lord. Maybe—Well, all he could do was try, he could act in good faith.

To prove his good intentions, he took the bottle of vodka to the sink and poured it out, every drop, down the drain.

She said, "Uh—"

He felt better already. Now they were working on a problem together, the first time they had been together on anything in a long time.

She said, "Uh—"

He said, "It's a start, anyway. We have to start somewhere."

So now it was all gone, the vodka. It hadn't seemed like a great idea, even at the time, a little impetuous, pouring out that whole bottle. Because now there was no vodka in there. None in the house. Not a drop. He had poured it all out. That idiot had poured all her vodka down the fucking kitchen sink, a half bottle of vodka. Emptied the bottle, rinsed it out, and threw it in the garbage can. Thoroughness personified. Didn't he know how wasteful that was? How compulsive and self-serving and thoughtless? No vodka! All she had in this house was those two measly goddamn beers, for God's sake? Two beers? And her daughter missing? Jesus! She was going to need a lot more than two beers.

Well, but wait. Was Katy missing or wasn't she? Who ever said she was missing? She looked up and down the empty street again. She wasn't there, but well, so what? She couldn't keep her mind on Katy, or even on being afraid, for thinking about needing a drink.

This, too, was a thought that seemed new enough to give Ruth McNaughton pause. In that pause, she thought, Katy is probably in her room. I didn't even look there. I only screamed for her. I only stormed around the house a little, a few rooms. She never comes when I call her, anyway. Maybe she's not lost at all. She's probably in her room, playing with a doll.

Ruth McNaughton went back inside, much calmer now. She called, "Katy? Honey?"

Katy was not lost. She was nearby. Very safe. She was only hiding for now. In her room, up on the second floor of the house, in the back of her closet, behind her dresses and loose wire coathangers and a few hanging plastic bags where her mama stored a few winter things, behind a false panel that could be taken out and replaced, Katy was sitting alone in a crawlspace in the rafters with the bird she called Sister.

Louis had taught her about the secret hiding place, had showed her how to take out the panel, how to replace it once she was inside so no one would know she was in there, how to duck down so she wouldn't crack her head in the low space, how to crawl back into the rafters and not put your foot down on the insulation and fall through. In summer, how to crawl out before you got so hot you fainted. He had given her a candle stub stuck with wax onto an old saucer, and a box of wooden kitchen matches to light the candle so she could see. He had taught her how to spit on the tip of the match for safety, when the candle was lighted. Louis had a place just like this behind the closet in his own room where he sat sometimes and read comic books.

Katy didn't care much for comic books, so she usually

only went inside the crawlspace to sit in the dark. She loved to sit in the dark. In this darkness she became invisible.

With the panel replaced, and the plastic bags hanging down, and the closet door shut tight and the candle not lighted, the secret hiding place was perfect darkness. An absolute blackness, like a grave. No light at all came in, not even the smallest hint, even in the bright middle of the day.

Katy could sit in the darkness for two hours. She thought of eyeless fish in underwater caverns. She thought of blind people. She thought of dead people. She saw what the fish saw. She saw what the blind saw, what the dead saw.

Today she was thinking of Hydro. She knew about his death, the funeral today. She knew he had drowned. In Katy's mind, Hydro was an underground cave fish. She pretended she was Hydro. She envied Hydro. She held up her hand in front of her and looked at the spot where she knew it was. She saw nothing. She held her hand up so close to her face that her palm touched her nose. She opened her eyes as wide as they would open. She still saw the same thing—nothing. She held out her finger now, pointing outwards. She said, "My fingertip sees the same thing as my eyes see." She said, "I am invisible."

But today she wanted to see. She needed some light. She was sitting, a little uncomfortably, on one of the rafters, a two-by-four, with her feet propped on another rafter. It was her usual seat. She felt between her feet, down in the soft insulation between rafters, until her hand touched the matchbox. She lifted it out of its place and heard the soft rattle of matchsticks inside it as she pushed open the little drawer of the box and took out one match. She closed the box again, for safety, as Louis had shown her. She struck the match on the side of the box and watched it flame up and illuminate the tiny rafter space, the raw pine boards and insulation, and she smelled the burning of the sulphur. She dragged the candle stub and its saucer towards her and touched the flame of the match to the wick and watched it gutter and spew and catch fire.

Her brown lunch bag was beside her, the top neatly folded over. Inside the bag was the dead bird, the wild canary. She had brought it with her from the refrigerator, as she had each day since the storm. She kept it in a brown paper bag in the vegetable crisper, no one ever noticed.

The dead bird was her best secret. Even Louis didn't know about Sister. She never told him that one of the drowned birds didn't wake up that night, didn't fly away, out the big window, into the sunshine and the trees the next day. Even Louis didn't know she had kept one bird to play with.

She uncreased the neat fold in her paper bag, and reached in with her hand, and felt the stiff little creature in the bottom, its feathers coarse against her fingertips. She closed her hand around it, gentle, and brought the bird out of the bag and held it out in front of her to look at. Even in the dim light of the guttering candle flame, the bird's feathers still were bright, the yellow-green of life.

She sat for a long time, holding it, sometimes bouncing it lightly in the palm of her hand. The bird was beginning to get a little rumpled looking, but it was holding up pretty well in the refrigerator, where it stayed most of each day and night. The little eyes were closed. The lids were lightest green.

She heard her mother's voice, the almost indiscernible sound through the walls. "Katy? Honey?"

She looked at the bird. She felt a little annoyed with her mother. Until now she had only sat with the bird, named it. Once or twice she sang to it: *Hush little baby, don't say a word.* Once or twice she told it a story: *And the birds ate up all the bread crumbs that Hansel had dropped, and they were lost in the deep woods.*

Today she had thought she might take all its feathers off.

The soft, muffled voice of her mother: "Honey? Are you hiding? Is this a game?"

She wanted to see the bird naked, she was not sure why. Her plan was to start just below the yellow beak, just at the bird's tiny neck, and strip all the feathers away, all the way down the bird's stomach and back, until the bird was completely naked. She might leave the tail feathers just as they were. The tail and the head would be normal; the rest of the bird would be naked. Maybe the wings would still have feathers, too. Maybe she would bite off the head. She thought of the bird's head inside her mouth.

Her mother said, "Honey, you're scaring me. Come out, honey, please, please come out for Mommy."

She put the dead bird back in its bag and folded the top over and made its neat crease. She was very angry at her mother. She waited until her mother's voice was too dim to hear, in another part of the house, downstairs maybe, and then she blew out the candle and wet her fingertips and squeezed the wick for safety, as Louis had shown her, and heard the soft hiss of the steam between her fingers. It burned her hand a little, but she didn't care.

She removed the wall panel and came out of the crawl-space and then replaced the panel neatly. She stuffed the paper bag with the bird in it into a shoebox for now, in a corner of the closet, and came out of the closet and shut its door behind her. She had been thinking of stripping the bird's feathers and biting off its head for a long time, since the first day. Now she was ready to do it, and she couldn't get any privacy.

She walked out of her room and down the stairs and up towards the front of the house. She made her voice sweet. She said, "Mommy?" Her mother was out on the porch, looking up and down the street again. Katy said, "Were you calling me?"

Ruth McNaughton's hands were shaking badly now, and a beer would have probably helped, but she was not thinking about a drink right now.

At the sound of the child's voice, Ruth startled, and turned quickly . She saw her through the screened door. She said, "Oh, Katy! Oh! Where *were* you? I've been calling and calling."

Katy said, "I was hiding."

Ruth knelt down in front of her and put her hands on Katy's shoulders.

She said, "Oh, honey, please, please, please, don't ever do that again. Oh, I was so scared, baby. Promise Mommy, okay, promise you won't ever, ever scare Mommy like that again. Do you promise?"

Katy said, "Okay."

She said, "Oh, honey." She hugged her now, held her tight. Katy allowed herself to be held without resisting.

Her mother said, "I'm going to quit drinking, okay?"

Katy said, "Okay."

Her mother said, "For you. Just for you. Because I love you so much. Okay? Does that make you happy? Are you glad Mommy's going to quit drinking?"

Katy said, "I'm happy." She tried to make her voice sound a little happier. She said, "Happy, happy, happy."

Her mother released her and looked at her at arms' length again. On her mother's face was a brave, sad smile. She said, "Okay, that's what I'm going to do then. So you'll always be happy. That's what I'm going to do, I'm going to quit drinking. In fact, I've already stopped. Three days ago."

Katy said, "Yay!"

Ruth said, "But you have to promise me you won't ever scare me like that again, okay? Really and truly promise, you know? Because I don't know what I would do if anything ever happened to you. I just really don't know what I would do. So promise me, okay? Will you do that right now, right this minute? Cross your heart and hope to die?"

Katy squinched up her eyes and put her hand on her chest. She said, "I hope I die."

She held her daughter close again. She said, "Oh, thank you, darling, thank you, thank you, thank you. You're a good girl, you are Mommy's good, good girl."

18

After the memorial service, the congregation of mourners filed sadly out of St. George by the Lake. Mr. Raney and a few family members from out of town had left the church first and were standing in the cypress shade to receive expressions of sympathy. Some stopped to speak, in low voices; they asked whether Mr. Raney had any plans, would he still keep the fishcamp open; they said Hydro would be greatly missed.

Mr. Raney said, "I hope you can make it out to the fishshack. Help us eat up some of that food."

Others went on out to the parking lot and opened the doors of their cars to let out some of the heat, and got ready for the drive over to Roebuck landing to the funeral launches. Some said they had to stop by home first to pick up the covered dishes of food they were taking out to the island. There was always a lot of food at a funeral wake.

The Prince of Darkness had made special preparations for the motorcade. Even though there was no body to be transported—Mr. Raney hadn't decided yet what to do with Hydro's ashes; he might bury them in Carroll County next to the boy's mama, or he might sink them in Roebuck Lake, he couldn't make up his mind right now—the Prince of Darkness led the parade in the big black Cadillac hearse, fitted out with black crepe streamers; Mr. Raney rode in the second car, another Cadillac, owned and driven by Mr.

William Tell himself, who appeared suddenly, out of nowhere it seemed, especially for the funeral. He was always fond of Hydro. He was getting on up in years, and had a broad, open freckle-face like a little boy.

Mr. William tell said, "I didn't see the sharpshooter at the funeral, Raney, or Aunt Lily neither one."

Mr. Raney said, "They're moving, is what I heard. This whole ordeal has been hard on the both of them."

Mr. William Tell said, "It ain't been easy on nobody."

It was taking forever to move the cars out of the lot.

Mr. William Tell said, "I blame myself."

Mr. Raney looked at him. He said, "You ain't to blame, Tell. Don't be silly. You ain't done nothing but own a store. You ain't done nothing but be a friend."

Mr. William Tell said, "I don't know. Look like I could have predicted something like this happening. Prevented it somehow."

The hearse pulled out of the parking lot, and Mr. William Tell aimed the nose end of his own Cadillac behind it and eased forward. The others followed behind, car after car, with their headlights on, in the middle of a bright day, beneath the endless blue sky. Webber Chisholm led the motorcade, real slow, away from St. George by the Lake, out onto the highway, in the Arrow Catcher patrol car, with the red light on top going zoop zoop zoop.

Mr. Raney said, "I don't hold it against you for owning a store that got robbed. Or for not being a fortune teller neither one."

Mr. William Tell said, "Look like Aunt Lily might have

predicted it." This was a joke, so Mr. Raney looked at his old friend, and they shared a quiet laugh in the car.

Mr. Raney said, "Count on you, Tell. You ain't never knowed how to leave foolishness alone."

Mr. William Tell said, "That crystal ball of hers—"

Mr. Raney said, "Don't get started, Tell, I mean it. I don't want to arrive at my own son's wake laughing my big butt off."

Mr. William Tell said, "It don't pick up nothing but "As the World Turns" and "Secret Storm."

Mr. Raney said, "Really, Tell, don't get started. I'll end up disgracing myself."

Mr. William Tell said, "She's the only colored woman in town who knows what Bob and Lisa's marriage plans are."

Mr. Raney was laughing. He said, "Tell—"

Mr. William Tell said, "I run into her at a cock fight a while back, hadn't seen her in two years, and she said, 'Ellen Stuart's done come out of her coma, but she's got amnesia.' First words out of her mouth. Hadn't seen her in two years. Cock fight, out on Phillipston."

Mr. Raney said, "Tell, you are a mess in this world."

They didn't have far to go in the cars. At the landing, down on Roebuck Road, the Prince of Darkness parked the hearse, and Mr. Willliam Tell pulled in behind him, and then the rest of the cars found places to park, up and down the blacktop. The Prince of Darkness got out of the hearse and was the first to walk down to lakeside, to the funeral launches he had moved in the day before. He stomped around in the grass, scaring off any snakes that might have crawled up in there in the morning sun.

The funeral launches were wide, flat-bottomed boats with high gunwales and twenty-five horsepower Evinrudes with electric starters on the back. They were all new boats, aluminum, and were painted black. The Prince of Darkness had made special arrangements with a dealer in Leflore, so mourners could be transported out to the island. The launches were also draped in black crepe.

Mr. Raney said, "The Prince of Darkness outdone hisself this time."

Mr. William Tell said, "Remember when his mama died?"

Mr. Raney said, "Don't get started, Tell, I mean it, I don't want to be laughing when I step in that funeral boat."

Mr. William Tell said, "He had a line of twenty-five crop-dusters, pulling black banners, to fly over the cemetery in formation."

Mr. Raney said, "Don't get started, Tell."

Mr. William Tell said, "He planned to spell out some kind of message in black smoke."

Mr. Raney said, "I mean it, Tell—"

"Something about the Resurrection, but—"

The Prince of Darkness saw to it that all the motors started up and were idling smoothly; the boys he had hired to pilot the other boats all knew what they were doing. They waited patiently as the launches filled up with mourners. They lent a hand to those stepping in.

The Prince of Darkness directed Mr. Raney and Mr.

William Tell and a few old aunts and other family members and close friends to sit in the first launch; this one the Prince of Darkness piloted himself, in his black suit. The other boats filled up as well, helter-skelter. Some brought their own boats—johnboats and ski boats and bass boats and a runabout. Many were carrying food with them, dishes and bowls and baskets, fried chicken and ham, sweet potato pies.

When they pulled away from the landing—the launches with black crepe, the Prince of Darkness himself at the helm of the first, and the lesser vessels as well, in single file, headed out into Roebuck Lake, slow as could be, with lake water lapping at the gunwales—the funeral flotilla was long and dignified and impressive.

Monkeys chattered in the trees overhead, and wild birds, parrots and stranger beasts, with their bright wings and red tails like capes. Alligators sank beneath the surface of the water. Then the launches, with the deep-throated voices of the slow-running Evinrudes, left the shade of the gum trees and the danger of cypress knees and lesser stobs, and pushed their way out into the greater water, black and shimmering, wide, incredible Roebuck Lake. The smaller boats bucked and lurched in the wake of the larger ones. Women held onto their hats. Men gripped the sides of the boats.

Mr. Raney stood alone in the bow of the leader, and might have been the carved wooden figurehead of an ancient sailing vessel, so still he stood, in such beauty, as he regarded the water where his son took his life.

The dolphins swam alongside the lead boats. They dived,

surfaced, they blew spume from their blowholes, they wheeled, they showed their oily humps. Mr. Raney called them by name, St. Elmo, Carlos, Django, Boo-kay Jack, My Taliesin, and all the rest. Mr. Raney focused his eyes on the trees rising from deep water, the tree houses, in search of tree people, and saw none, of course. He saw their rotting sofas, their gas stoves and propane tanks, the trapdoors and ladders. But the tree people were gone. He supposed they were never coming back. He thought they had been a happy people. He strained to see the farther shore, the wild buffalo, the looseherds of wild horses, and they too were vanished, of course, as they had been for so long. Still, he heard the drumbeat of their hooves, he saw their dust, smelled the musk of their flesh and hide and rutting, heard the high-pitched whinny of their animal lust and joy. Boatloads of mourners followed behind.

The wake was a good one, it turned out. The fishshack was not small, there were many rooms, and it was crowded on all its levels. Children climbed up and down the rope ladders, in and out the trapdoors. Parents kept saying, "Be careful." They kept saying, "I don't think Mr Raney wants you to be playing on that."

Mr. Raney and Desiree Chisholm had cleaned the place good—Desiree came out the night before—swept all the floors and knocked down wasp nests from the eaves, scrubbed the linoleum in the kitchen and cleaned the stove, made the two beds, hung the hooked rugs out on a line and beat the dust out of them with a rug beater. A bottle of bonded whiskey and another of white whiskey they had stashed in the linen closet of the bathroom, for anybody who wanted a discreet nip. Mr. William Tell had supplied the whiskey. Mr. Raney pushed the old refrigerator, with the bullet holes in it, off to one side, out of the way, so there would be more room. Desiree had hosed down all the decks and workspaces on the dock, washed fish scales and old slime back into the lake.

The day was hot. Mourners crowded the house and spilled out onto the dock, where they stood and talked. It was so hot, a bird dropped down out of the sky and walked in the shadows of the mourners to cool off. There was lively talk, gossip, sometimes laughter. A typical Southern wake.

Food was plentiful, almost too much of it, on top of the stove, in the oven, along all the counters, on the table in the kitchen and on the dining room table as well, in the refrigerator, the one that had never been shot. People stood around eating off china plates and paper plates and sometimes no plates at all. One man ate an entire apple pie, one slice at a time, right out of the pan.

There were ham and chicken and collards and cold sweet potatoes, there were blackeyed peas and cornbread, potato salad, baked beans, sausage and biscuits. Somebody had even brought chitterlings—chitlins—though this was the only dish that diminished little in supply during the course of the day. A child named Henry Hightower, convinced by an older brother or sister to eat one of the boiled chitlins, found that he could not swallow the morsel and that, instead of diminishing in size, it seemed to increase with chewing, and so he ate the same chitlin all day long, until nightfall, when he had to go home and be convinced to spit it out. Henry's mama said, "You didn't get no nourishment to speak of, but you got plenty of exercise."

Mr. Raney was tired, just dog-tired all of a sudden. He had been talking to folks out on the dock when he realized just how bone-weary he was. He eased away, nodding to old friends, speaking for a moment, here and there, to others, in singles or clumps. He watched the children playing. He made his way inside the fishshack, where he did the same, speaking to folks, hello, oh fine, fine I guess, holding up, well as to be expected, still a little numb, still can't quite believe it's true, you know. He took a bite of somebody's peach cobbler with cream, and set the rest back down on a table.

Mr. Roy and his wife were there, the mailman. Mr. Roy said, "Raney, it ain't your job to entertain, you know." Mrs. Roy had thought to close off the sleeping porch for Mr. Raney, in case he needed some time alone, and so that's what he decided he would do, he went back to lie down for a while, take a load off, maybe close his eyes for a minute or two.

He sat on the edge of Hydro's bed, the cot where the boy slept in the summertime, in this weather, where there was a good breeze through the windowscreens, and pulled off his good shoes and rubbed his feet for a little while, and then swung his feet up on the bed and stretched out. His head he laid back on Hydro's pillow and let himself sink back, almost like becoming a part of the bed.

He could hear the sounds of conversation and laughter outside the closed door, his friends, decent people. He lay like this for a while.

He had not changed the linen on Hydro's bed. His head was resting on the exact spot where Hydro had laid his own big head, where he had lain on the last night of his life. Mr. Raney realized this when he turned his face to one side, to get comfortable. In this position, he could smell the familiar, manly fragrance of his son's living body on the pillowslip.

He did not open his eyes, not yet; he only lay like this a while longer, breathing. He did not breathe too deeply at first, in fear of breathing up all that remained of his son. He wanted to ration it, make it last.

Outside his door the voices were mostly a blur, conversation with a sound like static in it, or like ocean waves at night, the running surf, soft for a while, and then loud, maybe a laugh or two, like a gull's cry, then many voices together, sometimes the sweeter sound of a woman's voice, a woman's laughter, which made him think of his dead wife, how he missed her.

Now and then there was one voice, or maybe two, that rose above the others, a word, two words, not much more, that he could recognize. He heard his old friend Mr. William Tell. His voice carried better than the others.

Tell always had something going, some joke, some silliness, even at a funeral. Mr. Raney listened from where he lay. Mr. William Tell was doing Red Skelton routines for the other mourners. Raney lay on his back, smiling, picturing his old friend out there. He was doing Freddie the Free-loader, and George Appleby, and Klem Kadiddlehopper.

Tell looked a lot like Red Skelton, tall, his red hair going white, maybe sixty years old. He put his hands up in his armpits, to make pigeon wings. He flapped them a little. He got this silly look on his face. People were already laughing, before he said a word. He said, "Wait, wait—" He said, "Gertrude and Heathcliff—"

Mr. Rancy hauled himself up off Hydro's bed, slow as a cow. He sat on the edge of the bed, looked around. On Hydro's table were a few things, a crookneck lamp, a little portable travel iron Hydro was learning to use to press his shirts, a flashlight for reading comic books under the covers late at night, a few postage stamps—had his son ever really written a letter?—who did he imagine writing to? Hydro's favorite wanted posters, a hit-and-run with a scar down one side of his face, and a murder-and-kidnapping wearing a nice suit. Armed and Dangerous. Mr. Raney held the posters in his hands for a while, and then put them back on the table.

Outside the door, laughter broke out. He heard Mr. William Tell say, "Gertrude and Heathcliff, flying over the beach—" Mr. Raney imagined the silly look on Tell's face, the way he leaned to one side and looked down from the sky at the picnickers on the pretendlike beach.

Mr. Raney got up from the bed now. He walked over to Hydro's closet and opened the door. In the bottom of the closet sat Hydro's laundry basket, filled with dirty clothes. Mr. Raney picked up a T-shirt and held it to his face and breathed in a perfect memory of his son.

Laughter, again, outside the door.

Still holding the cotton T-shirt to his face, Mr. Raney bent his knees, slow, slow, and eased down onto the linoleum floor of the sleeping porch. He heard Mr. William Tell, he heard the monkeys and the parrots in the trees. He curled up on the floor and breathed and breathed. He dropped the T-shirt. He promised himself never to do this load of laundry. As long as he had it, he would have Hydro.

Quiet applause from outside the door, the restrained clapping of hands. Mr. William Tell had finished a routine.

The pain that gripped Mr. Raney caused him to writhe on the floor. He wallowed like a hog in a loblolly. He made grunting sounds, he squealed like a pig. He called out for his own daddy, who had been dead a long, long time. He buried his head in the laundry basket. He said, "Daddy!" He thought of the letter he'd gotten when he was a boy and how proud his father had been. He stuck his head in Hydro's laundry basket and tried to inhale not just the smell but the clothing itself, the fibers, straight into his lungs. He collapsed again, he banged his head twenty times against the floor. He found Hydro's toothbrush and put it into his mouth and tried to taste Hydro's dried spit. He tore out his hair with his hands. He punched himself in the face with his fists. He licked the linoleum floor with his tongue and felt the grit between his teeth. He called, "Daddy!" His throat felt like a hot knife had just passed through it. He made puking motions and got only dry heaves. He moved across the floor using the rocking motion of a dolphin in the water; knees up, knees down, slide, again and again; he didn't even use his hands. He turned on his back and flopped like a fish out of water. He stopped. He lay on the floor, still. He did not move, not even to wipe sweat out of his eyes. He stood apart from his body and looked down upon himself. The physical representation of himself that he saw, beastlike and hideous, he understood to be the image of his inner life for many years to come.

He continued to lie there. Then he got up. He stood in the center of the room for a while. He picked up Hydro's hairbrush from a deal dresser and saw strands of Hydro's hair in it. He brushed his hair with the brush and looked at it again and saw his own hair mingled with that of his son. He picked up a couple of loose comic books and looked at their covers. One was *The Green Hornet and Speedy*, a man-boy team of costumed super-archers, who caught crooks even the G-men couldn't catch. The other was one Mr. Raney did not expect, called *Young Love*. On the front was a picture of a man flirting with a woman in an elevator, and another woman standing to the side of the elevator looking dejected. In the balloon above her head, the second woman's thoughts were, "A week ago he was French-kissing me in the elevator, and now he doesn't even recognize me." Mr. Raney imagined Hydro sympathizing with the rejected woman, promising himself that he would never treat anyone in this way.

Outside the door, Mr. William Tell was doing the routine in which Red Skelton pretends to put on a woman's girdle. It was mostly a silent routine, but Mr. Raney could recognize it by certain clues, the comic grunts, the rustle of clothing, a word or two, the laughter. He saw the funny, scrunched-up face, the rubbery arms reaching around, the pretense of arranging the stays and the garter snaps. He saw Mr. William Tell turn his back to the audience and look back over his shoulder. He heard the laughter. He saw Mr. William Tell bend over and stick his fanny out at the audience as he pretended to try to pull the elastic up over his rear end.

Mr. Raney sat back down on the edge of Hydro's bed. He had already taken off his shoes. Now he took off all his clothes and slipped between Hydro's sheets naked. He thought of his son's body having lain there, his skin having touched these sheets. For a moment he almost believed Hydro was there in the bed beside him, and then that he himself was Hydro. He slept and dreamed of a hacienda in Old Mexico, with señoritas and sombreros and hot sun and treeless ground. He dreamed of clear rivers where deer stood in the shallows and drank. He dreamed of a circus train unloading tents and animals and trapezes. He knew the strange mixture of despair and exhilaration Hydro had felt when he slipped over the side of the boat into the water.

Then he woke up. He lay and listened to the quiet laughter from the other side of the door. He couldn't tell which routine Mr. William Tell was doing now. Maybe he had worked up a few new sketches.

He got up out of bed and dressed again. He checked himself in the mirror and thought that he would see the writhing, wallowing, grunting, squealing beast, but saw only himself, Mr. Raney, a little rested from his two-minute nap. He combed his hair with his fingers. He thought: *This is the way I will look, the other is the way I will feel. All right.*

He heard someone just outside the door say, "It looks like Hydro was the sharpshooter instead of Morgan." For some reason this filled Mr. Raney with strange pride and made it easier to go on.

He opened the door and walked out into the crowded area of the wake. Mr. William Tell was wearing a dress now, over his regular clothes. He had on a tiny pillbox hat with a veil. In anyone else, this would have been disrespectful. In Mr. William Tell it seemed natural, even at a wake. His audience was in hysterics. Where he had come up with this costume, Mr. Raney could not even guess.

Mr. Raney slid quietly into the crowd and got a place to stand, where he could see. People were scrunched in, elbow to elbow, and standing on tiptoes to see Mr. William Tell, who was by far the funniest man Mr. Raney had ever known. He noticed that Mr. William Tell also had a little purse dangling from one arm by the strap, and white gloves on his hands. Mr. William Tell was bringing his knees up in a funny kind of walking motion, walking in place, as if he were wearing high heels that he could not manage. He looked like he might fall over at any minute. The expression on his face—well, Mr. Raney started to laugh, along with everybody else.

Mr. William Tell was walking and adjusting his girdle and putting on lipstick at the same time. All with this earnest expression on his face. Except every now and then Mr. William Tell would step out of character just long enough to cut his eyes out at the audience and laugh his fool head off, and then start into his act again. It made what he was doing seem all that much funnier, to be able to share a laugh with the comedian. There was a loud roaring in Mr. Raney's head, that he knew was the sound of grief and that it would not go away for a long time, maybe forever, but he also felt his heart fill up with love for his old friend.

Out the window, Mr. Raney could see Louis McNaughton and his father as they were leaving the wake. Dr. McNaughton steadied himself with one hand on one of the creosoted pilings, out on the dock, and stepped down into one of the launches. Dr. McNaughton looked like an old man. It was Louis, though, whom Mr. Raney was really looking at. He thought he would ask Louis out sometime, get to know him better, maybe give him Hydro's collection of comic books.

He looked at the little boy, getting into the launch, and imagined that Louis, too, was hearing some kind of roaring, maybe the same one as himself, the sound of inexpressible grief and the foreknowledge of lifelong pain that no one else could ever hope to understand or share.

Just at that moment, Louis looked back up towards the fishhouse. He saw Mr. Raney looking at him. He lifted his hand and waved a small wave, only his fingers moved. Mr. Raney waved back, in the same way. Louis turned and sat down in the launch, which was ready to cast off. The deep-throated outboard started up, and in a minute they were gone.

Mr. Raney turned back to the fishhouse, the wake, and saw Mr. William Tell, the purse, the high heels, the lipstick.

Then, just when Mr. Raney thought he might bust out

laughing in spite of himself, he saw something he did not expect to see at all. He saw an image, maybe even a vision, of the sharpshooter and his mama, Morgan and old Aunt Lily, barreling on down the road, some road, some highway, in Morgan's raggedy old truck, with blue smoke blowing out the tailpipe, up under wide blue Western skies. They were singing "The Yellow Rose of Texas." They were singing "The Eyes of Texas Are upon You." They were singing every Texas song they knew. They were clapping their hands in the chorus. *The stars at night are big and bright, clap clap clap clap.* They were singing "Deep in the Heart of Texas." Morgan was saying, "Are you happy, Mama? Are you glad to be getting out?" Aunt Lily was saying, "Git on down the damn road!"